The Serendipity of Catastrophe

The Serendipity of Catastrophe

Lisa Fellinger

For Logan
Thank you for choosing me to be your mama

Chapter 1

Anita Lorello saw the question in her therapist's eyes: how much longer would she go on like this, breathing but not living? With the one-year anniversary of her husband's death approaching, she'd been asking the same question. The pressure to move on intensified each day, but she still hoped to wake up and find this had all been a nightmare, that Victor hadn't really died the day before they were supposed to leave for the trip of a lifetime to celebrate their fortieth anniversary.

"What's going on in there, Anita?" Meredith asked, her voice warm and comforting, nudging her back to the present. She was young, probably in her mid-thirties, and she watched her intently with her deep brown eyes.

Anita shifted in her seat and played with the diamond rings still adorning her left hand, her wrinkled hands barely recognizable to her anymore. "Just thinking about Victor," she said. The way he smiled at her and his brown eyes sparkled. The way his hand found hers right before falling asleep. The mess of student papers he always left on the kitchen table. That table had been far too clean the past year.

Meredith sipped her coffee and raised an eyebrow. "What about him?"

Anita sighed and her shoulders slumped forward. "Nothing new. I just miss him. I miss him every day and it's been almost a year, and I have no idea how to move on with my life." She paused, considering the past year, how quickly it went and how very slowly at the same time, kind of like when her daughter had been an infant.

Meredith cleared her throat and set her coffee mug back down. "I did have an idea," she said slowly, as if testing the waters. "The trip you and Victor were supposed to take."

She bristled, not liking where this was headed. "What about it?"

Meredith shrugged, and Anita sensed she was trying hard to be so nonchalant. "What if you went through with it?"

"I couldn't."

"Why not?"

She looked away, as though the answer hid in one of Meredith's abstract paintings, and thought about the trip she and Victor had planned. Four weeks in Europe—London, Paris, Barcelona, and Rome. They'd been trying and failing for decades to follow through on some version of this trip, this most recent attempt being derailed less than twenty-four hours prior by a careless teen speeding through the Walmart parking lot.

Anita ran her fingers over the familiar sofa, tracing the green plaid pattern. "I want to go," she said, though her voice lacked conviction. "But when I think about the logistics of it all—the flights, the language barriers, the navigation..." She paused and closed her eyes. Her heart rate sped up just thinking about it.

Meredith nodded, but her expression remained neutral. "It would be a learning experience, for sure. But I think following through on this trip would provide you with some closure, an opportunity to make peace with Victor's death and begin moving on."

Anita bit her lip and reached for the glass of water on the table beside her. She knew moving on would require a foray beyond her comfort zone, but this seemed too far. And yet, she was running out of options. The grief support groups she'd attended hadn't helped. She had become increasingly isolated the last few months, but she couldn't find the energy to reach out to friends. They didn't understand what she was going through, anyway, and though they tried to support her, Anita didn't know how to explain her emotions to them. Without Victor, life was empty and meaningless.

"I've never even been out of the country," she protested further, wishing she hadn't opened this line of discussion. "At least before, Victor would have been with me. He was in charge of the travel arrangements, so I didn't have to stress or worry. I can't do it by myself."

"So then bring someone with you."

Anita let out a small laugh. "Like who?" All her friends had lives and families of their own. No one could leave everything behind to tag along with her to Europe for an entire month.

Meredith tilted her head, and Anita practically saw the lightbulb above her. She really was quite the actress. "What about your daughter?"

She froze. "She wouldn't be able to. She has a job." And there was no way Carrie would agree to a trip overseas. Not with her. Meredith of all people knew that.

"She's been to Europe before, yes?" She smiled, clearly pleased with the brilliance of her idea.

Anita nodded slowly, at a loss for a counterargument.

"Perhaps she could take some time, get you situated and comfortable, and then you could continue on your own?"

Did Meredith hear herself? "You know she'd say no. A

whole month together in Europe?" Anita shook her head. "She hasn't even come home once since Victor's funeral. She has her own life now, and I'm not part of it. Not since Victor died. Not even really before that." Carrie worked as a talent agent across the country in Los Angeles. Her career was demanding, but she'd found the time to visit home while Victor had been alive. Since his funeral, however, she'd had plenty of excuses for not being able to make the trip back to Buffalo.

Meredith leaned in. "Is that how you want your relationship with your only daughter to be?"

Anita broke eye contact, again turning to the paintings. It wasn't what she wanted, but what difference did that make? She was who she was, and Carrie was who she was. And who Anita was pressed on Carrie's every nerve despite her best efforts. Carrie had only tolerated her before for her father's sake.

She turned back to Meredith and shook her head. "I can't ask her to do that," she insisted again, dodging the last question.

Meredith gave her that look, the one she gave when Anita said she couldn't do something. She braced for another lecture about the word "can't," but instead Meredith only smiled and said, "It never hurts to ask."

———

After her appointment, Anita stopped at the Chinese restaurant near her house for an early dinner. Despite the number on the scale creeping higher, cooking for one was too depressing most nights. Takeout was far easier.

"What can we get you today, Nita?" The young Chinese woman behind the counter asked, her sleek, black ponytail bouncing from side to side as she zipped over to the register. She always forgot the A, but Anita couldn't take offense; after all this time, she still didn't know the other woman's name.

"Vegetable lo mein, please." She pulled a ten-dollar bill from her purse.

The woman took her money, then disappeared into the back to prepare her food, leaving Anita in the tiny dining area with her thoughts. Outside, the sun was shining, the temperature perfect for the end of August. While most of Western New York was out soaking up the last of the beautiful weather before fall quickly turned to blizzards and negative windchills, Anita had been holed up in the house watching crummy daytime television and eating far too much cookie dough ice cream. The routine brought some semblance of comfort, but now she realized she'd missed the entire summer. And spring. And winter.

When her order was ready, she thanked the girl and headed out with her bag. She stepped off the sidewalk to cross the parking lot, digging around in her purse for her car keys. How did they always fall to the very bottom in a matter of minutes?

A car horn blared, and Anita jumped back. A Jeep Cherokee flew past, the driver giving her the finger. Her keys jangled in her hand as it shook, and her takeout bag slipped from her grasp, landing with a thud on the sidewalk.

A young man on the other side of the car lane rushed towards her, and Anita's breath caught in her throat. With his brown hair and slender build, he looked so much like a young Victor. Even his glasses were similar.

"Ma'am? Are you all right?" he asked, coming up beside her.

Anita nodded, unable to find words.

"I saw the Jeep. He was going way too fast."

She found a full breath and bent down for her bag, her hand still shaky. "I didn't see him," she said, her voice barely above a whisper. Hadn't she checked both ways?

Anita looked ahead at her car. It was no more than fifteen paces ahead, but her feet were stuck. The man inched closer.

"Do you want me to help you to your car?" he asked.

Anita didn't relish the attention, but attempting to get there alone seemed impossible. "I'm right there," she said, pointing but avoiding eye contact.

The man nodded, then offered his arm for her to loop hers through the way Victor used to. He guided her to the edge of the sidewalk, waiting for another vehicle to pass. They crossed the parking lot, and he opened her car door for her. She slid into the driver's seat, clutching the steering wheel to steady herself, and inserted the key.

"Are you okay?" His eyebrows bunched together. Victor's always did that when he was worried about her but didn't want to flat out admit to it.

"I will be," she said, though she wasn't sure she believed herself. "Thank you."

"No problem." The man smiled, then jogged back towards the Chinese restaurant. A sense of calm came over her as she watched him leave. Was this a sign from Victor, some way of him letting her know he was still here for her? Or maybe it was just her brain playing tricks on her, always searching for him even though he was gone.

———

Anita entered her small kitchen and set the takeout bag on the counter, pushing aside a pile of unsorted mail. She'd stopped shaking long enough to drive the three minutes back to her house, but her appetite was gone. She grabbed a glass of water and finished it in a few gulps, then set the empty glass beside the sink.

Steadying herself on the counter's edge, she took a few deep breaths. How had she not seen that Jeep? Since Victor's accident, she'd been so vigilant, and yet she'd almost met the same fate. She shook her head at her stupidity.

Walking down the hall, she intended to lay down in her bedroom, but Carrie's old room caught her attention. The door was open a crack, though Anita swore it had been closed that morning. She opened it the rest of the way and stood in the doorway. Her stomach ached at the sight of the suitcases she'd stashed in the corner when she'd returned from the hospital the night Victor died. She had avoided this room for months so she wouldn't have to look at them.

Anita peeled her hand from the doorknob and entered the room, curiosity getting the better of her after talking about the trip with Meredith. She lifted her dark purple suitcase onto the bed and unzipped it. Inside were all their travel guidebooks, along with the notebook she'd bought to journal their adventures, the pages still blank.

She still tasted the Riesling she'd been drinking when the police officer called to inform her there'd been an accident and Victor was being transported to the emergency room. Within a few hours, she'd gone from being anxious over a flight to facing the rest of her life without her partner, her rock. Instead of realizing a lifelong dream to see Europe, the next several months had been a black hole of despair, of nights that blurred into days through tears and unyielding grief.

Anita grabbed the London guidebook and flipped it open. Victor's handwriting greeted her from the margins in blue ink beside a photo of St. Paul's Cathedral. *Must see!* he'd written. A high school history teacher and architecture buff, he had a list of churches in each city he wanted to visit. "They don't build them like that anymore," he'd said years ago as he mulled over a travel magazine.

While Victor filled their list of must-sees with churches and museums, Anita had sought out the highest-rated cafes from those with the best views to those with exceptionally gorgeous-looking pastries. She'd stumbled upon a macaron cooking class in Paris and squealed with delight to Victor; she'd never been able to master the delicate cookies, but here was her chance to learn from an actual Parisian chef!

Anita closed the book and her shoulders deflated. Despite her fears, she'd been looking forward to finally experiencing all this with Victor. The cathedrals, the art museums, the Eiffel Tower. The wine in Rome, the fish and chips in London. All her life she'd felt she was missing out by not traveling more. When friends talked about their European vacations, she was overcome with envy. There'd been an unending number of reasons they hadn't traveled overseas sooner, but she and Victor were finally going to make it happen. They finally had the time and the money, and with him beside her, she'd get through the tough parts.

Then her life crashed to a halt.

The airline had been sympathetic to her situation and accommodated her as best they were able, but the credits they issued were only good for one year. The rest of the money they'd saved for the trip had been refunded to their separate savings account, ready to spend at any moment. But if she didn't use the vouchers soon, she'd be out the cost of their airfare. Adding yet another obstacle likely meant she'd never follow through.

Minutes passed, the seconds ticking off noisily on the old wall clock that still hung above where Carrie's desk once stood. In spite of herself, she couldn't get her mind off the possibility of going to Europe after all. It felt impossible to proceed without Victor, but he wouldn't want her to miss out on this simply because he couldn't be there with her. His sudden death should have been a wake-up call, a reminder that tomorrow was never guaranteed, but instead she'd wasted almost a year lost in grief and depression instead of living her life. And today she'd come close to missing her opportunity as well.

But what if something went wrong? Anita's mind raced through all the potential scenarios, all the problems she might encounter. What if she got lost? What if her passport went missing? What if there was a terrorist attack? There was no way she could do it.

Her eyes settled on a photo of Carrie—her fearless, brave, unrelenting daughter—and Meredith's words rang through her mind once more: *It never hurts to ask.*

The irony wasn't lost on Anita that she was, once again, considering a trip overseas as a means to overcome grief. She thought back to the day Victor came home with a handful of travel brochures from a rep who'd been in the faculty lounge at school. He'd proposed a trip to Europe as a spontaneous, fun idea, but really it was a mission to convince her they could be happy together without children, that three miscarriages didn't have to mean the end of the world.

Anita fought him on the idea initially, insulted that he thought vacations could replace her desire to be a mother. But eventually, she began pulling out the travel guides while Victor was at work and allowed herself to imagine them in Europe. She pictured them leisurely sipping espresso in Italy, window shopping in Paris, or even catching a glimpse of the royal family in London. How she longed to see the queen in real life! She thought of the amazing food they would eat, all the good wine they'd enjoy, and the opportunity to explore new places together. None of it was a replacement for the family they'd been unable to start, but planning a trip gave her some semblance of hope, something to focus her energy on and take her mind off the pain of losing her babies before she'd even held them.

They ultimately decided on Paris as their first of many adventures, but before they put down a deposit with the travel agent, Anita learned she was pregnant once again. Instead of planning visits to Notre Dame and the Louvre, her focus turned back to baby strollers and car seats, onesies and sleep training theory. Paris would always be there.

But all these years later, Anita barely knew that daughter. With Victor gone, her link to Carrie disappeared. Her phone calls home were infrequent and short, and she never shared anything about her life other than the most basic facts. Anita hadn't pressed her for more, desperate not to widen the fissures in their relationship further, yet perhaps she'd inadvertently done just that.

As much as the thought of never seeing Europe devastated Anita, the thought of losing her daughter completely crushed her heart. A month together in Europe was likely Carrie's worst nightmare, but if by some miracle her daughter agreed to the trip, she couldn't think of a better opportunity to improve their relationship, to prove she could be the mother she'd always intended to be.

She rose and went back into the kitchen for the phone, the London travel guide still in hand. Meredith was right. Worst-case scenario, Carrie would say no. In fact, it was almost guaranteed she would.

Anita drew a deep breath, trying to keep her hope in check. She punched in Carrie's cell phone number and prepared for her daughter to turn her down.

But what if she said yes?

Chapter 2

Carrie Lorello tapped a pen on her desk in her home office, willing an email notification to appear. Her biggest client had a red-carpet premiere tonight for his most recent rom-com, *One Last Love Story*, and they hoped to announce his next role would be in the new Marc Ryan movie. After several phone calls, Marc's assistant had promised her an answer one way or another before the premiere.

Carrie switched her attention from her computer to her iPhone and back again, wondering which would receive the message first. She needed this deal to go through. Adam Hartley had the most potential of any client she'd worked with, and she hoped to impress her agency's partners by landing him a breakout role. At thirty-two, she was the perfect age to shine as a talent agent, old enough to have experience but young enough so the barely legal clients she often represented didn't consider her a dinosaur. Still, the industry was a cutthroat one, and even though she'd secured Adam as her client, dozens of others waited in line for her to slip up.

It was almost five o'clock. The premiere began at nine, and Adam needed to be there by seven for photos and interviews, which meant Carrie needed to have this deal sorted soon. She imagined the smile that would spread across his ruggedly handsome face when she gave him the good news, then quickly pushed the image aside. He was her client. No matter how attractive she might find him, her agency had very strict rules against personal relationships with clients. And beyond the agency, it went against Carrie's own better judgment. Men like Adam Hartley—handsome, charming, and confident—would always leave you heartbroken. But her career would never cheat on her.

Her phone buzzed with an incoming call, and Carrie sucked in a breath. She groaned when she saw it was only her mother and contemplated sending it to voicemail. She was busy and would get back to her when she had a spare moment. But her father's sudden death made her superstitious about missing calls from her mother, just in case. She didn't need that bad juju in her life.

"Hi, Mom," Carrie answered, trying to keep her tone curt. Quick check-in, make sure there was no disaster, then get back to her regularly scheduled evening.

"Hi, honey. How are you?

"I'm fine. Just trying to get some things sorted before a premiere tonight. What's up?"

"Oh, I didn't mean to interrupt you." Something in her voice sounded off, like she wasn't quite sure why she'd even called.

"So, what's up?" Carrie asked again, antsy to get back to obsessing over her email.

"We can talk later. I don't want to hold you up."

"You're not holding me up," she said, refreshing her inbox with a click of her mouse. Would she get to the point already?

"Well, I had a weird idea I wanted to run by you, but if you can't do it, I understand."

"What's that?"

"You know the trip your father and I were supposed to go on?"

"Uh-huh," Carrie said, biting her tongue. Was this a serious question?

"Well, I was talking with my counselor today—you know, Meredith—and she suggested I should still go on the trip."

Carrie paused, trying to picture her anxiety-ridden mother traveling overseas alone. She'd hardly been able to picture her going a year ago with her dad.

"The thing is, I don't think I can do it by myself," her mother continued. "Your dad was in charge of most of the details, and I don't think I can handle them on my own." She cleared her throat. "So, Meredith suggested maybe you would go with me instead. I would pay, of course." She paused again, then quickly added, "But if you can't get away from work, I understand."

Carrie's pen stopped, and her hand fell away from her mouse. How was she supposed to respond to that? Even if she could manage the time off work, spending a month with her mother wasn't her idea of a vacation. An entire month of judgmental comments about her life in California, strained conversation, and coaxing her through panic attacks? No, thank you.

"Yeah, there's no way I could get away from work for that long."

"No worries," her mother jumped in. "I assumed that would be the case. I just figured it didn't hurt to ask."

Was she imagining it, or did she detect relief in her voice? "Sorry," she offered, at a loss for what else to say.

"It's all right, dear. I'll let you get back to work. Love you."

The line went dead before Carrie found a response. She stared at the black screen for a moment, trying to make sense of their conversation. Eventually she'd have to visit her mother, but she was content prolonging it as long as possible. Without her dad to serve as a buffer between them, Carrie couldn't imagine how awkward a few days together would be, let alone an entire month.

A ping from her computer drew her attention back to the evening ahead. Carrie skimmed the email, then let out a sigh of relief.

She grabbed her phone, a smile spreading across her face, but before she could find Adam's name in her contacts, her phone buzzed with another incoming call.

Adam.

"Hey there," Carrie answered, shifting her tone back to happy and bubbly. "I was just about to call you. You ready for some amazing news?"

"Carrie!" He cut her off, desperation in his voice. "Sophia just bailed on me for tonight."

She rolled her eyes. Of course she did. Why did he keep wasting his time with this girl? Adam was Carrie's age, and Sophia was at least eight years younger, flaky and clearly only looking for a thrill by dating an actor. But Adam kept sticking around for whatever reason.

"Jesus," Carrie muttered.

"I know," he said. "I really can't go to this thing alone, and there's no one else I can ask on such short notice."

Adam paused and Carrie held her breath. Was he about to ask what she thought he was? No, that would be...

"Will you go with me?"

...Absurd. "I..." What was she supposed to say? Adam *could* go alone, but Hollywood *was* fickle. It preferred dates and couples, even if it was the norm for celebrities to marry and divorce as though they were merely changing outfits. Carrie's mind raced, trying to come up with an alternate solution, but nothing came.

"Please, Carrie?" he asked again, his voice quiet and sincere.

"It would mean so much to me."

Carrie pictured Adam's face as he asked, his baby-blue eyes sparkling, his eyebrows raised slightly as he waited for her response. "I really shouldn't," she protested weakly.

Adam sighed heavily. "I understand. Anyway, what was the amazing news? Is it what I think it is?"

She sat up straight in her desk chair, snapping back to business. "You got the part!"

"Carrie, that is amazing! Thank you!"

"Hey, you're the one who did the hard work. I just set up the audition. Of course, my countless follow-up calls didn't hurt."

"You really are the best, you know that? Well, I need to get ready. Are you sure you can't go with me? You can ditch before the after-party if you need to."

Carrie took a deep breath and looked around her bare apartment. The thought of an evening out all dressed up did sound more appealing than the takeout and catching up on work she had planned.

"Fine," Carrie said. "But just for the premiere."

She could defend standing in as Adam's date for one evening. Tomorrow, their relationship would go back to strictly professional, but tonight she'd allow herself to dabble in the glamour of Hollywood.

One night of pretending wouldn't do any damage, right?

———

"I still don't know how you did it!" Adam said, shaking his head as he sat across from her in the limo. It seemed a bit excessive to Carrie to have an entire limousine for just the two of them, but that was part of the magic of Hollywood: big expenses to keep up appearances.

"Seriously, Carrie. Thank you." Adam's enthusiasm was contagious, and yet he portrayed humility, a trait many of her clients lacked. Talent would only carry someone so far in this industry, especially in the era of social media and viral videos, and Adam had the qualities to become a real star given the right opportunities.

Carrie took a sip of her champagne and smoothed her maroon evening gown. It was all she had on such short notice that seemed to fit the occasion, a leftover bridesmaid dress from a friend's wedding a few years ago. Another friend who'd gotten married, had kids, and disappeared into the suburbs.

"Want a top off?" Adam asked, tipping the champagne bottle in her direction.

Carrie shook her head and held up her hand. "I shouldn't."

"Come on. A little more won't hurt. Let yourself enjoy the evening." He shook the bottle a bit, then flashed his gorgeous smile and raised his eyebrows, as though inviting her to something she shouldn't agree to.

"All right," she said, his eyes doing her in. "But just a little more. One of us has to stay sober tonight."

"No fun in that when there's news to celebrate!"

The champagne fizzed as Adam refilled her glass, his bicep bulging beneath his suit jacket, and Carrie feared her cheeks were turning red as they locked eyes. She took a small sip and reached for her phone, searching her email for something else to focus on. Why did she suddenly feel like a grade-school girl with a crush? She'd lived her entire adult life around actors and gorgeous men. But there was something about Adam's quiet confidence that Carrie had been drawn to since the beginning, and sitting here alone with him, all dressed up, it was hard to deny that underlying attraction.

It didn't help she was fresh off a breakup, if she could even call it that. Until last week, she'd been sort of seeing a journalist she'd met through an interview for another client. They hadn't been exclusive—Brian had been clear on that—and while it had been nice having someone around who understood the demands of her career, the chemistry just wasn't there. She was far from heartbroken over it, but perhaps the loss had her shaken up more than she'd realized.

Carrie tensed and looked out the window. What had she gotten herself into?

They pulled into the line of waiting limousines outside the theater, and she checked her makeup one last time in her travel-size mirror. Many of her clients dreaded red carpet events, and she was beginning to understand why. She'd never been on this side of them before, and the anticipation of so many eyes on her had her palms sweaty and her mouth dry.

Their turn finally came, and Carrie ran her hands through her brown hair. She'd had no time to do anything with it other than pull out her hair tie and run the straightener through it.

"You look amazing," Adam said, his voice sincere. "Thank you for coming with me tonight. You have no idea how grateful I am."

She returned his smile, and a sense of calm replaced her nerves. This was just Adam. What was she so worked up for?

The limo door opened, and Carrie followed him out where the crowd and the cameras awaited them. It took a second to find her balance, and she scolded herself for giving into his offer of more champagne.

Adam took her hand and led her down the carpet towards the interview area, a natural at navigating the chaos. First up, a reporter from *People* magazine. Carrie recognized her from a few events she'd attended with Brian. Her name was Sara something. She waited for a hint of recognition from the reporter but didn't see one.

"Adam Hartley," Sara began, quickly referencing her

notepad. "You are on an amazing hot streak right now. Can you tell me what's next for you?"

Carrie's lips turned into a small smile, excited she was here to witness him sharing his big news.

"I actually learned today I'll be the lead in the next Marc Ryan film," he told her, his eyes sparkling.

Sara's eyes widened. "Wow, that's amazing!"

"It is," Adam agreed. "And it's all thanks to my amazing agent, Carrie Lorello." He reached out and grabbed Carrie's hand again, tugging her towards him.

"What are you doing?" she whispered, her eyes darting around the crowd. They should have discussed ground rules before she'd agreed to this.

The photographer beside Sara picked up his camera and began snapping photos of the two of them.

"This woman is incredible," Adam told them. "My career wouldn't be where it is today without her."

Carrie forced a smile and tugged at her dress. If Sara hadn't placed her yet, she certainly did now. She scribbled on her notepad. What mess would Carrie be in tomorrow when this story broke?

But then Adam snaked his arm around her waist, pulling her even closer to him. She smelled his cologne and closed her eyes for a moment, a longing passing over her that she hadn't felt in a very long time.

Screw what her boss thought. She was always the professional one, the one who went above and beyond to ensure she didn't cross a single boundary. But she'd just launched their client towards A-list status. So tonight, she'd allow herself to let loose a little. She could easily talk her way out of this in the morning.

Chapter 3

Carrie opened her eyes and took in her surroundings. She was in a bed lower to the ground than her own, with a navy-blue comforter she didn't recognize pulled over her. She blinked a few times, adjusting to the sunlight beating into her eyes. When had she last slept so late the sun blinded her when she woke?

Rolling over, she found Adam passed out beside her in only his boxers. She gasped, then quickly covered her mouth. She couldn't risk waking him.

Carrie's head pounded, and though the details were fuzzy, there was no doubt last night involved a fair amount of alcohol. She pressed her hand against her forehead, trying for a momentary reprieve from the pain, as images from the previous night filtered into her mind and all hope of this being a horrible dream vanished. She remembered Adam convincing her to go to the premiere with him, the limo, him shouting her praises to a crowd of reporters. But how had she ended up back at his apartment, in his bed, with—oh God—only her underwear and no bra on in the morning?

Then it came to her. As they watched the movie in the dark

auditorium, Adam had reached over and squeezed her knee. An almost insignificant gesture, but it had made her simmer with the expectation of something more. By the time the movie ended and he asked her one more time if she wanted to go with him to the after-party, she'd convinced herself it wasn't the worst idea in the world.

It had been a while since she'd drank more than a glass of wine or two with dinner, and after her first gin and tonic, there was no stopping her. Hours later, she'd grabbed her cell phone for an Uber, but Adam offered to have his car service take her home. Apparently, she hadn't made it.

The rest was a blank, but she couldn't waste time figuring it out further. She needed to get the hell out of here. She looked at Adam once more, evaluating the odds of sneaking out without waking him. Her clothes were strewn about the bedroom floor, forming a path back towards the door. She crept out of the bed, thankful for the memory foam mattress, reached for her bra and snapped it on, then took a few steps and scooped her dress off the ground. She threw it on before scurrying out of the bedroom and sneaking out the front door.

Outside in the blaring sunlight, her disgust with herself intensified. She glanced back at the apartment building, hoping Adam had drunk enough that he wouldn't remember they slept together or she'd even been in his apartment to begin with. She would need to pass him off to someone else at the agency without drawing attention, which sucked, but she had no choice. Not after crossing that boundary.

Carrie ordered an Uber to meet her a block down and cowered behind a palm tree, eyeing pedestrians strolling up and down the street until her car came. The driver gave her a once-over, taking in the dress as she climbed into the backseat, but Carrie just smiled politely and kept quiet. Surely this wasn't the strangest thing he'd ever seen, not in LA.

After she got home and took a long, hot shower, she avoided her computer for another hour by sorting the pile of unopened mail on her kitchen counter. Once the clutter was cleared, she drew a deep breath and sat down at her desk, coffee mug in hand, and searched Adam's name. "Is Adam Hartley Getting Too Friendly with His Agent?" the first link asked. Carrie cringed but clicked it anyway.

Lined up in narrative progression of the evening were three photos: one of Adam with a genuine smile as he squeezed Carrie's waist on the red carpet, one of them at the after-party sitting much too close on a lounge couch, and finally one of them entering his building together hand in hand.

The article was written by Sara Wallace.

Carrie slammed her laptop closed and fell back into her chair. When her boss saw these images, she was screwed. She'd witnessed Sherilynn fire others for lesser offenses than getting drunk with a client and going back to his apartment. Her mind raced with how she could spin this so it wasn't as bad as it looked.

As if on cue, her cell phone pinged with a text message from Sherilynn.

My office, one hour.

Carrie tipped her head back and groaned. She'd been hoping to meet with Sherilynn today, but this wasn't to congratulate her on landing Adam the Marc Ryan role.

————

An hour later, in skinny black pants and a tailored gray blazer, her hair in a pristine bun, and her stomach rumbling with knots of doom, Carrie entered the office and walked past her coworkers. Sherilynn stood in the doorway of her office, her arms folded. "Carrie," she said, her tone flat. "Come in."

Sherilynn moved to the side and let Carrie enter before her. She sat across from the large white desk and waited for her boss to join her. Sherilynn made up for her lack of height by wearing the most ridiculously high stilettos, which forced her to walk slower than everyone else in the office. She wore her shiny blond hair in a sleek, low ponytail and maintained a French manicure. She was fierce, which was no doubt how she'd worked her way to the top before turning forty. Carrie respected and admired her, and being on her list of problems to deal with made her feel even worse about last night.

Sherilynn took her seat and tapped something out on her keyboard before focusing her attention on Carrie, her hands folded on her desk in front of her. "I assume you saw the gossip sites this morning."

She nodded and swallowed hard, trying to clear the giant lump in her throat.

Sherilynn's mouth drew into a straight, tight line. "I'm sure I don't need to tell you how appalling the headlines were to me."

"No, you don't. I'm appalled as well."

She waited, allowing Carrie an opportunity to explain herself. The denial sat on the tip of her tongue, waiting for her to speak the words, but she couldn't bring herself to lie. Every ounce of her wanted to, but she'd done what she'd done. Lying to her boss wouldn't fix that.

At her silence, Sherilynn nodded. "How long has this relationship been going on?"

"There's no relationship. Last night was... a huge mistake. I truly don't know what happened."

Sherilynn raised an eyebrow. "So last night was a booty call?"

"No, it's not like that either." She clutched the edges of her chair.

"Then what happened last night, Carrie?" Her tone was somewhat softer, but her expression remained no-nonsense.

She inhaled, sank back into the chair, and looked off to Sherilynn's right. "Adam called me right before the premiere. His date flaked on him, and he didn't want to go alone. I thought we could keep it professional, but then I stupidly agreed to go to the after-party. There was a lot of alcohol and overall poor judgment on my part."

Sherilynn held up her phone screen. A photo of her and Adam on the red carpet stared back at her, a different one than she'd seen in Sara's article earlier. In this one, Carrie was turned in towards him, looking ever the part of his girlfriend. They both flashed genuine smiles. What might last night have meant to Adam?

"An after-party doesn't explain this one," Sherilynn said, snapping Carrie back to her present reality.

"Oh, that was nothing!" she exclaimed, relieved to have a valid excuse for this one at least. "He was just excited I'd secured him the role in that upcoming Marc Ryan film." Maybe if she threw that in, Sherilynn would be more lenient.

Her expression remained unfazed. She pierced Carrie with her stare as though waiting for her to make all of this un-happen.

"I know I have to pass Adam off to someone else," Carrie said, her voice shaking. Her hands were clammy, and she struggled to keep her head up.

"Carrie, this is beyond passing him off."

She gritted her teeth, wanting to be indignant but knowing better.

"I'm so sorry, Sherilynn. I don't know what came over me. It was a complete lapse in judgment, and I swear to you it will not happen again." Carrie had her dignity and her pride, but she would grovel to keep her job. She'd helped shape this agency, given it her heart and soul for years. She couldn't imagine working anywhere else.

And yet, she'd slept with her client. After getting blackout drunk with him. There was a good chance she *wouldn't* work anywhere else after that.

"You're right," Sherilynn said. "It won't happen again. I'm so sorry to see you go, Carrie. You've been one of our greatest assets, and I was pleased to hear about the Marc Ryan role." She shook her head and shrugged. "But I don't believe we can continue our professional relationship considering your behavior last night."

Carrie forced a smile despite wanting to cry. This hit harder than any breakup she'd been through. This wasn't some replaceable man; it was her career and her reputation. She wanted to hunker down in the chair and fight for her job, to not move from this office until she convinced Sherilynn to let her stay, but arguing wouldn't change things.

"Thank you for everything you've done for me," she said, looking her in the eyes. "I truly appreciate the opportunity to have worked with you."

Sherilynn offered a sad smile. "You're one of the best there is." She leaned back in her chair and fiddled with a pen, the most relaxed Carrie had ever seen her. "I'm sorry to see you go, truly. But I know you understand I have no choice."

She wanted to say no, she didn't, but her respect for Sherilynn forced her to smile and nod, then rise from her chair and leave the office where several coworkers hovered by the door.

"Don't worry," Angela, a newer agent, said. "I'll take great care of Adam for you. Maybe we'll see each other at events since you're his new girlfriend? Oh, that was just a hookup, wasn't it?"

Carrie turned to the young girl, snide comments running through her mind, but she smiled and walked towards her desk. The chatter continued around her at a whisper, but Carrie knew what was being said. She'd been the one saying the same things in the past. *What an idiot*, they were saying. *She had everything going for her and threw her career away on a man.*

What an idiot, indeed.

———

Carrie headed straight back to her apartment and crawled into bed, silencing her phone and burying herself beneath the covers. When she woke at nearly six o'clock, the room was dark as a rainstorm had moved in and hidden the sun. The events of the past twenty-four hours floated back to her, and she wanted to vomit.

She grabbed her phone and saw five missed calls: three from Adam Hartley and two from Jack, her best friend who'd moved to London the previous summer. There was a text from Jack as well: *Is what I saw on People.com true? Are you all right?*

No, she wasn't. She couldn't imagine she would ever be again, actually. In one day, she'd gone from one of the agency's top agents to a cliche. She was about as far from all right as it got, but she didn't want to get into the details with Jack just yet. Talking to him about it would make it real, and she wasn't ready for it to be real.

She went into the bathroom in search of Motrin. Her head pounded even worse than when she'd awoken this morning, something she didn't think possible. She tapped out a couple pills and swallowed them, catching her own eye in the mirror, her hair a disaster and makeup smudged across her face.

Carrie didn't recognize the woman reflected back. The person she thought she was would never have allowed this to happen. She was confident, professional, and on top of her game.

Right?

She had friends—well, acquaintances—who were the same age and clearly did not have their lives in order. They partied all the time, or had married and divorced already, or had a husband and kids but complained and were miserable. The spectrum of togetherness in the early thirties seemed vast and diverse, but Carrie always placed herself securely towards the together side. She'd had a plan in place for her life since high school—where she would live, what she would do, who she would be.

Oh, God. She sounded like her mother.

Her voice ran through her mind, the "I told you so" Carrie was sure would come once her mother learned about this. If only she'd pursued a more stable career, one with a more reasonable workload, a more consistent schedule. One that allowed her to settle down and have a family. Preferably back on the east coast.

Carrie tapped out a third Motrin, tilted her head back, and swallowed it. She steadied herself on the sink. What was she supposed to do now? She needed a new job, but who would hire her while a photo of her galivanting with her top client was going viral?

Perhaps if she got away from LA for a little while, allowed the rumor mill to die down, and kept her distance from Adam-freaking-Hartley, she'd have a shot of preserving her reputation and getting in with another agency. But where would she go? Her savings account was smaller than she was comfortable with given she still had rent to maintain and other expenses. She never considered what she'd do if her career were pulled out from beneath her. She'd been on a steady path, and in less than twenty-four hours everything changed.

Carrie returned to her bedroom, flipped the light switch on, and surveyed the room. A couple books waited on her night-stand, a glass of water beside them. Her comforter, usually pulled neatly at each corner, was crumpled up in the center of her queen bed, shoved against the wall as a clear indicator she was single and alone.

Her phone pinged with a text message, and Carrie grabbed it off the nightstand. Another message from Jack. *Just checking in. Worried about you. Call when you can.*

Sinking into the mattress, she thought of her mother's offer of a paid tour of Europe as though she and fate knew what Carrie would need before she did. London was on the list of cities they'd planned to visit, and she could certainly use a Jack hug right about now.

She leaned back into her pillow and groaned. Was this really her only option? A month traipsing through foreign countries with her mother? It wasn't ideal, but the writing on the wall was clear: without her career, she didn't have a life in LA. And if her only hope of preserving her reputation enough to continue working here was going to Europe with her mother, then she'd have to suck it up and get through it.

Tears collected in the corners of her eyes as though her body was mourning the loss of her life here with or without her permission. She grabbed her phone and dialed her mother before she changed her mind. "Hi, Mom," she said when she answered, swiping at her eyes and holding back a sniffle. "I have some good news."

Chapter 4

Thursday evening, Anita waited at the baggage claim of the Buffalo airport, blending into the background as those around her reconnected with loved ones, each happy reunion increasing her nerves. She picked at her fingernails as passengers poured down the escalator, alternating between relief and disappointment each time an approaching woman proved to be a stranger and not her daughter.

Her mind was still playing catch-up after Carrie's call the other night. How her daughter actually managed the time away from work remained a mystery, but bigger yet was the shock that Carrie had asked in the first place. Anita had accepted her initial no, had been prepared to go back to Meredith and report that she'd tried but it didn't work. Yet here she stood, waiting for her daughter to come home so they could make plans to spend a month overseas together. Perhaps there was hope for them yet.

Anita couldn't recall the last time she'd picked Carrie up from the airport. It had almost always been Victor who collected her from her flight while she waited at home, preparing a meal Carrie usually declined. When she came back for Victor's funeral, she'd insisted on taking a cab to the house. She hadn't wanted to trouble her, or so she said.

Anita had acquiesced to her place as second-best parent over the years. Carrie was always a daddy's girl, but the study abroad incident during her junior year of college officially sealed Anita's place. If she could go back in time, she'd like to think she would have handled things differently. But, if she were honest with herself, she handled it the only way she was able to in the moment.

Nevertheless, she couldn't turn back time; she could only move forward and attempt to repair their relationship now before she lost her daughter for good. This trip dangled before her as a shiny promise that things would change. They had a whole month together to hash out their problems. Surely, that was enough time to start anew.

A roar of cheers and applause interrupted Anita's thoughts. To her right, a young couple returned to a group holding a sign congratulating them on their engagement. Behind the couple, Carrie stood out in the crowd of leggings, oversized hoodies, and sloppy buns. Instead, she wore a pair of dark skinny jeans, a white T-shirt, and a gray blazer, and her hair was in a pristine ponytail. She hardly looked the part of a weary traveler.

Carrie's eyes found her, and she smiled and waved. The friendly gestures calmed Anita's stomach slightly. As she came closer, however, there were dark circles under her eyes, and her smile was pained. Carrie stopped a few feet from her, fidgeting with her carry-on bag, leaving enough space between them so it would be awkward for Anita to lean in for a hug.

She cleared her throat. "How was the flight? You look exhausted."

Carrie straightened and tugged at her shirt. "I'm fine. I was just up most of the night packing. Maybe coming back today had been ambitious, but I'm here now."

Anita forced a smile and kept her mouth shut. Those eyes suggested far more than one night of missed sleep, but pressing her would only result in an argument.

They moved to the baggage carousel and waited for the sluggish belt to produce Carrie's bags. Carrie remained glued to her phone, likely catching up on all she'd missed while in the air, but Anita sensed by her stiffness something was troubling her. Still, she knew better than to comment. A mother's intuition might be spot on, but Carrie was never all that interested in her input on her life.

Finally, the bags appeared, and they headed out into the crisp September evening and walked to the car in silence.

Anita navigated to the highway, dusk chasing away the sunshine ahead of them. "How did your premiere go the other night?" she asked.

Carrie shifted and looked out the window. "It was good."

"I still can't believe you were able to get this time off," she continued. "But I suppose you deserve it. You work so hard."

Carrie simply nodded and went back to scrolling through her phone.

Anita fixed her attention on driving, unsure what else to say. The last time she'd seen her, the silence between them seemed appropriate. There'd been no words for the loss they'd endured. Now the silence lingered, a brutal testament to the relationship they truly shared.

As they pulled into the driveway, the dark house stood as a harsh reminder that Victor wasn't there, and with Carrie here his absence was new and overwhelming once again. They were no longer a family of three. There was no Victor inside to wrap Carrie in a hug and start her talking. Anita struggled to catch her breath as she turned off the car, feeling as though she'd been punched in the chest, but Carrie didn't seem to notice as she jumped out to collect her bags.

She stared at the house another moment, then forced herself out of the car as well. "Do you want help with your bags?" she asked, trying to keep her voice as even as possible.

Carrie shook her head. "We'll leave the heavy one for now," she said, then headed for the side door ahead of her.

Carrie flipped the lights on as she entered the kitchen, setting her bag down by the table.

"Are you hungry?" Anita asked, coming in behind her. "I could whip up some spaghetti."

"Not really," Carrie said, digging in her purse on the kitchen table for something.

"You really should eat something. You're looking rather thin." The words were out of her mouth before she considered them.

Carrie pressed her lips together. "It's called being fit, Mom."

Anita stiffened and glanced down at her own stomach, all the takeout this past year having left its mark. "I didn't mean anything by it," she said. Why did she never say the right thing?

Carrie stopped rummaging through her purse and looked right at her, visibly taking a deep breath. "Spaghetti sounds great," she said.

"Are you sure?"

"Oh my God, Mom. Yes."

"Okay, then." Anita quietly set about pulling out pots and ingredients. The silence grated on her, and she searched for some neutral topic. "When do you think will be the best day for us to leave?" Though they were on a time crunch given the expiring airline credits and Carrie's need to get back to LA sooner than later, they'd agreed it made the most sense for her to get back to Buffalo and then work out their specific travel plans from there.

"I'm not sure yet," Carrie answered. "We'll have to look up

the flight schedules and compare prices." She rubbed at her temples. "Do you have any ibuprofen?"

Anita set a large pot in the sink and turned on the water. "Sure, it's in our bathroom vanity. Second shelf, I think."

She disappeared down the hall, and Anita sighed. It was bound to be a little awkward at first, but it would get better. This was new territory for both of them.

After a few moments, Carrie walked back into the kitchen, an orange pill bottle in her hand.

"Why do you still have this?" she asked.

It was one of Victor's old prescriptions. His thyroid medication. "Oh, I didn't realize that was in there," Anita responded, turning her attention back to the sink.

Carrie stared at her. "It was right next to your toothpaste."

She shrugged as she lifted the pot of water from the sink. "I guess I hadn't noticed."

"Dad's entire nightstand is still covered with his things."

Anita forced herself to make eye contact with her daughter. "I haven't found time to sort through everything."

"It's been over eleven months."

She dropped the pot down on the stove harder than she'd intended, and a little water swished out onto the stovetop. "I'm well aware of how long it's been."

"I'm just saying."

"I didn't realize you were the grief expert, but if it means that much to you, then just throw the bottle out."

Carrie rolled her eyes and headed back down the hallway. A door slammed, then she returned empty-handed. "I'm actually not hungry," she said, collecting her bags. "I am tired, though, so I'll see you in the morning."

"Carrie..."

She closed her eyes, and Anita thought she saw a tear slip out. "I just...can't tonight. We'll talk in the morning." Without giving her a chance to explain further, Carrie turned and headed down the hallway to her old bedroom and shut the door.

Anita picked the pot back up off the burner and dumped the water into the sink. She set the empty pot in the drying rack and stood at the counter, trying to determine how the evening had gone from awkward to nasty so quickly. She felt naïve for expecting anything different. It wasn't like Victor being gone would magically make Carrie want to open up to her mother.

Her own appetite gone as well, she went into her bathroom and opened the medicine cabinet. The empty space beside her toothpaste mocked her. No matter how hard she tried to hold on to the way things were, nothing would bring Victor back.

In the trash can beside the vanity, the orange pill bottle lay on top of some tissues. Anita snatched it back out, desperate to put it back and continue pretending she didn't notice it there, continue pretending Victor still needed it. She clenched her fist over the bottle, stared at herself in the mirror, and then threw the bottle back in the trash can.

———

Despite her utter exhaustion, Carrie had a hard time finding sleep. She'd been eager to get away from LA, where she'd spent the past couple days holed up in her apartment, dodging calls from reporters and clients, but was a month away with her mother really her best and only option? What was that nonsense about her being too thin? She may have lost a bit of water weight the past couple of days, too distracted to eat properly, but if anything, it had done her some good. She'd been hanging onto a couple extra pounds since her father's funeral, so this just evened things out.

In the spirit of trying to make this work, though, Carrie had tried to be agreeable and move past it. But finding her parents' bedroom practically the same as she'd left it last year triggered more grief than she'd anticipated. Somehow, in the whirlwind of getting out of LA as quickly as possible, she hadn't fully considered what it would be like to come home to a house that looked like her father still lived there even though he'd been gone almost a year. She missed their ritual stop at Denny's on the way home, a quick little catch-up over pancakes, bacon, and a milkshake to share before heading back to the house.

Her last conversation with her father ran through her mind, the shame still fresh over the anger she'd taken out on him. If only she'd known. But there was no way for her to suspect that would have been their last conversation.

He'd called just as she got back home after dinner with Jack, her head spinning after he told her he took the job with Google. In London. Which meant in three and a half weeks, her best friend, her surrogate sibling, would be moving overseas.

"I just don't know why you guys are wasting your money," she told her dad after he confirmed they were still set to leave for Europe in just two days. "Mom will be miserable every day worrying about a bunch of silly nonsense. And she'll only stress you out too much."

"I told you there's nothing to worry about," her dad said. "I'll be fine."

Carrie sunk into her couch cushions and stared at the ceiling fan above her. Between increased work demands recently with new clients being added to her roster and Jack leaving, she didn't have the energy to worry about her dad. But after he'd shared with her that his doctor was "highly concerned" about his blood pressure, all she'd been able to do was worry.

"Dad. You need to tell Mom about your blood pressure."

He paused. "I have it under control," he said, his voice quiet and measured.

"No, I won't stop until you promise to tell her. I love you too much to risk your health because you're worried about coddling Mom's anxiety. I won't let her kill you!"

Her dad's silence confirmed she'd gone too far.

He drew in a deep, slow breath. "Marriage is often about keeping your spouse's best interests before your own," he said. "Someday you'll understand."

"Dad...I didn't mean to..."

"It's okay," he interrupted. "We'll talk tomorrow."

Before Carrie could say another word, he hung up. She tried calling him the following evening to apologize, but her call went to voicemail. The next call she received was her mother, hysterical, telling her there'd been an accident, and she needed to get back to Buffalo immediately.

Carrie let out a breath, sat up, and turned on the bedside lamp, surveying her old room. It looked much the same as it once had, though some of her parents' things had found their way in here over the years—her mom's old sewing machine, stacks of secondhand books her dad collected but hadn't sorted. Despite the strain earlier with her mother, this room was like a giant hug, the consoling "there, there" she needed as though her father were hiding in the shadows. Had he been with her out in LA and she'd just been too busy to notice, or was he here all along, waiting for her to come visit?

In search of a distraction, Carrie climbed out of bed and opened her old closet. A small bin labeled "Carrie" caught her attention. She pulled it out from beneath a couple other boxes as though removing a Jenga piece, then pulled off the lid. Inside were souvenirs from her childhood she hadn't wanted to throw away but couldn't justify lugging out to California. One item was her first Barbie doll, blond with a sleek, royal-blue evening gown. She ran her fingers through the doll's hair and recalled how she'd brushed it out each night before bed. When it came time to pack up her room for college, this had been the only childhood toy she'd saved. Though kids had been the furthest thing from her mind when she was eighteen, somewhere in the back of her mind she'd pictured her own daughter one day playing with this same doll.

A sob caught in her throat as she reflected on that optimistic young woman about to leave for California. For the past ten years, she'd focused on building her career and time slipped away. She watched as most of her friends married and started families and discussions of home renovations and childcare over coffee replaced dramatic dating stories shared over cocktails. Carrie listened and feigned interest, but she never wanted to be them. She was happy with her career, happy with the freedom being unattached brought.

She swallowed hard and stuffed the doll back into the bin. Shutting the closet door, Carrie crawled back into bed and propped up her pillows. She pulled her laptop from her carry-on and opened a fresh Word document. Feeling sorry for herself wouldn't get her career back on track. She needed a plan, even if she wasn't ready to execute it just yet. Carrie tapped away at the keyboard, brain dumping every possible contact who might be able to offer her a position once she returned.

After several minutes, she took a deep breath and looked over her list, pleased with the results. With over ten years in this industry, she knew a lot of people. One of these would pan out. It had to.

Chapter 5

Anita woke the following morning to light streaming through her bedroom window. The sounds of dishes clinking and pattering feet wafted down the hallway, and it took a moment to remember it was Carrie, not Victor.

She stayed in bed and watched her ceiling fan spin for a few minutes. Once she left her room, she would have to be conscientious of every word she spoke. She'd have to decipher her daughter's sighs and eye rolls and find a way to avoid blowing this whole plan up before it even got off the ground.

Anita finally pulled herself out of bed and grabbed her robe off the back of her bathroom door, then made the bed before heading into the kitchen. Part anxiety and part avoidant behavior, but if she didn't make the bed, it would bother her all day.

In the kitchen, she found Carrie at the table staring at her MacBook Pro and sipping from a Starbucks takeout cup. The travel guides and a copy of Anita and Victor's original itinerary were spread out on the table beside her. She glanced down at her bathrobe and marveled at how productive Carrie had been before she'd even woken up.

"Good morning," she ventured, her tone quiet and cautious.

"Morning." Carrie didn't look up from her laptop screen. "I got you a coffee. It's on the counter."

"Oh, thank you." Anita found the Starbucks cup, pulled the lid off, and added a scoop of sugar and a dash of creamer. She took a sip. Why did people spend several dollars on this when her home-brewed coffee tasted better and she didn't need to leave the house for it? Still, she was grateful for the jolt of caffeine and the gesture.

She joined Carrie at the table, trying to gauge her daughter's mood. "Where did you find the itinerary?" she asked.

Carrie squinted at her over her laptop, her hands suspended above the keyboard. "Oh, I had a copy saved in my email. Dad sent it so I'd know your plans while you were away."

Of course. What else had Victor taken care of that she had been oblivious to?

The weight of navigating this new phase of life with Carrie sat on Anita's chest. Carrie seemed to have forgotten their tiff from the night before, although it was possible her intense concentration on trip planning was a means of distraction. Either way, pretending it hadn't happened worked just as well for Anita. She shifted in her seat and forced herself to open a conversation. After all, Carrie had said they'd talk in the morning, so here was her opportunity. "How are the plans going?"

Carrie took her hands off the computer long enough to reach for her coffee. "I'm still pricing out tickets to London," she said. "But it looks like Tuesday will be our best option."

Anita ran her finger along her coffee cup lid. Four days. It seemed so far, yet so close. She'd been here before, on the precipice of leaving, and a sense of déjà vu overtook her.

For all the preparation she and Victor had put into their plans, it had never felt real to her that they would actually get there. She couldn't see them strolling through Gaudí's park, or window shopping on the Champs-Élysées, or eating authentic pasta in Italy. She worried her inability to visualize the trip was an omen but shook off her concern and pressed on. In hindsight, should she have taken her concerns more seriously? That was the tricky part about anxiety; she never knew what was legitimate.

Anita made a mental note to discuss this with Meredith on Monday. She smiled at the thought of her expression when she told her they were leaving for London the next day. She wouldn't believe she'd followed through. Anita could hardly believe it herself.

"What can I help with?" she asked, leaning over the table slightly, trying to decipher Carrie's notes in the itinerary's margins.

"I think I've got it covered." She continued typing.

"Oh." Carrie was likely trying to be helpful, but she and Victor had this trip planned to a T. They had detailed schedules for each day, down to their wake-up times. After decades of planning, their list of sights to see was long, and having a solid plan in place was the only way to guarantee they'd see everything they wanted to. If Anita was going to summon the courage to fly overseas, she certainly wasn't coming home feeling as though she'd missed out on anything.

"Do you have the list of the places we wanted to go?"

Carrie pointed to the itinerary. "Yeah. A week each in London, Paris, Barcelona, and Rome."

Anita shook her head. "No, I mean all of the sights we wanted to go to in each city."

Carrie waved a hand haphazardly. "Yeah, we'll figure that all out afterward."

"It's just...there were a lot of places on our list."

"I know, Mom. But we need to sort out our dates and transportation between cities first. Then we can figure out the rest."

She had a point. Of course it was jumping the gun to start

planning all of the sights before they had nailed down their specific travel dates. Still, Anita's stomach clenched thinking about the possibility of not seeing everything she'd wanted. If she continued to press the issue right now, though, she would only tick Carrie off. But she needed something to keep her busy and her mind off of the planning process.

"How about some breakfast to go with your coffee? Maybe some waffles?"

Carrie's eyes darted up from her computer screen. "With chocolate chips and whipped cream?"

"You've got it!"

Anita stood and pulled the mixing bowls from the cupboard like she used to when Carrie was younger, doing elementary school homework at the kitchen table on a Saturday morning. Victor would walk in any moment smelling of soap and mouthwash. He'd kiss her on the cheek, then pour himself a cup of coffee and wait with Carrie for their waffles.

"I do have one question, actually," Carrie said.

"What's that?" Anita pulled the flour canister from the pantry.

"The way it lines up now, it looks like we'll be in Barcelona for...the anniversary. Was there something specific you wanted to do that day? We could rearrange the order of the cities if we need to."

Anita set the flour on the counter, the canister suddenly heavier. How had she not connected that they would be in Europe for the anniversary of Victor's passing? As if that day weren't going to be challenging enough to get through, she'd now have the giant reminder of all he'd missed out on surrounding her the entire day. But she was committed now. And besides, maybe this was a sign from Victor. Maybe he would be there waiting for her.

Anita cycled through the list of sights they wanted to see,

and she smiled as she settled on Victor's biggest must-see. "Barcelona will be perfect. We'll go to the Sagrada Familia," she said. He had been overly enthusiastic to see the magnificent cathedral still in the process of being completed almost one hundred years after Gaudí's death. While every other cathedral on his list had long been completed, this one was an ongoing project, a blend of modern technology and past architectural genius.

Carrie nodded. "Sagrada it is."

She returned to her plans, and Anita paused a moment before continuing with the waffles. She was in for a roller coaster the next several weeks, no doubt. But when she closed her eyes to picture her and Carrie strolling down the streets of Barcelona together, approaching Sagrada Familia, an image appeared, and that eased her mind.

———

After a few days of tiptoeing around Carrie while she determined an itinerary, booked flights and train fare, and made hotel reservations, Anita settled into Meredith's office Monday afternoon, still in disbelief it had only been a week since their last conversation.

"How has your week been?" Meredith asked as she sat in her armchair and reached for her coffee mug.

Anita beamed with nervous excitement, anticipating the stamp of therapeutic approval for a job well done. "Well, I need to cancel our appointment next week," she said as casually as possible. "In fact, the next four appointments." A giant smile spread across her face. "Carrie and I leave for London tomorrow."

Meredith's eyes widened, and she dropped her mug to her lap. "Are you serious?"

Anita nodded. "I called her after our appointment last week, figuring you were right. The worst she could say was no. And she did, initially, but then she somehow managed to get the time off from work, and she called me back. She flew in Thursday evening and quickly got everything rebooked." Anita shook her head slightly. "I'm still amazed she actually got the time off work."

"Wow. That's incredible. You must be so excited."

The smile slipped from her face. "I am excited. But also nervous."

"About the flight?"

"The flight, the language barriers, the navigation." She paused and let out a sigh. "But mostly, I'm nervous about spending so much time alone with Carrie."

Meredith's forehead creased. "Why does that make you nervous?"

"We've never spent this much time alone together. Never. There's always been tension between us—I worry for her well-being, and apparently I overdo it, and that upsets her." Anita looked down at her lap and rubbed her hands on her jeans. "Without Victor here to be our buffer, it's just harder to pretend." The admission was like a stab through her own heart.

"Well, she wouldn't be here if she didn't want to be," Meredith said. "Arranging a month away from her job couldn't have been easy."

"That's true," Anita said, though she still didn't fully buy it.

"And now you have this incredible opportunity to resolve your issues and repair your relationship."

She swallowed a lump in her throat. "I have no idea how to even begin to do that, though."

"Well, you take it one step at a time." Meredith grabbed a pen from her side table and propped her notepad up on her lap. "Let's break it up into smaller goals. What's your overall goal?"

Anita cleared her throat. "To have a better relationship with my daughter."

Meredith nodded and transcribed her words onto the piece of paper. "Great. So, what's one small thing you can do to work towards that goal?"

"Aren't you supposed to have the answers?" Anita teased. She knew the therapy drill by now, but she never stopped hoping Meredith would wave a magic wand and fix everything.

"I could have a conversation with Carrie," she said, serious again. "A real conversation about something important to her. We haven't really talked about anything of substance since she got back to Buffalo."

"Perfect," Meredith said, again transcribing her goal onto the notepad. She ripped the sheet off and handed it to Anita. "Now, bring this with you as a reminder to yourself. You've got this. Ask some questions, listen intently. Honestly, she likely needs her mother more than ever right now, so just be there for her and let her come to you."

Anita folded the sheet of paper and slipped it into her purse. She could do this, she assured herself. Just let Carrie come to her.

"And Anita?" Meredith asked.

"Hmm?"

Her mouth widened into a giant smile. "Have fun!"

———

Anita returned from her therapy appointment to an empty house. Carrie had texted to let her know she was running out to grab food, a welcome relief as she still had packing to do and didn't feel like making and cleaning up dinner. Besides, her appetite had been held hostage by her nerves all day in anticipation of their flight tomorrow morning.

She tossed her keys and purse on the kitchen counter and grabbed a glass of water, reveling in Meredith's approval. It felt good to have made some progress, to have her pleased with her initiative and to have a plan in place to work towards improving things with Carrie.

She pulled the paper Meredith had written her goals down on from her purse, then went to her bedroom where her suitcase sat on her bed, taunting her. Carrie must have put it there while Anita was out. She froze a moment, memories of the night Victor died flooding her mind, but then forced the thoughts away. They needed to leave by four a.m. tomorrow to get up to the Toronto airport in time. The short drive up was worth the significantly lower airfare and direct flight into London, but the early departure meant Anita didn't have the luxury of getting lost in her feelings tonight.

She opened the suitcase and pulled out a water-colored notebook. She opened the cover and exchanged the sheet from Meredith with the folded paper she'd stuffed in there last year. Her original packing list. She laid the list out beside her suitcase and worked her way through the items. Toothbrush—check. Toothpaste—check. Face wash—check. Voltage adapters.

Anita picked the list back up and sat on the bed, the two little words staring back at her. Every item above this had a checkmark beside it from last year. Her life had stopped with the reminder of the item she'd forgotten to buy, and now her heart felt like it was going to seize.

Abbey Road had been playing on the bedroom speaker, the little Bluetooth gadget Carrie bought them the previous Christmas. Anita still had no idea how to operate the thing, but that was what Victor was for. They stood on their respective sides of the bed, stuffing their suitcases in silence until Anita came to the voltage adapters.

"Darn it!" she'd said.

Victor looked up, the wrinkles around his eyes deepening as he squinted at her over his reading glasses. "What's the matter?"

"I forgot to pick up another voltage adapter."

"But we have two already."

"I know, but I wanted to have a third in case anything happens to one or we need an extra." Anita sighed and reached for her car keys off the nightstand. "I guess I'll run out to Walmart."

"I can go," Victor offered. "Why don't you get dinner started, and then we can come back to this after we eat?"

Anita agreed and went into the kitchen to preheat the oven. How could she have forgotten the voltage adapter? To be fair, her mind had been a frazzled mess the past few days. Between trying to remember everything she needed to pack and constantly calming her mind about their upcoming flight, she should have been amazed this was the only thing she'd forgotten.

Victor came into the kitchen with his brown leather jacket on and keys in hand. "I'll be back," he said.

They kissed quickly, a little peck that had become so routine over the years. "Love you," she said as he headed out to the garage.

"Love you too."

Anita had busied herself with making dinner. She pulled an already opened bottle of Riesling from the fridge and grabbed a couple of wineglasses from the cupboard. They had a few glasses left in the bottle from last night, and it needed to go. Besides, anything to help calm Anita's nerves was appreciated.

Half an hour later, the chicken breasts were done, and Anita put one on each of their plates, then scooped some broccoli and rice beside them. Surely Victor would be home momentarily; Walmart was only about five minutes from their house. He'd probably gotten overwhelmed comparing the different options and lost track of time. Or ran into an old friend and was chatting away. Anita set the plates on the table and picked up the house phone to call his cell, only to hear the chirping sound of Victor's ringtone coming from the living room where his phone sat charging.

She poured the last of the Riesling into her glass and sat at the table, waiting for him to come through the door, apologizing for whatever had held him up and caused dinner to go cold. Another few minutes passed, and then the house phone rang. Probably a telemarketer. They were the only ones rude enough to call during dinner hours. Anita downed the last sip of wine and grabbed the phone.

"Is this Mrs. Lorello?" the voice on the other end asked.

"This is. Who's calling please?"

"Ma'am, this is Officer Watkins with the Amherst Police Department."

Anita straightened in her chair. She looked at the door, willing Victor to walk through so she could see he was all right, that this call was something silly and not what she knew in her gut it was.

"There's been an accident. I'm afraid your husband is being transported to the emergency room at Millard Fillmore right now."

"Is he...is everything okay?"

There was a pause, the heavy kind that sobers a person instantly so the two glasses of wine were no more than a distant memory for Anita along with all the plans she and Victor had made for their future.

"You should get there as quickly as possible," the officer said.

The front door opening jarred Anita from the memory. She sniffled and folded the list back up, slipping it onto her night-stand as Carrie appeared in the bedroom doorway.

Carrie tilted her head to the side, her hand on the doorknob. "You okay?" she asked.

She nodded, though her head felt like it was moving too quickly. "Just packing."

"I grabbed some Chinese for dinner," Carrie said.

"I thought you hated Chinese food."

She smiled. "No, Dad hated Chinese food. *I* think it's amazing."

Anita chuckled. "Dad did hate Chinese. I'll be right there."

Carrie disappeared, and she took one last look at her suitcase before following her. This wasn't the same as last year. One way or another, that suitcase would be packed, and she and Carrie would fly out to London tomorrow morning. She just had to push past the memories.

Chapter 6

Despite the early hour, the Toronto airport buzzed with passengers awaiting their flights. Families huddled together, animatedly discussing which sights they were most excited to see on their vacation. Businessmen typed away at smartphones and laptops, their destination less important than whatever meetings awaited them. Anita longed to join in the excitement, but something gnawed at her. This was all wrong.

She closed her eyes and tried to tune out the surrounding noise. A young couple opposite her struggled to calm their infant, and Anita prayed she and Carrie would be far away from them on the seven-hour flight. Trying to calm her racing thoughts and oncoming waves of anxiety would be challenging enough without adding a crying baby into the mix. While she was grateful they'd found a direct flight to avoid several takeoffs and landings, the thought of being suspended above the ocean for several hours with no control over her fate had Anita in a tizzy of anxiety.

Carrie, on the other hand, seemed entirely calm, as though this were any routine morning. Beside Anita, her nose was buried in a book she had picked up at a stand on their way to the gate.

She cleared her throat. "Did you ever get around to booking the baking class I mentioned?"

Carrie lifted her head from her book, her eyes heavy. "Baking class?"

Had she seriously forgotten? "Yes, the macaron class in Paris." Anita tried to keep her tone calm, but her knee began bouncing.

"Oh, right. I didn't yet, but I'm sure we can book it once we're there."

Carrie returned to her book. Case closed, discussion over. The class might not be important to her, but it was one of the highlights Anita had been looking forward to. She'd spent countless hours finding the best one and signed up months in advance. She had a list of potential backups if their original option was booked on such short notice, but she'd left it at home assuming she wouldn't need it.

But Carrie wasn't the plan in advance type. And she wasn't much into baking either.

What had Anita been thinking going through with this? She'd be lucky if she and Carrie lasted the month without making things far worse between them. Her hope that this would improve their relationship now seemed far-fetched. Carrie appeared oblivious to Anita's anxiety building like a tsunami wave about to crash over her, or maybe she was fully aware of it, waiting for her to jump out of her chair and run back home. A large part of her wanted to do just that, but Carrie had asked off work to join her for this trip, and that alone gave her a small speck of hope to cling to.

Besides, she was so close to finally making it to Europe. She was generally a homebody, content to stay within her comfort bubble and stick to her routine. But there was something about finally realizing this dream that made her want to overcome her nausea at the thought of flying and her discomfort with her daughter to finally stand in the places where the history she'd read about had taken place. To stand in Italy where her grandmother had been born. To sit in cafes where her favorite authors may have written and pondered life. She was too close to following through on the trip of a lifetime, but while she should be overjoyed, instead her chest constricted and breathing became difficult.

Not here.

She stood, hoping to make it to the privacy of a bathroom stall, but dizziness overtook her and blurred her vision, and she dropped back into her seat. Her heart pounded, and Anita pressed her hand against her chest in a futile attempt to slow it down.

"Mom?" Carrie asked, her eyes wide.

She pointed at her purse, and Carrie hurriedly passed it over. She riffled through it until she found the orange pill bottle. "Water," she said.

Carrie gave her the bottled water she'd bought after clearing security. Anita swallowed a pill and closed her eyes. *In and out, in and out.*

Her heart rate began slowing, and she opened her eyes. "Thank you," she whispered to Carrie. Her poor daughter looked shell-shocked, though everyone else nearby didn't seem to have noticed, all of them carrying on with their conversations or their focus trained on a phone or laptop.

"Mom?" Carrie's voice had a childlike quality, worried and nervous. She hadn't heard that voice in a very long time.

"I'm fine," Anita answered. She wanted to offer more assurance, but it was all she could muster in the aftermath of the panic attack.

Carrie's eyebrows scrunched together. "Are you sure?"

"Ladies and gentlemen, we're about to start the boarding process," the gate agent announced over the speaker system.

Anita smiled as wide as she could. "I guess that's our cue," she said. She gathered her bag, passport, and boarding pass. If she couldn't feel calm and collected, she could at least look the part. Inside, she screamed this was a terrible idea. The thought of taxiing down the runway and then being launched up into the sky for several hours made her breath hitch in her throat. But the images in her mind of them bonding over croissant and espresso, however unlikely, were enough to resign her to whatever fate awaited them on this flight.

Carrie stared at her a moment longer, then led the way to the gate. Anita handed her ticket and passport to the gate agent. Could this young woman even fathom how momentous this occasion was for her? Likely not. To her, it was just another workday. People flew overseas all day, every day. Anita was merely one more passenger.

"Enjoy your flight." The woman handed back her ticket and passport, a polite smile plastered on her face.

Anita followed Carrie down the corridor and onto the plane, awkwardly maneuvering herself and her carry-on down the narrow aisle until she stopped at their row.

"Do you want the window or aisle?" Carrie asked, hoisting her carry-on into the overhead compartment.

"I'm fine with either one."

Carrie's jaw clenched as she stared at her. "Mom, I'm fine on planes. Is the window going to be better or worse for your anxiety?"

Anita's cheeks warmed. She hoped no one else heard, though the man who was all but on top of her likely did. She turned to find a line of agitated people waiting for her and Carrie to clear the aisle. She spoke softly, feeling like a chastised child. "The window would probably be better."

Carrie reached out her hand. "Let me take your carry-on."

Anita rolled her bag to her, then settled in beside the window. She looked down at her wedding ring, a simple solitaire with a white gold band. Nothing would have been different had Victor been here instead, but it seemed less shameful to rely on her husband so heavily.

Carrie sat beside her and jammed her oversized purse beneath the seat in front of her with her foot. "Do you need anything?" she asked.

Anita shook her head, unable to speak or look at Carrie. She needed a hand to hold and someone to tell her in a soothing, calm voice everything would be fine, but she couldn't ask those things of her daughter.

"Mom, I'm sorry I snapped at you. I just didn't want to hold up the line."

"It's fine, dear." She cleared her throat and rubbed her hands over her jeans.

Carrie rubbed her forehead, then dug out her book again.

The plane reversed slowly, and the flight attendant's voice came over the loudspeaker to rattle off the emergency instructions as the plane taxied to the runway. Anita pulled out the safety booklet, then stuffed it back into the seat pocket and grabbed the Oprah magazine she'd purchased instead, her mind mellowing as the Xanax kicked in. She'd already been through the worst of tragedies. If her plane were to crash, she wasn't certain she wanted to know how to get herself out alive.

———

Once they were in the air and the Xanax took full effect, Anita put her magazine away and tried to sleep. But every jolt of the plane brought her back to full consciousness, and when they finally hit a smooth stretch, the baby started crying.

Carrie seemed to have no trouble sleeping, though. Shortly after takeoff, her book sunk into her lap and her head drooped. She looked peaceful, the opposite of how she'd seemed since she arrived in Buffalo. Anita took the book, slipped the bookmark between its pages, and tucked it away. It brought her back to when Carrie was in elementary school; all the nights she had gone into her room to check on her and found her passed out on top of a book. Though she insisted Carrie not stay up reading past bedtime, how could she be mad her daughter loved to read? There were worse ways she could have spent her evenings.

This was the first time since Carrie came home that Anita could sit and study her daughter. Every other moment they'd spent together so far, she had to watch her words, watch her staring, watch everything. She couldn't recall the last time she had felt comfortable and able to be herself with Carrie, but it was probably around the time she'd found her passed out with books in her bed.

How had this person who Anita's world had once revolved around become such a stranger? As a stay-at-home mom, there'd once been nothing that happened in Carrie's life that she didn't know about. But then Carrie had gone off to preschool, and while her world expanded, Anita's grew lonelier. With each year that passed, she was edged out a bit more. Her advice was less and less welcome until one day it wasn't sought at all. And then eventually her daughter stopped sharing anything about her life with her, and she was left to learn it all secondhand from Victor.

"You have to stop projecting your anxiety into your conversations," he had told her once many years ago, shortly before Carrie left for college. "Carrie's a bright girl. She'll make her mistakes, but they're hers to make."

While Anita didn't disagree with Victor, his advice was easier said than done. Carrie was absolutely a bright girl, but she put too much trust in things working out in her favor. She didn't seem to realize the world wasn't fair, that just because you wanted something didn't mean it would be yours.

A ding overhead brought Anita's attention back to the present.

"Ladies and gentlemen, the captain has turned on the fasten seatbelt sign. Please remain in your seats for the remainder of the flight. We will now begin our descent into Heathrow Airport."

She returned her seat entirely upright and clutched the armrests. Her seatbelt had remained buckled around her waist the entire flight other than one trip to the restroom, no longer than absolutely necessary. She lifted the window shade and looked down at a landscape that appeared not much different from the one they'd flown away from several hours ago.

"Wow, we're here already?" Carrie asked, stretching her legs and leaning forward to see out the window. She covered her mouth as she yawned.

Anita glanced over at her daughter, envying her rested, calm demeanor. She had held hope of some mother-daughter heart-to-heart conversation on the flight now that the planning was out of the way and they could focus on other things.

Let her come to you. Anita replayed Meredith's advice in her mind like a mantra. There was plenty of time.

The plane inched closer to the ground and shook as the wheels emerged from hibernation. She inhaled sharply and reminded herself this was a routine part of the process.

"You okay?" Carrie asked.

"I will be." Anita sipped her water, then stuffed the bottle back into her bag. She'd taken another Xanax about an hour ago when Carrie was sleeping, but it didn't seem to be a match against this anxiety.

They moved closer to the ground each second, the plane's

speed now obvious as trees and buildings flew past the window. Anita closed her eyes. As much as she wanted the flight to end, anticipating the plane bouncing as it met pavement made her agitated.

Finally, the wheels touched down, and the plane screeched to a stop. Anita opened her eyes, amazed. For all her worrying, the landing was one of the smoothest she'd experienced. Other passengers clapped, and she let out a breath. "I can't believe we're here," she whispered.

"See? The scary part is over," Carrie said.

If only her daughter understood. The flight might be behind them, but for Anita there would be no end of hurdles to overcome for the next month. Unfamiliar cities, menus she couldn't read, metro systems. It was all intimidating.

Next up: immigration. She clutched her passport as they deplaned and followed the crowd.

When they approached the immigration desks, the line was shorter than Anita anticipated. Passengers breezed through the turnstiles, quickly moving on to their destination.

"Next!" an officer called from one of the windows.

She hesitated.

"Mom, go ahead," Carrie said, pointing haphazardly at the open window, then returned to fiddling with the zipper on her bag.

Anita approached the officer and handed over her passport, a tentative smile frozen on her face as he examined first the book, then her.

"Reason for your visit?" he asked as he inserted her passport into a machine.

"Oh, um." Anita drew a blank. She forced her smile wider, trying to remember what she and Victor practiced last year.

"Business or leisure?" the officer prompted impatiently.

"Leisure," Anita said, relieved to have the correct answer provided. "I'm here with my daughter." Her stomach tightened.

The officer turned his attention back to his computer screen, then stamped the first page of her book and handed it back. At her age, she felt silly being excited about a fresh passport stamp, but it was her first ever. Until last year, she'd never owned a passport.

"Welcome to London," the officer said.

Anita smiled, then pushed her way through the turnstile where she was reunited with Carrie.

"Ready?" Carrie asked, tucking her passport back into her purse.

She straightened as she fell into step beside her, full of resolve. She was through the flight, and immigration was less intimidating than she'd expected. Maybe this wouldn't be so challenging after all.

Carrie led the way outside to the taxi stand, the crisp air and sunshine welcome after the stuffiness of the plane and airports. They slid into a waiting cab, Carrie gave the driver the hotel address, and they settled in for the half-hour cab ride.

Out her window, Anita took in her first glimpses of Europe as the sun began to fade into evening. She was in a country hundreds of years older than the United States, yet it didn't *feel* old. There were old buildings, but more modern ones filled the spaces between them. Pedestrians passed by one another on the sidewalks, dressed much like people back home, checking their phones as they walked. Public buses exhaled to a stop in front of designated signs. New moms walked along with their strollers, couples passed by with dogs, and life continued on much the same as in Buffalo.

Anita smiled to herself, unable to believe she'd expected this to be terrifying. It was different, of course, but she was overcome with excitement, not fear. But wasn't this precisely what she always did—built things up in her mind to the point she had no choice but to be terrified?

She looked over to Carrie, who stared at a text message on her phone. "Catching up on work?" Anita asked.

Carrie's head shot up, and she blinked a few times before seeming to understand the question. "Oh, yeah. Just some loose ends to take care of."

"Will you have to work a lot throughout the trip?"

"I don't know, Mom," she snapped, closing out of the message and tossing her phone in her purse.

Anita turned her attention back to the window and bit her lower lip. She'd thought work would be a safe topic of conversation, but she was wrong once again. She should probably get used to long stretches of silence. That was better than constantly having her head bit off for saying the wrong thing.

The cab moved to the side of the road and stopped in front of their hotel. She recognized it from the photos she had seen online when she and Victor booked it originally. Carrie hopped out with the cab driver to collect their luggage from the trunk, but Anita took a moment to collect herself first.

Finally, she stepped out onto the sidewalk and a young woman zipped past her to join a group of people gathered at an outside table at the pub a couple doors down. Carrie already had their bags on a trolley.

"Mom, do you have your card?" she asked, watching her expectantly.

Anita nodded and fiddled with her purse, trying to undo the locking system on the anti-theft bag Victor had bought her for a birthday present last year. It was a bit bulkier than her other purses, but it promised to be slash-proof and RFID blocking to protect her passport information.

Carrie tapped a foot, her eyes wide and her lips drawn into a straight line.

"Got it!" Anita declared when she finally freed the zipper and found her card. She handed it over with a flourish, pointedly not looking at her daughter. The driver quickly processed her payment, then Anita followed Carrie into the hotel.

"Reservation for Lorello," Carrie said as they approached the front desk.

While Carrie handled checking in, Anita turned around and surveyed the hotel lobby. Other guests passed through, seemingly carefree and enjoying their vacation while a dark cloud followed her. She closed her eyes a moment and pictured Victor beside her instead. How things would have been different had they made it here last year. She was grateful to be here now, but every ounce of excitement was tinged with sadness at what should have been.

"All set," Carrie said, holding up the key cards. They found the elevator and rode to the fourth floor in silence.

They entered their room and Carrie immediately tossed her bag on the bed and flung it open.

"You really should check the bed first before you do that," Anita said, unable to stop herself.

Carrie stared at her blankly.

"For...bed bugs." She shook her head. "Never mind. That's silly."

"No. I just didn't think about it."

Anita placed her own bag on the provided luggage rack but noticed Carrie didn't move hers, nor did she check the bed for bugs.

Carrie pulled a cosmetic bag from her suitcase. "I'm going to take a quick shower, then we can venture out for some dinner."

Anita glanced at the clock. It was already past eight o'clock, and her stomach was aching, but another thirty minutes or so wasn't worth triggering an argument their first night here.

Carrie disappeared into the bathroom, and the shower

turned on, followed a moment later by the curtain closing. Anita lifted the blanket on her bed, then pulled back the sheets, inspecting for any sign of bugs. She did the same with Carrie's, then sunk onto the bed and looked out the window. The pressure of figuring out what to say and how to say it lifted temporarily, and she exhaled, gearing up for the evening ahead.

Carrie's phone vibrated on the nightstand where she'd left it plugged in. Anita peered over, then forced herself to look away. Something was off with Carrie since she'd arrived in Buffalo, but she had been reluctant to talk about it. Still, prying and snooping on her phone wasn't the way to connect with her daughter. Of course, if Victor were here, he'd have coaxed it out of her by now. He likely wouldn't have even had to ask; Carrie would have gladly volunteered the information to her dad all on her own.

There she went again, envying her dead husband. The reality was he wasn't here and wouldn't be here ever again. Anita stared out the window where the city lit up as dusk took over.

It was her fault her husband wasn't here to see this alongside her. And that was something she needed to learn to live with.

———

Carrie let the hot water trickle down her back, wishing she could send all her stress down the drain with it. She'd forgotten how long a day of travel always felt, and her mother certainly hadn't made it any easier. Seeing her gasping for air this morning brought back memories Carrie didn't want to revisit and left her wishing she'd chosen a different way to deal with her job loss. She would earn her free trip over the next several weeks, that was for sure.

At the moment, though, her most pressing concern was figuring out her next step. The entire drive up to Toronto this morning, she'd gone over her list of contacts in her mind, weighing the pros and cons of reaching out immediately or waiting a couple of weeks for things to blow over. Ultimately, she decided waiting a couple of weeks was the best option, but the idea of sitting in career limbo unnerved her. At least she would have some sightseeing and touristy adventures to keep her mind busy.

She turned off the shower and wrapped a fresh, fluffy towel around her long brown hair. She rubbed moisturizer on her face, the bags under her eyes surprising her, evidence of the toll this week had taken. She threw on some makeup, adding extra concealer beneath her eyes, then left the bathroom, a trail of steam following her into the air-conditioned room.

"It's your turn, Mom." Carrie looked over at the far bed where her mother was fast asleep.

Smiling, she rummaged through her bag for yoga pants and a T-shirt. The city lights outside the window caught her attention as she got dressed. This was her third time in London, but the city hadn't lost its ability to amaze her. Traveling always humbled her, magnifying how small her role in the world and human history was. She was simply one more person trying to make it through without leaving behind a complete mess.

She grabbed her iPhone off the nightstand. One more missed call and numerous text messages from Jack. She sunk onto the bed, staring at his messages. What kind of best friend was she? She hadn't even told him she was coming to London, still debating if she wanted to see him. A large part of her wanted to continue avoiding him, avoid speaking aloud everything that had happened and all the ways she'd managed to mess up her life, and continue living in a bubble of denial. But it had been six months since she'd last seen her best friend, and she missed him. She hadn't fully appreciated the hole his absence left in her life until now. She'd been too busy working. The story of her life.

Her brain was too jet-lagged to get into everything tonight, but she couldn't avoid Jack any longer. Not if she wanted to avoid irreversible damage to their friendship.

Sorry for ignoring you, she responded. *It's been an interesting week. I just got into London with my mom. No, I'm not joking. It's a long story. Let's meet up tomorrow?*

She set the phone back on the nightstand, a weight lifted now that she'd replied to Jack. She grabbed her book and a granola bar from her carry-on and snuggled into her bed, her hair still damp as she didn't want to wake her mother with the blow dryer. Her stomach rumbled. She could use a proper dinner, but the possibility of a quiet evening to relax and recharge before jumping into the role of European tour guide was more enticing.

She ripped open the granola bar and took a bite, but her phone pinged with a notification before she could open her book. It was a Facebook reminder to look at her memories for the day. She opened the app and a photo of her and Dad from last year appeared. She had been home for a visit, and they'd gone out for dinner at their favorite Italian restaurant downtown. The visit ended up being the last time she saw him in person, the photo the last one taken of the two of them together.

Her heart became heavier as she took in the photo and thought about that last trip home before his accident. Living across the country had allowed Carrie to go back to life almost as usual after her dad's funeral, and so far, she'd avoided a total breakdown despite missing him. But after returning to her childhood home without him there and without the distraction of work, thoughts and feelings she'd been burying were starting to come up. Their last phone call, in particular, kept running through her mind. Had she told him she loved him before they hung up? She couldn't remember for sure, but she was pretty sure she hadn't.

She glanced over to her mother sleeping in the other bed. She'd successfully deflected any deep conversations so far, but with the two of them constantly together for the upcoming weeks, how would she continue evading questions about work and LA? The thought of telling her mother she had been fired horrified her. This wasn't the daughter she wanted to be, the one who threw away her career over a man. This wasn't the picture of her life she wanted to paint for her mother. She wanted to prove to her that her life in LA was something to be proud of, that she didn't need a traditional marriage and kids to live a full life.

If her dad were here, he'd be the one to break the news to her mom. He would absorb the judgmental look and calm her down before Carrie had to face her herself. But now it was up to her to handle her mother. She just had to pray she'd figure out her next step before she ultimately had to admit the real reason she had been able to come on this trip.

Chapter 7

Anita woke the following morning and blinked as she looked around, taking in the unfamiliar bedding and artwork. She looked to her left where Carrie lay sound asleep in the other bed, and her memory jarred.

She was in London. She'd made it.

She pushed herself up to a sitting position and propped a pillow behind her. Carrie was curled into the fetal position with her comforter wrapped tightly around her, the way she'd slept since she was a child. It brought her back to nights when Carrie was far too old to need to be checked on, but she had snuck into her room in the middle of the night anyway. After days when they had fought or days when Anita felt particularly left out of her daughter's life, it gave her comfort to see her sleeping the same way she once had in her crib, back when she'd been most dependent upon her mother.

Victor had caught her once after getting up to use the bathroom. "She's in high school, Annie," he said.

"I know. I just needed to see that she was all right."

Victor had raised his eyebrow and then dropped the conversation, clearly not understanding Anita's strange need to watch her daughter sleep. Victor and Carrie had their special bond, but he would never understand the physical pull a mother felt to ensure her baby was safe and sound, no matter how old that baby may be. Perhaps her constant need to check everything was as it should be, particularly when it came to Carrie, was a lingering effect of her miscarriages, but Anita would rather be safe than sorry. And yet, while the most important thing to her was ensuring her daughter's safety, it was that exact instinct that often grated on Carrie and pushed her further away.

Carrie stirred, opened her eyes, and looked at Anita. "Morning," she said, her voice crackly. "How long have you been up?"

"Just a minute. Sorry I fell asleep on you last night. I guess the week finally caught up with me."

"No worries." She climbed out of bed and gathered clothes from her suitcase.

Anita cleared her throat and sat up straighter. "So, what's the plan for today?" she ventured.

Carrie smirked, letting out a small laugh.

Anita hated the little laughs, the smirking. It made her feel like she was the butt of a joke she wasn't privy to. "What?" she asked, her voice sounding small.

Carrie shook her head. "Nothing. Just...you and your plans."

"Oh." She stared down at her hands.

"I just don't usually schedule my time on vacation."

"No, you're right." Anita bit her lower lip. "Let's just see where the day takes us," she said, the words painful to speak.

"Well, I showered right before bed, so I'm all set. You can use the bathroom first."

Anita searched through her bag for her shower kit, resolving to get unpacked and organized this evening before bed. As she shuffled through her belongings, she uncovered the travel guides she'd insisted on bringing with her. Carrie hadn't understood the need for the outdated guides, especially when everything could be found online these days, but these books were more than mere facts and information. They'd been pored over by her and Victor as they'd planned this trip, their margins holding the notes each of them added. Anita's handwriting was loopy while his was small chicken scratch, always in blue ink.

Those notes held the story of their planning and their lives over the years—the starts and stops in their interest and enthusiasm for the trip, all the hopes and expectations they held for the momentous adventure. The books taunted her now, full of plans she and Victor made over several decades, plans Carrie was undermining. She covered them back up and zipped into the bathroom.

As she showered, she gave herself a pep talk. It was okay Carrie didn't want to make a plan. Anita had been through their original itinerary so many times it was essentially burned into her memory. She knew most everything they wanted to see by heart, so she could discreetly guide her daughter in the right direction. After waiting decades to see these countries and these sights, she wouldn't let Carrie's carefree attitude deny her the chance to see everything she had come here to see.

After all, she knew more than most that tomorrow wasn't promised. She couldn't assume she'd ever have a second chance to be here.

———

After showering and getting dressed, they headed out for their first day of sightseeing, or wandering, as Carrie referred to it. Anita had a game plan in mind, running through ways she could direct her daughter towards Buckingham Palace. She had a fascination with the royal family, a guilty pleasure Victor indulged, often picking up tabloids for her with stories of the royals on the cover. She'd probably faint if she happened to catch a glimpse of the queen while here. Or Prince William and Kate.

But their first stop, at Carrie's insistence, was the hotel Starbucks.

"I'll have a grande skinny caramel macchiato," she rattled off. "Mom, what do you want?"

Anita straightened and squinted at the menu boards. "Oh. Just a medium coffee, please."

The cashier responded, but he surprised her with an accent so heavy she couldn't understand anything other than he was asking her a question. Was that meant to be English? She froze, embarrassed to ask him to repeat himself.

After an awkward silence, Carrie jumped in. "What roast did you want, Mom?"

"Um, whatever the regular coffee is." She shrugged and tried a laugh. How was she incapable of ordering a simple coffee?

"Pike Place is fine," Carrie told the cashier, offering her card.

"No, I've got it," Anita insisted. She grabbed her purse and fiddled with the latch again, but her fingers couldn't open it quickly enough. Why did they make these so small? Her cheeks warmed as they watched her.

"It's okay, Mom." Carrie said. "I've got this one." She handed her card to the cashier again, who smiled and completed their order.

Anita followed her to the end of the counter to wait for their drinks. Carrie said nothing further, just started tapping away on her phone. "I don't go to Starbucks often," she said. "I didn't know they had different roasts."

Carrie nodded, but her eyes remained fixated on her phone where she had a map pulled up. "St. Paul's first?" she asked.

"Oh. Um, sure." Anita clenched her jaw. St. Paul's was on

their list, but it wasn't the palace. And it was in the exact opposite direction.

"Great," Carrie said. Conversation concluded.

The barista called out Carrie's name, and they collected their drinks and headed out. The sun was shining, the temperature perfect for a day of walking, but a cloud of negativity engulfed Anita as they walked down the sidewalk. If she couldn't even understand a barista in another English-speaking country, how did she expect to survive France, Spain, and Italy? She'd been so pleased with herself for getting through the flight and immigration yesterday without a hiccup. But their very first morning in London, she had already failed at communicating and failed to pay for her daughter, who she'd promised an all-expenses-paid trip to in exchange for her company.

She needed Victor here. They would have gone out for a proper breakfast rather than a dash into the chain coffee shop they could have gone to back home. Then they'd have headed straight to Buckingham Palace. They'd have dinner reservations, and Anita would be able to relax knowing Victor was there to guide her through everything rather than constantly being on edge and judged.

Beside her, Carrie halted. She stopped as well and glanced behind her. How had she gotten here? She'd been so lost in her thoughts she hadn't been paying attention as they walked.

Anita looked to the right and inhaled sharply. Across the street, St. Paul's majestic dome and intricate facade stood as a reminder that Starbucks orders and language barriers were trivial; she was in England!

She fumbled with her purse's zipper, scrambling to pull out her phone to take a picture. Tears threatened at the corners of her eyes, and she sniffled, trying to find a full breath.

"Mom? What's the matter?"

Anita closed her eyes, wishing she could have a moment alone to collect herself. "It's nothing," she said.

"It's Dad, isn't it?"

She paused a moment. "Yes." She let her purse hang at her side again, forgetting her phone, and instead stared at the ornate cathedral, images of her and Victor poring over travel guides filling her mind. All of that planning, yet here she stood without him.

"Should we start with something else?" Carrie asked as she eyed the cathedral.

The offer was tempting, but if Anita didn't face her despair head-on, this trip would be for naught. Besides, every stop on their sightseeing agenda was bound to evoke sadness. "I'll be fine," she said.

Carrie waited another moment, then took the lead across the street, always the confident go-getter. A group of tourists gathered beside Anita with guidebooks and cameras, pointing and talking amongst themselves. She and Victor would have been with that crowd, happy to stand back and observe before proceeding rather than rushing right in.

Had Anita once been such a go-getter as well? Perhaps before the world dragged down her spirit? She couldn't recall being so confident and adventurous, though she hadn't always been this reserved. Regardless, she'd come here to experience Europe, and she certainly wasn't going to experience it standing on the sidelines the entire time. With one last glance at the cautious tourists, she followed her daughter.

The enormity of the cathedral left Anita awestruck as they walked in its shadow towards the ticket counter. She glanced at Carrie, who was looking up at the cathedral, taking in the sight for herself, and her heart ached. Her daughter was right beside her, yet she felt a thousand miles away.

"So, what's new with work? Any new clients I might

know?" Anita asked, searching for a safe starting point for a conversation. Work was really all she knew about her daughter's life these days.

Carrie straightened and cleared her throat. "It's been fine. No new clients recently."

There was that wall again. Was it really asking too much for a simple conversation? After all, she had paid for her daughter to come with her on this trip. Carrie could at least pretend like she wanted to talk to her.

They approached the ticket counter in silence, but Anita had her credit card ready to go before Carrie finished telling the attendant how many tickets. A small victory.

They handed over their tickets at the entrance, then walked into the nave of the church. Tourists milled about, foreign languages and accents blurring their conversations into one big, garbled mess of background noise. The checkered floor reminded Anita of her mother's bathroom, but the high arches lining the length of the cathedral towards the dome pulled her eyes upward.

"It's beautiful," Carrie said, her tone reverential.

Anita blinked and looked around. To be standing in a cathedral she'd dreamed of seeing for years felt surreal. "It really is."

The tension between them dissolved, and for a moment it seemed they'd found a door in the wall. Then Carrie reached into her purse and pulled out her phone. She opened it and stared at a message, her eyebrows bunching in a worried expression.

"Who's that?"

Carrie drew a heavy breath. "It's Jack. He wants to meet for drinks tonight."

Of course! How had she forgotten Jack had relocated to London? She'd always loved him, and though Carrie never let on, she had long suspected there were feelings between the two of them. Not that she would ever tell Anita if there were. She'd love to see him again and catch up. It might even help loosen things up between her and Carrie to have a third party present.

Carrie looked up from her phone, her lips twisted into an apology. "Would you mind terribly if I went?"

"Oh," Anita said, trying to hide her disappointment. Of course they didn't want an old woman joining them for a night out. But where would that leave her for the evening? "No, of course not. Tell him I say hi."

"Thanks, Mom." She typed out a response as they walked on, a skill Anita would never master.

She followed Carrie down the aisle of the cathedral, holding back a sigh. Perhaps it wasn't personal, but she couldn't help feeling edged out the first official night of their trip, the one *she'd* been looking forward to for decades.

Chapter 8

Carrie found the pub she and Jack agreed to meet at around the corner from the Tower Bridge and paused outside, her palms sweaty and her forehead throbbing with a slight headache.

Why was she nervous? It was just Jack. In their more-than-a-decade-long friendship, he'd witnessed her do many stupid things. They'd swapped dating horror stories, supported one another through career missteps, and talked each other through family dramas. But this felt different. Admitting she'd messed up her career over a one-night stand with a celebrity was embarrassing, and she worried Jack would now see her as the failure she was. Despite him seeing her at her lowest moments over the years, she never expected he'd witness her at the bottom of her career. She'd never expected to be anything but at the top at her agency.

Carrie gathered her nerve and entered the pub. Jack, as expected, was already seated at the bar with a beer in hand. She maneuvered through the crowd in the dimly lit room and approached her best friend from behind. In a terrible British accent, she said, "'Ello there, gov'na."

Jack turned and took her in, the creases around his eyes deepening as he laughed. He set down his beer and stood from his barstool, and as he wrapped his arms around her, she felt lighter. Maybe this wouldn't be so bad after all.

"How are you, sunshine?" he asked.

Carrie smiled at the old nickname. "I'm okay," she said, hoisting herself onto the stool beside him and blinking away her emotions. The scene brought her back to their college years and nights out at the local bar discussing their recent hookups. If only life were still that uncomplicated.

"What can I get you, miss?" the bartender asked, setting a cardboard coaster on the bar before her.

"Could I have a gin and tonic, please?"

The bartender nodded and walked away. Carrie set her wristlet and phone on the bar and turned to Jack with an exaggerated sigh, taking him in. His face was a tad more filled out than the last time she'd seen him, with creases that hadn't been there before now present, and was that a shock of gray hair she saw? She sensed London had been tough for him, but his smile was still radiant, the same safe space for Carrie it had always been.

"So, what brings you to London?" Jack asked over the top of his glass as he prepared for another sip. "With your mom no less?"

Carrie laughed. He was never one to waste time on silly pleasantries when there were real issues at hand. Part of why she preferred his friendship over other females. Men had a way of being direct and cutting through the gossip to the heart of the issue.

"It's wild, I know. She called me the night of the *One Last Love Story* premiere. Apparently, her therapist suggested she go through with their Europe trip on her own, but of course going by herself was impossible. So, she offered to pay for everything if

I went with her. But there was no way for me to get away from work for an entire month."

"Nor did you want to," Jack interjected.

Carrie chuckled. "Exactly. So I told her no."

The bartender returned with her drink, and she paused for a long sip.

She shrugged, as though the rest were no big deal. "Then everything happened, and suddenly I had a lot of free time and a desperate need to get as far from LA as possible."

Jack took a swig of his beer, but his expression remained serious. "So, you and Adam Hartley. Not soulmates?"

Carrie let out a small, sad laugh and hung her head. "I don't know what happened there."

"Really?" His eyebrows raised. "I mean, he's Adam Hartley. What's there to be confused about?"

Carrie swallowed hard, thinking back to just one week ago. Jack was right, Adam was insanely good-looking and sweet and kind to top it off. And he'd shown an interest in her at a moment of weakness. But still. As Sherilynn had pointed out, that wasn't a good enough reason to cross the line.

"You know me," she finally said. "I don't mix personal and professional."

Jack held up a finger like a schoolteacher correcting a student. "You don't *have* personal to mix with professional."

"Really?" Carrie asked, keeping her tone playful. "The first time I see you in six months and you attack me right off the bat?"

He placed his hand on her forearm. "I've been worried about you," he said. "And you know I'm right."

Carrie pulled her arm back under the guise of wanting another sip of her drink. "I have a personal life," she said, though even to her, the protest sounded weak.

"When was the last time you were in a relationship?"

"You know I just ended things with Brian."

Jack cocked his head. "I'd hardly call that a relationship. When was your last *serious* relationship?"

Carrie pursed her lips, left without an answer.

"My point exactly."

"I still don't see what that proves." She took another sip of her drink, her guard going up as Jack struck a nerve she hadn't been aware of.

"You've always been a workaholic," he continued. "But you've become completely absorbed with work since I left. How often do you go out with friends without me there to drag you out on the weekends?"

"I go out."

Jack stared directly at her. "Then why was Gina asking me a few weeks ago if I'd heard from you because she hadn't been able to get ahold of you?"

Carrie flinched, recalling several unreturned calls and texts from their college friend. "I attend a lot of events for work, so when I'm off I want some downtime."

"There's downtime, and then there's hiding out."

She turned away, breaking eye contact. Perhaps she had been more antisocial since Jack left, but the accusations sounded worse coming from the person who knew her best.

"Okay, know-it-all," she said. "Then tell me why I gambled my career and slept with my client."

Jack shrugged. "I mean, I wasn't there, but my best guess is you were starved for some attention. Oh, and drunk." He winked and smiled, but the nonchalance only made the observation more unbearable.

Carrie downed the rest of her glass, then signaled to the bartender for another. It was such a simple explanation, and yet she hadn't wanted to believe it could be so straightforward. "You suck when you're right, you know that?"

Jack laughed. "I've missed you, sunshine."

"You should move back to LA."

"Are *you* moving back to LA?"

Carrie flinched. "Why wouldn't I?"

"I don't know. It seemed like maybe this getaway was a way of figuring out where you wanted to go next."

"I left to give time for the rumors to subside," she said. "So I can go back and get another job."

He nodded and sipped his beer.

"I'm going back to LA. I love my life there."

"Really?"

"Yes."

"Okay."

"Why don't you believe me?"

"I didn't say I don't. You're the one getting defensive about it."

The bartender came back with her second drink, and Carrie took a large sip, inhaled deeply, then looked back at Jack. "Anyway," she said. "How have *you* been?"

His eyes shimmered. "I didn't mean to come at you so strongly. I guess I was getting even for you dodging my calls for a week straight."

"I'm sorry for that. It's been ridiculous between, well, getting fired and then preparing to come to Europe with Mom. Wow. Two things I never thought I'd say. This really has been a hell of a week." Carrie lifted her glass and clinked it against Jack's bottle. "But I made up for it by flying all the way to London to see you!"

He chuckled. "That you did."

They moved on, leaving LA and Adam Hartley out of their conversation going forward, yet later that evening as Carrie walked back to the hotel, Jack's words kept playing in her mind. She had been getting defensive with him, but why?

She loved her career; there was no doubt about that. She'd attended UCLA, her dream college since middle school, and landed a job with her firm upon graduation. She had been working her way up at her agency, and there was no debate that career-wise she'd been doing amazingly well. But outside of her work, what kind of life did she really have in LA? Most days, she woke and went to the gym, then headed straight to the office where she worked a minimum of twelve-hour days, picked up takeout for dinner, and fell asleep watching Netflix. Alone.

After Jack left last year for London, there was no one remaining she'd been willing to give up her minimal free time for. Even weekends were mostly spent at the office or attending work events. Her apartment was tidy, but that had more to do with the fact she was rarely there than because she maintained it well. She'd considered adopting a cat a while back but decided against it since she wouldn't be home enough to care for it. Even then, Jack pointed out that cats were generally self-reliant, and what did it say that she didn't even have time for a cat?

She hated when he was right.

Carrie's head was fuzzy after a few gin and tonics mixed with a reality check courtesy of Jack. He was usually spot-on in his assessments and observations, but he wasn't right about this. Was he?

She'd never considered a different life for herself than the one she'd made in California. But what if she couldn't find a new job? If LA was done with her, then what?

Perhaps she had more to figure out in the coming weeks than she'd realized.

———

Anita stared out the hotel room window at the glowing lights of London as the sun set, trying her best not to feel resentful at being cooped up in the room while Carrie went off for drinks with Jack. Carrie had asked what her plans were for the evening as she headed out earlier, and Anita shrugged her off and said she was tired, that she'd probably just turn in early and rest for tomorrow. In reality, she wasn't the least bit tired, but the idea of venturing out of the hotel on her own was enough to trigger her anxiety.

But at least being abandoned for the evening meant Anita had time to call Meredith. It was eight o'clock in London, which meant it was still the middle of the workday back in Buffalo. Fortunately, she was available when Anita called her office.

"How was the flight?" Meredith began, her voice filled with hopeful anticipation.

"Oh, it was nerve-wracking, but I survived." The flight into London seemed eons ago.

If Meredith seemed surprised by her reaction, she didn't let on. "So, how's everything going?"

Anita sighed and sat in the armchair by the window, relieved to put down the facade. "I just don't know what I'm doing here."

"What do you mean?"

"Why did I go through with this? I'm not the kind of person to fly off and have adventures on a whim. That's not me. So, what am I doing here with my daughter who wanders around until she finds something interesting and finds everything about me offensive?"

"You're growing," Meredith replied as though it were obvious, as though it didn't take a doctoral degree to answer that question.

"I don't know how to grow, or change, or evolve, or whatever you want to call it. I told myself coming here would prove I could change, but it's not that easy."

"No, it's not," Meredith agreed.

"And everywhere I look, all I can see is Victor. I thought the point of doing this was to move forward. How can I do that if I still see him everywhere I look?"

"It's not easy to move past grief, but you've taken the first step and should be proud of that. It won't be an overnight transformation. Changes and grieving...they take time."

"But it's so much harder than I thought it would be," Anita said, her eyes stinging with the threat of tears. "It feels wrong being here without Victor."

"I know. But we talked about this. Victor wouldn't want you to sacrifice this opportunity because he had to. And now you have a chance to reconnect with your daughter. I may have never met him, but I know he's cheering you on from above."

Anita smiled at the thought. She hoped Victor was watching her from afar.

"So, the other day we discussed working on your relationship with Carrie. Have you attempted a conversation with her yet?"

Anita leaned back in the armchair and looked out the window. With London sprawled out before her, she shouldn't complain, yet everything felt overwhelming and unmanageable. "I've tried, but she shuts me down every time."

"What have you tried talking to her about so far?"

"Work, mostly."

"Okay, so let's try something else. What else could you talk about?"

Anita was quiet a moment, searching her mind for any other bit of information she knew about Carrie's life these days. "Well, she's having drinks with her best friend, Jack, tonight. I can ask her about that tomorrow."

"Perfect. I think that's a great idea."

She sighed. "But what if she shuts me down again? What if she doesn't want to talk with me the way she used to talk with Victor?"

"She probably won't, but that's okay," Meredith said. "Your relationship with Carrie is and should be different from the one she had with her father."

"I know she loved him more. If she'd been able to choose, I'm sure she'd rather I have died last year." The words were like stabs to her heart. This was the first time she dared to speak them aloud, yet there was catharsis in finally releasing her biggest fear.

Meredith was silent, and Anita checked her cell phone to make sure the call hadn't dropped. "Hello?" she asked.

"Anita, what happened to Victor is a terrible tragedy, and I'm sure Carrie is struggling with the unexpected loss of her father. But I'd bet anything she wouldn't have wished this on either of you. It sounds like you're both handling your grief differently, but this could be a wonderful opportunity for you. She may have been closer to Victor over the years, but she needs her mother right now whether she'll admit that or not."

Anita wasn't sure Carrie had ever needed her, especially now. If that were true, why hadn't she visited since the funeral? Why did weeks pass without even a text from her daughter?

"My next appointment is here, so I have to get going, but I think asking about drinks with Jack is a great opening for a conversation. Hang in there. I have faith you can do this."

After they hung up, Anita grabbed a tissue from the bathroom and dabbed her eyes. The possibility of being turned down by her daughter yet again was frightening, but the thought of continuing the status quo horrified her more. She took a deep breath and exhaled. Today had been an adjustment, but tomorrow she'd work on the first step towards her new life.

Chapter 9

arrie sensed her mother wanted to say something as they headed downstairs the following morning, caught the side glances and inhales that preceded a question or remark. She was equally curious as to what she wanted to say and thankful she wasn't saying it.

Her forehead pulsed with a mild headache, the result of a bit too much alcohol the night before and spending half the night awake turning Jack's comments over in her mind. They stopped at the hotel Starbucks first again, and Carrie ordered a venti caramel latte with an extra shot of espresso.

"You're rather quiet this morning," her mother finally said as they waited on their drinks.

Carrie closed her eyes. Her luck had run out. She hated statements like that, observations that were meant as questions. Couldn't she just ask whatever it was she wanted to ask?

"I'm just thinking," Carrie answered, tapping her foot as though doing so would speed up the barista.

"How were drinks with Jack last night?"

She straightened and looked towards the door. "Drinks were fine."

"Just fine?"

The eagerness in her mother's voice was obnoxious. For years now, she'd been implying that Carrie and Jack should get together, and no matter how many times Carrie told her they were just friends, she'd been relentless.

"It was good to see him again. It's been a while."

"Carrie!" the barista called as she placed two takeaway cups on the counter.

She lunged toward the counter and grabbed their drinks. "Thank you," she said with a smile, relieved to escape outside where hopefully sightseeing would distract her mother from being nosy.

"Where do you want to go first?" her mother asked as they stepped out into the sunshine. It was just past eight o'clock, and the sidewalk was already a solid mix of tourists and locals about to begin their day.

Carrie took a tentative sip of her coffee, then recoiled as it was still too hot. "I don't care."

"Are you sure you're okay this morning?"

"Mom, I'm fine," she snapped. "Let's just walk around a bit until we decide what we want to do."

Her mother nodded, and they continued down the side-walk. Carrie felt a twinge of guilt for her harsh tone, but she appreciated the silence it brought.

After a few minutes, they'd walked an entire block, though Carrie couldn't recall any of it. They stopped at a street corner, waiting for the light to change. Across the street, a Five Guys restaurant beckoned to them, and for a moment she felt as though she were back in LA.

With Jack's comments still at the forefront of her mind, thinking of home brought on a wave of sadness and unease. Before last night, she'd had no doubt her plan was to find a new job and go back to LA. But after talking with Jack, she was wavering. If she wasn't happy with her life there, why was she so eager to return to it?

"Do you think I'm happy in LA?" Carrie asked, the words tumbling out before she realized she was speaking aloud.

Her mother stared at her, her face twisted with confusion, and she wished she could snatch the question back.

"I don't know how to answer that," her mother finally said.

Carrie shook her head and refocused on the traffic light. The longest light ever. "Never mind. It was a silly question."

The light changed, and she took off, leaving her mother no choice but to follow. A group of young tourists crowded them, making conversation impossible. Bullet dodged, at least momentarily.

After several minutes without another word between them, Carrie paused on a pedestrian bridge. She rested her elbows on the railing and looked over the Thames, the sun reflecting off the water. Carrie reached up for her sunglasses, but she must have left them in the room.

Her mother leaned against the railing beside her. "I wasn't trying to brush off your question," she said. "You caught me by surprise is all."

Carrie took another sip of her coffee, trying to look nonchalant. "It's not a big deal."

Her mother didn't take her eyes off of her. "You seem happy in California, but I'm not there. And I don't know what your life is like other than what you tell me." She paused and cleared her throat. "Which isn't a whole lot most of the time."

Carrie's head shot up, surprised by how honest and direct her mother's statement was.

"Do *you* think you're happy in LA?"

She took a deep breath, let it out, and repositioned herself along the railing. "I am." She squinted at a boat coming towards the bridge. "I definitely am. Jack just said some things last night."

"What did he say?"

Carrie looked down at her coffee cup and swallowed hard. It had been a long time since she'd been so vulnerable with her mother, and it felt foreign. She was the last person she wanted to have this conversation with, but she was also the only person she had right now, and if Carrie didn't get some clarity around this, she would continue to drive herself batty. "Just things," she said, shrugging. "Mainly that I don't have a personal life. But work keeps me busy."

Her words were defensive again, but why? She didn't need to defend her life. Her work wasn't just a job; it was the dream career she'd aspired to. She worked hard, but she loved the thrill of landing a client. She loved negotiating contracts, loved being in charge, loved the possibility of discovering the next breakout star. It was a demanding career, but she'd been willing to make certain sacrifices, specifically along the starting a family line. So why was she surprised to realize things were missing from her life?

Her mother kept her eyes on Carrie, giving her space to say more, but she didn't know what more to say without giving away everything. If she knew the actual reason Carrie had been able to get away from work for this trip, her disappointment and judgment would be more than she could handle when she was so close to the brink herself. But how long did she believe she could keep her mother in the dark? Eventually this trip would end, and then what?

Carrie opened her mouth to speak again, but a commotion at one end of the bridge pulled her attention away as a group of protestors approached. She had read about the protests taking place throughout Europe the past few months, and as much as she believed they weren't in any danger, her mother would likely panic at being swept up in a crowd.

Her mother turned her head. "What's going on?" she asked, standing up straighter. Anxiety had crept back into her voice.

"It's fine. We should probably just go this way." Carrie began walking again, waving to her to follow.

They hurried down the bridge, and voices came over loud-speakers as they passed by the crowd. She glanced at her mother. Her arms were wrapped around herself, her eyes wide and on alert. Of course something like this would happen the moment she let her guard down a bit.

And yet, Carrie was thankful for the distraction.

———

Anita stared up at the giant twinkling Ferris wheel and swallowed hard. She and Victor had read all about the London Eye and its magnificent view of the city, but he understood it was a no-go for her. She never even liked those tiny Ferris wheels at the county fair. There was no way in hell she was getting on one almost four hundred and fifty feet tall.

But earlier in the day, they had walked by it after lunch at a pub around the corner, and Carrie was childlike in her infatuation with the ride.

"I wanted to go on it when I came to visit Jack, but we just didn't get around to it," she had said. "I've heard the views are incredible."

Anita nodded but remained quiet, taking the last sip of her coffee.

"Especially at night when everything is lit up," Carrie continued.

She eyed the Ferris wheel. Was this some kind of test? Carrie had to know she'd never get on that thing. Of course, she wasn't officially asking, but Anita felt pressured nonetheless. Here Carrie was showing interest in their trip, in actually doing something together rather than abandoning her for the night again, and she was going to turn it down on account of being a scaredy cat?

The London Eye wasn't a typical Ferris wheel. Instead of open-air seats, it had enclosed pods large enough to walk around in, and it moved much slower. She and Victor had read it took about thirty minutes for the wheel to make a full rotation. The pods certainly didn't look as tipsy as the seats at the fair. Maybe it wouldn't be so bad.

And her daughter really wanted to do this.

"Well then, let's do it," she said, forcing cheerfulness.

Anita wished she'd had her camera ready to capture Carrie's surprised expression. She hadn't seen that one coming, that was for sure. But Anita's victory was short-lived. Now as she stood here once again staring up at the giant wheel, she wondered what she could have been thinking. It moved slowly, for sure, but slow was worse. Slow dragged it out. Slow prolonged her panic.

Carrie stood beside her, mindlessly tapping away on her phone. Somewhere between this morning and now, she'd shifted back to her usual closed-off self, the one who wanted nothing to do with her mother. Perhaps she sensed Anita was about to bail on the ride and was just waiting to say, "I told you so."

"Okay," Carrie said, closing out of her messages and stowing her phone in her purse. "Ready?"

Anita swallowed a lump in her throat. She'd taken a Xanax half an hour ago, inflating her courage to an extent, but her feet remained glued to the sidewalk.

Carrie turned around, already a few steps ahead of her, and cocked her head. "Mom?"

Anita cleared her throat. "Yeah, I'm coming," she said,

though she couldn't convince her feet to move. She closed her eyes and told herself to breathe. She could do this. She'd made it through the plane ride here, and that was more terrifying than a carnival ride and lasted longer.

Following her daughter to the ticket booth, she tried to calm herself by counting how many pods the wheel contained. But she was too distracted to properly distract herself and kept losing count.

Once Carrie purchased the tickets, they stood in line, surprisingly short given it was one of London's biggest attractions. Was a short line better or worse? Probably better. It offered less time for her to back out.

"Do you remember the first time Dad and I went on the Ferris wheel at Darien Lake?" Carrie asked, her eyes sparkling with the memory.

Anita chuckled. "How could I forget?" Carrie had been about eight years old and begged her parents to go on the ride with her. Anita had gotten out of it with some excuse or another, but Victor gladly took her. Once at the top, Carrie scooted over to the side, looking down to find Anita, and the top scoop of her vanilla ice cream cone, complete with rainbow sprinkles, fell off and landed right on the ride operator's head.

"The look on Dad's face when he realized what happened," Carrie said, laughing. "Then he looked at me so seriously and told me to finish the rest of that cone immediately so the guy didn't know it was me."

"Then you got off the ride and apologized to him anyway," Anita finished.

"Next," the operator called out, motioning her and Carrie to move forward.

She inhaled sharply, tensing again, and followed Carrie to the loading platform. Unlike the typical Ferris wheel, this one went so slowly it didn't need to stop to load passengers, and each pod held up to twenty-five people. A family of four filed into the pod ahead of them, excitedly chatting about the views that awaited. Anita looked up again, and the reality of just how high she was about to go sunk in.

The operator motioned them forward. She wanted to follow through, to prove to herself and Carrie she could do this, but the panic rose up and she shook her head. "I can't," she said. She took a step backward and stepped on the shoe of the young man behind her. Her cheeks warmed, but her embarrassment at backing out was minor compared to the panic attack that awaited at the top of the wheel.

"Mom, are you coming?" Carrie asked, her tone the familiar mix of concern and irritation Anita often received from her daughter, the same tone she'd used when they were boarding the plane a couple days ago.

"I can't do it. But you go. Enjoy the ride. I'll wait here."

"Um, okay." Carrie shook her head and continued into the pod.

Anita stepped aside to let the couple behind her move forward. "Don't spill any ice cream this time." She offered her daughter a weak smile.

She walked off to the side and found a bench. Her hands shook as she sat, and she blinked to keep from crying. She had come so close. Anita had so badly wanted to go up there with Carrie, to enjoy a mother-daughter moment without a care in the world, taking in the sights of London. What had freaked her out at the last moment? She couldn't even articulate it.

All she knew was she'd once again blown her opportunity to connect with her daughter. The anxiety won out yet again.

Anita watched as her daughter slowly ascended to the top. Would everything she wanted always be just out of her reach? Perhaps it was simply too late to change.

Chapter 10

The following evening, Carrie slipped away again to have dinner with Jack. She'd seen the hurt in her mother's eyes earlier when she told her about her evening plans and considered bailing, but her desire to see Jack and gain some clarity on their previous conversation won out. Besides, she had another three-and-a-half weeks to make it up to her.

"I've been thinking about what you said the other night," Carrie said as she and Jack looked over their menus. The restaurant he had chosen tonight had an intimate feel, with woodwork that reminded her of her grandparents' home, older but classic, and was more conducive to a deep conversation without other bar patrons attempting to squish between them.

"Oh, Carrie." Jack set down his menu and frowned. "I'm sorry about that. I didn't mean to lecture you or try to act like your..."

He let the sentence trail off, but Carrie finished it in her mind. Her father had the unique ability of reading her, of knowing something was up even when she tried her hardest to hide it. He pried things out of her with the right questions, the right amount of silence to allow her to open up. He'd have called her the same night and had the full story within a few minutes. She would have been embarrassed, but he'd also have known exactly how to comfort her.

Carrie turned her attention back to Jack. "It upset me in the moment, but I think you were right."

He pretended to faint into the back of his chair. "I'm sorry. Could you say that again?"

Carrie pursed her lips, finding his deepening accent endearing. She missed this now that he was overseas. Text conversations and FaceTime were simply no replacement for face-to-face.

"I'm serious," she said. "You were right about me not having a personal life in California. Maybe even about me wanting to leave. Though that's a big maybe, and I'd have no idea where I'd go."

"London?" Jack suggested with a smirk.

"London?"

He shrugged. "Not the worst idea I've had. There are some great talent agencies here, and I know one advantage London has over LA."

Carried sipped her water and raised an eyebrow. "Oh? What's that?"

"Me."

"Well, of course."

A look passed over Jack's face as their eyes met, and Carrie's stomach tightened. His expression turned from playful to serious, and she sensed this conversation was about to go somewhere she wasn't prepared for. This was more than an offhand comment.

"I wouldn't make the worst boyfriend, would I?"

Carrie blinked several times, trying to catch up. At one point years ago, she sensed Jack might have feelings for her, but nothing came of it. Their friends often commented about how close they were, alluding to the idea they'd make a good couple. But Jack was her best friend. She loved him, but there wasn't anything more to that love than platonic friendship.

Right?

"How long...I mean, when did you..."

"When did I start falling in love with you?"

He tossed the words between them as though they weren't the most monumental thing Carrie had heard in forever, and she fell into the back of her chair with their weight. She managed a small nod and waited for his next sentence to send a dagger to her heart.

Jack shrugged again, nonchalant or pretending to be. "I suppose it's been a while, a slow, steady spiral." He rubbed the back of his neck, a sign he was hiding his nervousness.

"Don't worry," he continued. "I don't expect you to say you feel the same. I just thought while we were being honest about our personal lives and all, I should probably come clean."

"I wish I knew what to say." Her mind circled through the last several years, trying to pinpoint something she'd missed, some giant clue she should have picked up but didn't. "So last year, when you offered to pass up your job offer and stay in LA after my dad died..."

Jack nodded. "Clearly, I'm horrible at expressing my feelings."

Carrie looked away, her mind scrambling to catch up with everything being thrown at her. "I feel like a terrible person."

He reached across the table and placed his hand over hers. "Carrie, please don't. I didn't say any of this to add to your stress, and I don't want this to change anything between us. You're the most important person in my life. I just wanted to be completely honest with you."

Carrie saw the desperation in his eyes, but she still couldn't find words.

"Please tell me everything is good between us," Jack said.

"Of course," she said. She couldn't lose her best friend, not now.

Now she just needed to convince herself everything was fine.

———

Carrie struggled to catch her breath as she walked back to her hotel after dinner. While she and Jack moved on and tried to act normal—whatever that meant anymore—she couldn't keep her mind off the bombshell he'd shared. She'd gone to dinner with the hope of making sense of her personal dilemmas, but instead she had left with even more.

Her mind raced, trying to pinpoint when Jack's feelings for her began and how she'd missed any sign of them. What kind of best friend was she to not notice something like that? She moved slowly, not exactly eager to return to the hotel room where her mother would hover and ask questions Carrie didn't have the brainpower to entertain.

She approached a pub, and though she wasn't one to drink alone, in a foreign country no less, tonight it felt like exactly what she needed. Between going in or heading back to the hotel, she opted for the pub.

"Evening, miss," the bartender said as she took a seat at the worn wooden bar. The smell of beer and stale chips hit her nose, and Carrie felt like she was back in her college days at the dive bar around the corner from campus. A pair of twentysomething women sat at the other end, and two older gentlemen sat separately but shouted to one another across the empty seats between them. Other than that, the place was quiet. "What can I get for you?"

"A gin and tonic please."

The bartender whipped up her drink, then left her with her thoughts. Carrie always marveled at bartenders' ability to read their patrons and know what they needed, chit-chat or silence. Tonight, Carrie appreciated the silence.

She downed the first drink within a few minutes, her mind once more dissecting her conversations with Jack the past couple of days. Everything she'd once known to be true seemed to be tipped upside down. Was she really miserable in LA? *Was* she looking for something different? And did she love Jack the way he loved her?

Until now, Carrie hadn't seen a problem with the life she had chosen. She'd had a plan since high school, and she was simply following it through. The absence of romantic relationships, parties with friends, or extravagant vacations didn't bother her. There were some things in life more important and establishing herself as one of the best talent agents in the industry was one of those things. Men would stab you in the back, but your career success would be there for the long haul.

Did it get lonely sometimes? Sure. Did she get tired of the same takeout night after night in front of her television? Without a doubt. But was she building a career she could be proud of? She'd thought the answer was a resounding yes, but if one evening's poor choices wiped out all she had worked towards, could she still claim it had been worth the sacrifice?

Or had her career simply been a cover, an excuse to avoid everything else? Jack wasn't wrong about her lack of romantic relationships. She'd dated over the years, but she tended to go for the men who were unavailable, like Brian who'd made it clear from the beginning he didn't want anything serious. Or a movie star who clearly was out of her league.

Carrie's mind wound itself precisely where she didn't want it to, back to the last time she'd gone all in on a relationship.

Oliver Wilson had been a TA in her Psychology 101 class

when she studied abroad in Australia. Though it was frowned upon for a TA to pursue a relationship with a student, Oliver insisted it was fine so long as they didn't label their relationship. Carrie had fallen for his broad muscles and charming smile instantly and had no problem carrying on a secret relationship if it meant she got to be with him. Oliver wasn't like the immature boys her age; he was older, well traveled, and intoxicating.

But after a couple of months, she caught him with another student. He hadn't even appeared remorseful or guilty, and Carrie wondered how many others there actually were. While she'd been considering moving to Australia for him, he had been banking on the fact she would return to the United States, and he'd move on to another girl.

While her friends told her he wasn't worth her thoughts, Carrie hadn't been able to shake the constant nausea that nagged at her the following week. And when one morning the smell of her roommate's coffee actually made her throw up, she walked to the corner store just off campus and bought a pregnancy test. She used the small bathroom tucked in the back of the store, and after three minutes, two pink lines changed Carrie's life forever.

To her surprise, no tears came. She quickly cleaned up the test kit and shoved it into the trash bin, then headed back to her dorm room.

But on her way back, a panicky feeling overtook her that she'd never experienced before. She sat down on a bench, but her heart continued thumping so quickly she wondered if she needed an ambulance.

When the panic subsided, she returned to her dorm room and called her parents, thankful her father answered. She begged him to let her leave Australia early and go back to LA, conveniently omitting the small detail about being pregnant, and when she returned, Jack was there to help her pick up the pieces and move on. Jack was always there.

Carrie ordered a second gin and tonic, then nursed a third. She wasn't generally a big drinker, not a fan of feeling out of control and disconnected from her own body, but this evening the more she drank, the clearer her thoughts became. And the clearer her thoughts became, the more they pointed to Jack as the answer to all of her uncertainties.

How easy would it be to fall for him? He was her best friend, a rock in her life. They could skip that awkward beginning-of-a-relationship phase when you were expected to devote all of your time to this new relationship. God, how she hated that phase.

And yet, if things went badly, if she lost Jack, she'd be left with no one. Carrie shut her thoughts off. She couldn't even consider that outcome.

Logically, nothing worth having came without a risk. If she wanted to have it all with Jack, that would mean taking some risk. She just didn't know if she was ready to gamble their friendship for the possibility of more.

An hour after she arrived at the bar, Carrie tipped the bartender and headed back out onto the London streets. She stood on the sidewalk a moment. To the left, her hotel awaited a few blocks away. But to the right, a bit farther off, Jack had returned to his flat. She hadn't even come close to sorting her feelings for him, but perhaps if she saw him, the answer would become clear.

Carrie turned to the right. She had a good sense of direction, and while she probably could have navigated her way to Jack's flat on her own—after all, they'd walked there countless times on her last trip—the insensible heels she'd worn didn't mix well with the alcohol, so she waved down a cab.

Ten minutes later, she stood in front of Jack's door, contemplating her motives. Was it only the alcohol that brought her here? No, it was deeper than that. Right? She knocked on the door, and though part of her wanted to run before Jack answered, her feet wouldn't budge.

The door opened. "Carrie? What are you doing here?" His eyebrows drew together, and he looked around the hallway as though expecting to find someone else with her. He looked ready for bed in sweatpants and a loose T-shirt.

He looked really good.

Carrie fiddled with her fingers. Did he think she was ridiculous showing up like this? "I've been thinking since we left dinner."

Jack raised an eyebrow. "What about?"

"Us."

He shifted and crossed his arms. "And?"

Carrie swallowed her nerves and forced herself to say the words aloud. "And I think I might have feelings for you too."

Her answer was hedged and uncertain, and Carrie was sure Jack would see right through her drunken idiocy and send her back to her mother. But to her surprise, he leaned down and kissed her, the weight of so many years of pining behind his lips. Then he pulled her into his flat, and they fumbled their way to the bedroom.

Chapter 11

Anita awoke to infomercials, the blackout curtains drawn so she couldn't guess the time. She pushed herself up carefully, her neck angry from sleeping at an odd angle. She must have fallen asleep waiting for Carrie to get back.

Carrie's bed was still in the pristine condition housekeeping had left it, her suitcase in the same spot on the floor. No sounds came from the bathroom. Anita fumbled around on the night-stand for her phone, and her heart sped up as she read the time. It was past five in the morning, and there were no missed calls or messages from Carrie.

Maybe she'd seen the movie *Taken* too many times, but such things did happen in real life. She called Carrie's phone, silently pleading for her daughter to pick up, but the call went straight to voicemail.

Her phone was off. That could just mean it had run out of battery. After all, she hadn't been back to their room since around lunchtime yesterday. But it could also mean someone had her and had taken her phone away.

What did she do next? What authority was she supposed to contact to report her grown daughter missing in a foreign country? She and Victor hadn't needed to prepare for this contingency.

She pulled out the first clothes she found from the dresser and threw on a pair of jeans and a sweater. She riffled through her luggage for her Xanax bottle and tapped a pill into her palm. As she was about to toss the pill into her mouth, the key slot clicked, and the door opened.

"Carrie!" she shouted as her daughter walked in.

She froze in the doorway. "Morning, Mom." Her voice strained with compensatory cheer.

Anita imagined she wasn't thrilled to find her mother sitting up waiting on her. She wanted to explain that she hadn't been, that she'd just woken up and found her missing.

Carrie crossed the room to her suitcase, wearing the same clothes she'd left for dinner in. Her hair was a bit disheveled, and her eye makeup was smudged. She had left for dinner with her male best friend the evening before and was now creeping back into the room before dawn like a teenager past curfew. The pieces came together, revealing an entirely different scenario than Anita had feared moments ago.

More than anything, she wanted to turn to Victor and scream, "Ha! I told you so!" While he'd been so certain nothing was going on between Carrie and Jack, Anita knew all along. Who knew their daughter best after all?

"So, you and Jack?" She tried to suppress a smile.

Carrie's face turned a deep shade of red as she continued pulling clean clothes from her suitcase. "I'm going to take a shower."

She escaped into the bathroom, and Anita's stomach clenched. She hadn't meant to chase her away, but she should have known better. Of course Carrie didn't want to talk about whatever happened with her and Jack last night with her mother. While Anita yearned to be Carrie's go-to person, she simply wasn't. But she saw in her daughter's eyes she needed someone to talk to, and with Jack being the object of discussion, perhaps this would be the opening she had been hoping for.

Between a slight hangover and the early start to the day, by the time Carrie and her mother left for breakfast at seven o'clock, all she wanted was to crawl back into bed. But she'd left Jack sleeping this morning, and as the time drew closer to the start of his workday, she anxiously awaited the fallout.

This scene was becoming far too familiar. What had she been thinking last night? Drunken sex was never the answer to a problem. Hadn't she learned this yet?

And yet, there was something there last night Carrie couldn't recall with any other man, a closeness she'd never experienced before. Was this what love felt like? Had she truly been overlooking Jack all these years? Or was that feeling just because she knew him so well? Despite the sex, or perhaps because of it, she still had no idea what she felt or what she wanted.

While they waited at their outdoor table for their breakfast orders, her mother's eyes searched her face, so many question marks within them. Carrie fiddled with her napkin and pretended to be occupied looking around and watching the other patrons. The last thing she wanted to do was discuss last night with her mother. She would fling the "I told you so" at her about her and Jack, and Carrie wasn't in a place to deal with that. Not when so many questions still floated in her mind.

The waiter finally approached and set plates down in front of them. The smell made her stomach churn, but she cut off a piece of the Nutella crepe and started chewing. "What's on the agenda for today?" she asked, directing the conversation before giving her mother the opportunity to do so.

"We haven't visited Buckingham Palace yet," her mother said. "And we only have a couple days left here."

There was hope in her voice. Though the day was somewhat overcast and threatened rain, she wanted to see the palace before they left. And if they were preoccupied with something her mother really wanted to do, there was less likelihood of a conversation Carrie didn't want to deal with.

"The palace it is," Carrie said. She sipped her coffee.

"Jack could join us if you'd like." Though her mother didn't lift her eyes from her plate, she felt them like daggers, waiting for her response.

Carrie forced herself to swallow her coffee and remain nonchalant. How had she walked right into this? "He's working."

"Well, he could join us later."

Carrie's phone vibrated on the table, Jack's name lighting up the screen. A wave of relief washed over her, quickly replaced by nausea. He wasn't exactly safe territory either this morning. "I'll be right back," Carrie said.

She grabbed her phone and walked off the restaurant's patio, across the street to a bench. Her mother would be watching, so she would need to keep her expressions neutral, but she'd rather deal with Jack than her mother's inquisition.

"Hi," she answered, working her best to keep her voice steady.

"So should I be worried that you pulled a Harry Burns on me and took off without morning cuddles?"

Carrie laughed, recalling the many times she'd forced Jack to watch *When Harry Met Sally* with her. "I'm so sorry," she said. "I needed to get back to the hotel before my mom woke up, which unfortunately I didn't quite manage." It was a partial truth. She *did* mostly want to get out of his apartment before her mother discovered she hadn't returned. But she also hadn't been able to face him. The thought of his eyes on her while she admitted she still wasn't sure about her feelings for him had almost caused her to throw up.

Jack paused, then lowered his voice and continued. "That's all this morning's hasty exit was about then? Getting back to your room undetected?"

Carrie wanted to reassure him, to tell him everything was fine and she was happy about last night. But she wouldn't lie to her best friend. "Jack, I feel horrible."

He was silent, and Carrie pictured him hanging his head, staring into his coffee. If it wasn't bad enough she hadn't been able to reciprocate his feelings when he shared them, she really had to go and make everything worse by showing up drunk at his flat? Who did that to their best friend?

"Jack..."

"It's fine," he said, though his tone suggested it was anything but.

"I just...I'm still not sure how I feel about us. Last night...I shouldn't have gone over there."

He remained silent, and Carrie searched for something to offer him to make this all better, though she feared nothing would. "I don't want this to come between us." Her voice was barely above a whisper, her greatest fear being spoken aloud.

"Never," he replied, though his voice still sounded off. "You're my sunshine. Nothing could change that."

Carrie wanted to call him on the lie, but what good would that do? Until she sorted out her feelings and what they meant, she had no assurances to offer.

"I should probably get back to my mom."

"Of course. We'll talk later?"

Carrie bit the inside of her cheek. She'd never heard Jack

sound so uncertain, so sad. Certainly not over anything she'd done. "Absolutely," she said.

They hung up and she crossed the street back to the patio where her mother waited, her head down and focused on her plate. Carrie shook off the conversation with Jack and slid back into her seat with a smile.

"Is Jack joining us later?" she asked.

Carrie took a sip of water. "No, he's busy tonight."

"That's a shame."

"It is." The hope went out in her mother's eyes. Hope that this was it, that Carrie had finally found love with her best friend and would settle down and start giving her grandkids. She was used to letting her down—she'd had years of practice— but this time hit particularly hard. This time, she had disappointed Jack as well.

Chapter 12

After a week in London, Paris was next on the agenda. While Anita had mixed emotions about finally seeing Paris, their mode of transportation was currently at the top of her list of things to fret over. Undoubtedly, the most efficient way to travel between the two cities was the Chunnel—an underseas railway that connected England and France. About twenty-three miles were under water, and even with the train traveling a hundred miles per hour, that still meant they'd be submerged for almost fifteen minutes. Combining her fear of being under water with her claustrophobia, Anita couldn't imagine enduring fifteen minutes in the enclosed space without losing her mind. But she'd managed the flight, and with the help of her friend Xanax, she was determined to overcome this as well. At least this was just a one-way trip.

Shortly after boarding the train, Carrie broke out her earbuds and became distracted with her phone. As the train windows shuttered and they entered the underseas tunnel, Anita was left alone with her thoughts, and she did her best to turn them away from the fact she was currently close to 250 feet below water.

An older couple sat a few rows ahead of them, the man doing a crossword puzzle while the woman read a novel. Anita watched them and imagined they were her and Victor. Going to Paris with Carrie instead of him felt especially cruel, and her daughter hadn't the slightest idea of why that was.

Over the years, Paris had meant different things to her, to her and Victor. What had started as a dream to one day see the Eiffel Tower in person had turned into a consolation prize, then somewhere they'd come so close to seeing but still so far. Ultimately, Paris had become a symbol for Anita of the final straw in her relationship with Carrie.

She could still picture that evening vividly, could still taste the bitterness on her tongue when she thought of it. She'd been standing at their kitchen counter, her knife suspended midair above a half-chopped onion, when Victor told her Carrie was leaving Australia early.

"What do you mean she's leaving?" she'd asked. There were still five weeks before her semester abroad ended. She was scheduled to fly from Sydney to Buffalo on December nineteenth, just in time for Christmas.

"She needs to come home," Victor said. Nothing more, just a simple statement.

"Why?" Anita demanded. "She begged us to go there."

Victor looked at her with pleading eyes, the look he gave when he hoped to avoid an argument and wanted her to drop it. "I remember."

She dropped the knife into the sink and wiped her hands on a towel. "Well then, what could possibly be so important that she convinced you to let her come home early after all we did to send her there?"

"Annie..."

"No, don't Annie me! I deserve to know what's going on in my daughter's life that could be this important."

"I can't...I can't tell you."

Anita narrowed her eyes. How did he think that was an acceptable answer? She pushed herself off the kitchen counter and snatched the phone from its cradle. She punched in Carrie's number in Australia, the phone shaking in her hand.

"What are you doing?" Victor asked.

"I'm calling Carrie."

He took three steps towards her and ripped the phone from her hand. "Stop it," he said.

"I deserve to know what's going on, Victor." Her voice was low and shaking. "If you won't tell me, I'll ask her myself."

"She's having some issues, and she needs to come home. That's all I can say."

"Fine." Anita put her hands up in surrender. "I'll find out when she gets here then."

Victor frowned. "Well, she's not coming straight here."

"Where is she going?"

"To LA."

Her cheeks heated up. "LA? Why is she going to LA?"

Victor held his hands out, helpless. "She asked to go there."

"You said she was coming home."

"I misspoke. She's coming back to the States."

"What is she going to do in LA until Christmas? She *is* still coming for Christmas, right?"

"I'm sure she is. Look, we didn't talk everything through. I just talked with her and told her I'd get her a plane ticket and call her back. She's going through something. Surely you can understand."

"What I understand is she *begged* us to go to Australia for the semester. She begged, and you caved. I told you it wasn't a good idea, didn't I?"

Victor offered a slight nod, a small concession. "You did."

"We used our Paris money on this, canceled our own plans, and she doesn't even care."

"She doesn't know we did that."

"Of course she doesn't. Because *you* didn't want to tell her." She jabbed a finger into the air towards him. "And we always do what *you* want us to. Well, guess what. She's not just *your* daughter."

"I know that." Victor set the phone on the counter and came towards her, his arms outstretched.

Anita evaded his hug and lunged for the phone, then dialed Carrie's number as she stormed into the living room.

She answered on the second ring. "Daddy?"

"Carrie, it's Mom."

"Oh, hi."

Did Anita hear her sniffling? "Dad told me you want to come home. What's going on?"

"I...um...is Dad there?"

She sat on the couch and tried to keep her voice even. "Honey, you can talk to me. I'm here for you. What's going on?"

"I just...I...Can I just talk to Dad please?"

Anita closed her eyes. She tried not to let her daughter's words sting, but how could they not? They brought back all the times over the years Carrie preferred Victor over her, all the times she was reminded she wasn't the favored parent, that she wasn't good enough to be let into Carrie's life.

She opened her eyes to find Victor leaning against the entryway to the living room, watching as though he knew Carrie was asking for him on the other side of the phone. It must have felt good knowing your daughter loved you most, that she didn't even want to tell her own mother why she needed to abandon her study-abroad semester.

Her heart rate sped up, and her vision blurred. She whipped the phone across the room at Victor. "There!" she screamed. "Talk to your daughter. Your ungrateful, selfish, self-centered daughter. Screw both of you!"

Anita shoved past Victor and ran upstairs, slamming the bedroom door behind her. She collapsed onto the bed and sobbed, her entire body shaking, her tears leaving a giant wet spot on the comforter.

A few minutes later, the door opened, and Victor sat beside her. He put his hand on her back, trying to calm her down, but it wasn't enough this time.

"What was that about?" he asked, his voice much calmer than she deserved.

Anita sat up and reached for a tissue from her nightstand. "She heard every word, didn't she?"

Victor nodded. "Are you that upset we didn't go to Paris? Because we could probably still make it work. Maybe not the full two weeks like we'd been planning, but maybe a week?"

"It's not about Paris."

"Then what was that all about?"

Anita looked at the door, unable to meet Victor's eyes. "What else did you want me to do? God only knows what happened to my daughter over there and I'm not allowed to know what it is? I'm her mother! You both have your special little club and act like I'm some outsider, but I carried her for nine months. She was a part of me for *nine* months, and now look at us. She hates me so much she can't even talk to me. If only she knew what she meant to me, what I went through to finally have her." Anita took a deep breath and looked back at Victor. "I think we need to tell her about the miscarriages."

Victor rubbed his temples. "What? Where is this coming from?"

"She's old enough now, and I think she needs to know. So she understands why I am the way I am."

"But that's all in the past. I don't want her to carry that weight."

The look on her husband's face told Anita everything she needed to know. Whether Victor had truly made peace with the miscarriages or not, he couldn't face them again by resurrecting the past.

Maybe it would have helped matters had Carrie known about the miscarriages. Maybe it wouldn't have made a difference. But it occurred to Anita now that Victor was no longer here. It was up to her whether she shared her story. She eyed her daughter sitting beside her and swallowed hard. It was time Carrie knew everything. Whether it would fix anything at this point, Anita didn't know. But she at least deserved to know where her mother's anxiety stemmed from, why she was always so protective of her one and only daughter. She deserved to know why Anita had been so upset that she'd left Australia early.

"Mom?" Carrie asked, pulling her earbuds out.

"Hmm?" She raised her eyebrows.

"Are you okay? You look a little pale."

Anita's immediate urge was to say she was fine, to cover up her emotions and not invite further questions. But she'd decided Carrie needed to know about her past, and the longer she waited, the higher the chance she would back out of following through.

"I'm just...not sure how to feel about going to Paris," Anita said, tiptoeing towards the potential conflict.

Carrie's eyebrows scrunched together, the creases between them becoming more pronounced. "Why?"

She shifted and cleared her throat. "Well, we actually came close to going to Paris years ago."

Carrie frowned. "When was this?"

"There were a couple times." Anita swallowed and gathered

her thoughts. "The day I got the call from the doctor that I was pregnant with you, we were supposed to meet with a travel agent to put down our deposit on a trip."

"Oh, wow. I never knew that."

Anita forced a smile, diffusing the situation before it officially needed to be. "The second time, we had the money set aside and the plans in place, and then, well, we used the money to send you to Australia instead."

Carrie's eyes widened, and she saw the dots connecting in her mind. Carrie opened her mouth as if to say something, then closed it again and looked away.

"I'm sorry," Anita said. "I know...well, I just thought you should know."

Carrie shook her head. "I didn't realize."

"Dad didn't want us to tell you."

"So why are you telling me now?"

Anita looked down at her hands. "I just thought it might help some things, help our past, make sense."

"Like that you blame me for you and Dad never going to Paris?" Carrie's voice was louder now, defensive.

"That's not what I meant. I don't blame you."

Carrie grabbed her earbuds again. "Okay, Mom," she said, her words dismissive, and slipped the earbuds back in.

Anita's heart dropped. She watched Carrie a moment, trying to find words to clarify what she'd meant but none came. Perhaps Victor had been right. A parent's sacrifice wasn't expected to be repaid, so what was the point in telling her? After all, he knew their daughter best. He always had.

———

A little before seven o'clock that evening, they took the metro to the Trocadéro square after settling into their hotel room. Sunset was approximately eight-thirty that evening, and Anita wanted to be at the square to watch dusk turn to night, to see the Eiffel Tower light up in its shimmering glory.

They hadn't said much to one another since her revelation on the train, and though the weight of hiding this particular truth from her daughter was lifted, it had been replaced by the fear she was only angrier with her than before.

As it was the tail end of rush hour on a Tuesday evening, the underground cavern swarmed with businesspeople rushing past, shaking off the workday and moving on to more exciting plans. The scene felt so familiar; if it weren't for the sea of French being spoken all around them, Anita could have believed they were in any major city back in the States.

But as they exited the metro station and resurfaced onto the sidewalk, the excitement was palpable. This wasn't just any city. This was Paris.

Groups of tourists flocked in the same direction, and as they walked, Anita's hands tingled with anticipation, her heart fluttering faster. The idea of a bucket list always perplexed her—writing out a list of life dreams only seemed a setup for failure—but if she had one, seeing the Eiffel Tower would be the top item. Beyond being a world-famous structure, it had become an icon in Anita's mind, a symbol of having finally made it to Europe, of finally becoming a person who was worldly enough to travel abroad.

They walked along a trail of trees, then turned a corner and the entire tower emerged before them. Anita froze in her tracks, amazed at how one step was the difference between seeing nothing and seeing it all.

Everyone told her she'd be shocked by its enormity in person. She hadn't believed them, convinced she was aware of its size, but standing at the top of the Trocadéro square, it was like a painting too big for the space it occupied, yet too beautiful to get rid of.

Carrie pulled out her phone and snapped photos, but Anita was too entranced to dig for her own phone. All those years of saying someday she'd make it here but never fully believing it. And now here she stood.

"Mom," Carrie said, pointing to a spot a few feet to her right. "Stand over there. I'll get your picture."

Anita shifted over, and her shoulders tensed. After decades of taking photos beside Victor, their arms looped around one another in the familiar pose they'd adopted, posing alone was intimidating. A piece of her seemed to be missing.

She smiled her best and waited for Carrie to take the photo.

"That's a good one," Carrie said, tilting her phone to show her.

It wasn't a terrible photo, but she saw the discomfort in her eyes. Her smile wasn't as vibrant as it had been with Victor beside her. Her hands rested on the front of her thighs, uncertain where to go. But the Eiffel Tower drew the eye away from her awkward pose at least.

Carrie turned her attention back to the tower. "It's incredible," she said.

"I never want to leave this spot."

Carrie looked around, then slipped her phone back into her purse. "I have an idea," she said. "Follow me."

Anita followed her through the crowd of tourists to a kiosk along the square's edge selling paninis. Carrie jumped in line, and Anita stood beside her.

"There're some benches over there," Carrie said, pointing towards the stairs at the square's edge. "I thought we could eat here and watch the sun go down."

It wasn't the exquisite Parisian dining experience Anita had in mind for their first evening here, but Carrie wasn't looking to find the first flight away from her after their interaction on the train, and that meant the world to her. "That's a great idea," she said.

After they ordered and collected their paninis, Anita followed Carrie down the steps to a bench with a perfect view of the Tower. As they unwrapped their dinner and settled in, an article she had read popped into her mind about people who committed suicide from the Eiffel Tower. How was it that where some people saw only beauty, others saw a means to end their suffering?

She'd contemplated suicide a few times herself since Victor's death. At moments when the grief felt too overwhelming to handle. Meredith assured her such thoughts were normal, that as long as she didn't begin crafting a definitive plan, it was nothing to worry much about. She didn't know what kept her from following through other than some vague hope things would get better. Sitting in Paris with her daughter, the possibility of improving their relationship dangling before her, she believed this was why she'd hung on.

She just needed to stop messing things up further.

Anita set her panini back on her lap and looked at Carrie. "I'm sorry about what I said on the train," she said. "I don't blame you for us not going to Paris. That wasn't what I meant. I just thought it might help you understand my frustration over the whole Australia incident." Anita paused. She closed her eyes and gathered her courage. If she wanted Carrie to be open with her, she needed to do the same. "I *was* upset that our Paris money had been used for Australia, and then you abandoned the trip. But the real reason I was so angry was because no one would tell me what happened that made you leave."

Carrie stared straight ahead and remained silent, but she didn't snap at the comment.

Anita continued, her voice softer. "I still wonder what

happened there to make you want to leave so suddenly. You don't have to tell me if you don't want to. But I'm here to listen if you ever do."

Carrie cleared her throat and set her own panini back down on its wrapper. She dusted off her hands, then looked at her. "So, what was Dad most excited to see in Paris?"

Anita let go of a breath. It wasn't the response she'd hoped for, but it wasn't a complete dismissal. Maybe her words were sinking in. Maybe her daughter would come around. For now, she'd roll with the change of topic. "Your dad, of course, was most excited for the Louvre. All that history in one place. He spent so many hours poring over books and devising the best plan to see everything he wanted to see. If it were up to him, we'd probably have spent the entire week there."

"The Mona Lisa?"

Anita laughed. "Nope. Pretty much everything but. He said it was a waste of time fighting the crowd to see such an overrated painting. But I told him I wanted to see it anyway, just to say I did. So, he added it to the list."

Carrie smiled. "That sounds like Dad."

She took another bite of her panini, but a sniffle drew her attention back to Carrie. "Carrie? What's wrong?"

"It's nothing," she said, wiping beneath her eye with her finger.

"It's not nothing. You're crying."

Carrie looked ahead at the Eiffel Tower, seeming to debate if she wanted to talk. Anita understood too well the simultaneous desire to talk and fear of doing so. She wanted to lean over and wrap her arms around her daughter, but something stopped her. It had been too long since her hugs had felt welcomed by Carrie.

"I was just thinking about Dad and how none of us ever know when it'll be our last day. When it's too late to do everything we always wanted to. And I just feel a little guilty now for being a part of the reason he didn't get to see Paris."

Anita's heart sank. She'd never intended to burden her with guilt.

"Carrie, I need you to listen to me and to understand one thing very clearly," she said. "Your dad and I, we did want to travel and see Europe. But more than anything, we wanted to be parents." Sharing the miscarriages was on the tip of her tongue. But she'd done enough damage for today. She couldn't add anything more. "Our greatest wish—your dad's greatest wish—was for you to be happy. We chose to spend that money to send you to Australia because you having that opportunity meant more to us than a trip to Paris. It's not your fault he never made it to Paris." *It's mine*, she added silently.

Carrie wiped away one last tear, then motioned to the wrapper in Anita's lap. "I can take that. I have to run to the bathroom."

She took their trash and disappeared to the other side of the square. Anita leaned back into the bench. If she could go back to this morning, she'd talk herself out of sharing those details with Carrie. Victor had been right after all.

The sun was disappearing quickly now, and Anita checked her watch. Almost eight-thirty. To her left, the crowd in the square had grown, camera phones and selfie sticks out in full force. How amazing that day after day, year after year, a structure still drew such a crowd.

Finally, Carrie came back. "Long line at the bathroom?" Anita asked.

She handed her a small bag. "I got sidetracked."

Anita peeked inside to find two macarons, one chocolate and one vanilla.

"I didn't know which one you'd want, so I grabbed both."

Anita chuckled. "Is there such a thing as a bad macaron?"

Carrie pulled a vanilla macaron from her own bag. "Not that I can tell."

She bit into the cookie, its meringue shell squishing between her teeth. "Hey, that reminds me," she said. "We need to book our macaron class."

"I already looked up openings on the train," Carrie said. "There's a class on Sunday we can get tickets for."

Anita smiled, touched her daughter had remembered the class on her own. "That sounds perfect."

Carrie grabbed the second macaron from her bag and took a bite, then nudged her with her elbow. "Look! It's lighting up!"

The Eiffel Tower had turned from iron to shimmering gold. "Oh, wow." She dropped her hands and stared. "It's incredible."

"It's even more beautiful like this. But it makes me sad Daddy never got to experience this with you."

"Me too." Anita glanced to her left, up on the raised square where couples held hands and snapped photos together, kissing in front of the icon of the romantic city, and a familiar aching filled her heart. And yet, she wasn't sorry to be here with Carrie, to share this experience with her daughter who'd never before wanted to share anything with her. There was a silver lining in all of this, some beauty nestled within the pain and suffering. She reached out and placed her hand on Carrie's. "But I'm so glad to share it with you."

Chapter 13

There were 130 swirls on the ceiling. Carrie had spent the last few minutes counting them. Before that, she'd been focused on the blinking red dot on the coffeemaker. She'd tried counting backward from one hundred by sevens. No matter what she tried, she couldn't fall asleep.

She rose from bed and quietly riffled through her bag in the dark for her sweatshirt and book. She grabbed her cell phone from the charger on the nightstand and snuck out of the room.

The lobby was empty except for two female employees at the front desk. Carrie settled into a plush maroon chair out of sight of the desk, but close enough to overhear their conversation, elated each time she understood a word or phrase in French.

Her mother's revelation on the train had her thoughts jumping all over the place. They had used money they'd saved for Paris to send her to Australia? Why hadn't they told her? Would it have made a difference if they had?

Her mother's offer to talk about what happened there sat heavily with her. On the one hand, she wanted to explain so she could stop guessing, stop wondering what had happened to her daughter over there. She'd never considered that she still thought about that. But Carrie wasn't sure that telling her mother she'd gotten pregnant by a jerk and had to go home to LA for an abortion was the answer she wanted to hear either.

A few minutes later, a text from Jack came through. What was he still doing awake? It was almost one in the morning here, almost midnight in London.

Hope you're enjoying Paris. I'd love to catch up with you again this trip, if possible. Let me know.

Carrie closed her book and sighed. She felt his uncertainty through his words. She wished he were here with her now, but as her best friend, not the Jack she'd complicated everything with by having drunken sex.

If this had been anyone other than him, Carrie would easily give some excuse about this not being a good time for a relationship or that they didn't have the spark she was looking for—anything to get him off her back and go back to life as usual. But this was Jack, her dearest friend, and they couldn't return to any sense of normalcy until she addressed what happened, until she determined what it meant and where her feelings stood.

She thought back to that night, to the way everything felt so comfortable, so right. But when she woke in the morning, all that flashed through her mind was waking up in Adam Hartley's bed and how she'd destroyed her entire life over a man. And now here she was, quite possibly doing it again.

Carrie went to her browser and searched for her name along with Adam's in Google. She'd avoided looking up any stories since leaving LA, convincing herself nothing good could come of doing so. But the late hour and insomnia clouded her judgment, and she caved. To her relief, there were no new stories posted within the past week. That was the thing about Hollywood—events tended to vanish into oblivion just as quickly as they surfaced. If only Sherilynn's memory operated the same way.

She clicked on the original article she'd seen and scrolled through the photos. She couldn't deny her smile in the one of them on the red carpet. She looked so happy, so relaxed. When had she last allowed herself to be so comfortable around a man? The better question, though, was *why* had she let her guard down that night? Had it really only been the alcohol mixed with loneliness that sent her home with Adam? Or had there actually been something there?

She closed out of her browser and opened her message thread with Adam. He'd been messaging her since that night, but she had left them all unanswered. She couldn't face him, couldn't face the reality of what she'd done. She had been driving herself up a wall trying to figure out why she'd torpedoed her career for him, but she didn't seem to have the answers. Maybe he did.

She calculated the time quickly—still only early evening back in LA—and called his number.

"Carrie!" Adam answered. "Oh my God. How are you? *Where* are you?"

Carrie forced a smile, hoping to mask the nervousness in her voice. "I'm good. I'm actually in Paris right now."

"Paris...France?"

Carrie laughed. "Yes. It's a long story, but I'm here with my mom."

"Wow. Well, I guess that explains why you haven't returned my messages."

Carrie hesitated a moment. "Partly, yes."

"Ah, so you *were* avoiding me." She pictured him smiling as he spoke, his lips turned up and his dimples deepening. They'd always had this teasing nature between them since they first started working together. She had never read much into it, but now she wondered if the signs had been there all along, if she'd been flirting with him and hadn't even realized. Was that delusional?

"I'm assuming you heard I was let go," Carrie said sheepishly.

"I did. I had an argument with Sherilynn about it, actually. That was a bogus reason to fire you after everything you've done for me and how amazing you are at your job. But now that I know you were avoiding me, maybe I shouldn't have gone to such lengths to defend your honor."

Carrie smiled. "I'm sorry but thank you for doing that. The agency has very clear guidelines about relationships with clients, though, and I most definitely crossed a line that night." She paused and cleared her throat. "Which brings me to the reason for my call, actually."

"You want to talk about that night?"

Did Carrie imagine it, or did Adam sound excited to discuss it? "I guess I'm looking to figure out what happened." She cringed. Did she sound too clingy? Too weird? "I don't usually mix personal and professional, and it's been driving me nuts trying to figure out how we ended up back at your place."

"I mean, you agreed to it..."

"Oh, I'm sure I did," Carrie added quickly. She hadn't meant to give him any concern she was looking to "Me Too" him. "Maybe this was dumb. I just...I can't understand why, and I thought you might have some insight."

This was definitely dumb. Who just called up a celebrity and asked them to explain why they'd crawled into bed with them? He was a sexy actor. Was there really any other explanation needed?

Adam exhaled. "I'm not really sure I know either," he said. "I thought maybe there was something between us, but then you mentioned some guy who'd moved to London last year, and I started to think maybe you were still getting over your breakup."

Carrie leaned back into the chair. Had she really been talking about Jack to him? In a way that made him think he had been her boyfriend?

"Jack wasn't my boyfriend," she clarified, though she didn't know why she felt the need to. "Just a really good friend."

Adam was quiet a moment, then continued. "Can I be honest with you?"

Carrie braced herself. "Of course."

"I was pretty bummed when I woke up and you were gone. I understand why you left, professional boundaries and whatnot. But I thought we had a great night."

Carrie pushed her hair behind her ears. "In the spirit of being honest, can I tell you something?"

"Go ahead."

"It was a great night, and I was attracted to you. But what we did cost me my job, which was the most important thing to me."

"I know. And you're an amazing agent."

"Thank you."

Their confessions hung between them in awkward silence for a moment before Adam cleared his throat. "So, are you going to a new agency? Because if so, I'll follow you, if you don't mind. This new woman they matched me with is driving me nuts."

Carrie laughed. "Who are you with now?"

"Angela something?"

She should have been more surprised they'd given Adam to someone so new, but it made sense. Angela was the new Carrie, the college grad who would stop at nothing to further her career. From this vantage point, she saw all the signs that she would lose her personal life to her career, just like Carrie had. She wanted to warn the girl, but of course, she wouldn't listen. Just like Carrie wouldn't—didn't?—believe anyone when she was that age either.

"Angela's young, but she's good." Carrie leaned back into her chair, her shoulders slumping with an exhale. "I'm honestly not sure what my next steps are."

"Well, keep me posted?"

"Of course."

"Take care, Carrie," Adam said, her name rolling out of his mouth in a soft tone.

As she ended the call, a part of her wished she were still back in LA, wished she were the type of woman who gave up her dreams for a man. But that wasn't her. That would never be her.

———

The following morning came around far too fast. Before Carrie knew it, she was being woken to the bathroom door opening, a beam of light spreading into the room as her mother came out from a shower.

"Oh, I didn't mean to wake you," she said. "I couldn't sleep any longer, so I thought I'd get a jump on showering."

Carrie pushed herself up and grabbed her phone off the nightstand. It was only quarter to seven. "It's fine," she said.

Her mother turned the bedroom light on, and Carrie squinted. Her head was pounding, likely the result of zero sleep.

She slipped into the bathroom without another word, wishing she could teleport back to LA. She needed time to process her conversation with Adam. A rising star actor told her he had feelings for her and thought they would be great together. It wasn't every day that happened. And yet, the only face that kept flashing through her mind was Jack's.

Carrie swallowed a couple ibuprofen and took a quick

shower, motivated by her need for caffeine. Her stomach grumbled as she got dressed. She finished putting her shirt on and popped back into the room. "Breakfast?" she asked.

Her mother held up the guidebook she'd brought with her. "I was just looking up options. There's a place nearby that's supposed to be good. Holybelly?"

Carrie shrugged. As long as there was food and coffee, she was good. "Works for me. What's the address?"

Anita rattled it off, and Carrie plugged it into her phone and set the navigation, then led the way out of their hotel and a few blocks over. The streets were mostly full of locals since it was still on the early side and damp from an overnight rainfall. The smell of rain still hung in the air, and Carrie welcomed the cloudy morning. It matched her mood.

The restaurant was smaller than an American restaurant, but bigger than a typical Parisian cafe, and packed solid with people. Carrie expected a wait, but the hostess seated them immediately at a table tucked into the back corner.

"May I have a cappuccino, s'il vous plaît?" Carrie asked as she slid into the booth side of the table. The hostess nodded, then passed her request off to their waitress. The surrounding tables were full of conversations in English and several people underdressed in sweats and leggings. Carrie guessed not a single local was among them, but the menu looked good, so she wouldn't snub her nose just yet.

"Is everything all right?" her mother asked.

Carrie opened her menu, not meeting her eyes. "I just have a headache."

Her mother fiddled with her napkin before turning her attention to her own menu. "What are you getting?"

She tapped her foot and bit her tongue. Was she serious? Carrie had opened her menu five seconds ago. And how hard was it to just look at the menu and decide what she wanted for herself? "I don't know yet," she replied as calmly as she could muster. She was extra cranky because of her headache, but adding a spat with her mother wouldn't make things any better so she'd play nice. "But the sweet stack sounds pretty good."

A few minutes later, the waitress came with Carrie's cappuccino and took their orders. Without a menu for distraction, the silence between them felt strained. But the harder she tried to think of something to say, the more her mind drew a blank.

"Have you talked with Jack at all since we left London?" her mother asked, steering the conversation in the exact direction Carrie hoped to avoid.

"I haven't." She picked up her cappuccino and took a sip, sad to mess up the beautiful floral design marked in the foam.

"Can I ask you a question?" she continued as if on cue. "Just to settle once and for all a long debate between your father and me?"

Carrie clicked her tongue and braced herself. "Sure."

"Did you and Jack ever date?"

"No, we didn't." She said it nicely, but her mother's smile fell.

Carrie should have left it at that, but the disappointment on her mother's face mixed with her lack of sleep made her a softie. She rubbed at the back of her neck and looked away. "But Jack did tell me in London that he's had feelings for me for a long time."

The shift was subtle, but Carrie recognized the triumphant look in her mother's eyes. "And how do you feel about him?"

The directness of the question caught her off guard even though she'd opened the door and had been pondering it for days. Her mother was never so direct with her; that had been her dad's role. She wanted to tell her it wasn't her business and end the conversation, but she was actually making an effort and withholding her judgment, at least aloud. Carrie thought back briefly to the past couple of weeks. Her mother seemed to be trying, making more of an effort at conversation, trying to get to know Carrie in a way she hadn't for a long time. She had long ago given up hope of improving things between them, but she had to give her some credit for trying.

"I'm not sure," Carrie said, the admission almost lost in the noisy restaurant. "Honestly, I don't even think I'd know how to recognize those feelings if they did exist anymore. It's been so long since I've had an actual relationship, I don't even know what to look for. God, that's so pathetic." She stared at the salt and pepper shakers, willing herself not to cry. The young couple at the table next to them didn't seem to speak English, but they were too close for comfort for such a personal conversation. Of all the places to have this conversation, she'd sure chosen a winner.

Her mother's eyes widened. "It's not pathetic. When it's the right person, you'll know."

"How did you know Dad was the right one?"

Chuckling, her mother fingered her napkin on the table. "I didn't immediately. It was a few months before I thought he was 'the one.'"

"If it took so long, why didn't you walk away?"

She tilted her head. "We had fun together. He made me laugh. I didn't know he was my future husband, but he made me happy. And if I hadn't given it time, I wouldn't have known. Sometimes you need to wait it out and give things a chance to grow into what they're supposed to be."

"I guess that's my problem. I never want to give things that long of a chance. I want a clear-cut answer right away."

"It's not a problem, but maybe something to consider working on."

Carrie squinted at her mother. Who was this perceptive being in front of her? "You sound like a therapist."

Her mother shrugged. "Just some wisdom I've gained over the years. The two best things in my life were worth waiting for."

"Two?"

"Your dad," she said. "And you."

Chapter 14

The rain was coming down hard, and Carrie marveled that a little red awning was enough to separate her from being soaked like the pedestrians scuttling by. The locals stood out easily, unfazed beneath their sturdy umbrellas. The tourists, on the other hand, were mostly ill-prepared and scurried beneath nearby awnings, ready to buy some shelter in the form of a drink or afternoon snack.

They had spent the morning at the Paris Opera house and Galeries Lafayette, both perfect rainy morning activities. After their stop for lunch and coffee—always more coffee—they were headed back to the Galeries for their macaron class. Her mother hadn't stopped talking about it all morning. Carrie still didn't understand what the big deal was, but it seemed to mean a lot to her, so she was looking forward to crossing this off their list. For Carrie's part, all she could focus on was her phone. After her mother went to bed last night, she'd pulled up the list she brainstormed of potential contacts and emailed several of them, doing her best to put a positive spin on her current situation.

As she finished the last sip of her cappuccino, her mother excused herself to the restroom, and she whipped out her phone. She refreshed her inbox, watching the circle spin around and around. Still nothing.

Carrie tipped her head back and let out a small groan. Each day that passed without a lead on a new job made her increasingly anxious and kept her from relaxing and enjoying her time here as best she could.

She again pulled up her list of contacts, staring at the names and wondering who, if anyone, would be gracious enough to give her a chance. All she needed was a shot to prove she wasn't the screwup she seemed to be that night. Still, Jack's words rang through her mind. Should she be considering options outside of LA?

"Work?"

Carrie jumped as her mother walked up behind her, then quickly closed out of her email and stuffed her phone back into her small black purse. "Yeah," she said. "Nothing urgent." She stood up and clapped, feeling like a kindergarten teacher. "Ready?"

Her mother eyed her a moment, and Carrie worried she was about to call her out. Had she seen the list on her phone? No, she'd closed it quickly. And even if she had seen a list of names, she wouldn't know who they were or what it meant. Finally, her mother nodded and grabbed her umbrella, and they headed back out onto the sidewalk.

The rain had slowed enough so their umbrellas were sufficient to keep them from getting soaked on the ten-minute walk back to the Galeries.

They walked in silence, the pattering of the rain on their umbrellas their soundtrack. After several minutes, Carrie looked around. Something didn't look right.

She looked over at her mother, who was also looking around at the buildings.

"Did we go the right way?" Carrie asked. She generally took

pride in her ability to navigate a city, but Paris was proving to be confusing. Its many angled streets had her getting mixed up constantly the past couple of days.

"Oh dear," her mother said. There was worry in her eyes, the crinkle above her nose giving away her concern. She looked at her watch. "We're going to be late now."

Their class started at four p.m., and it was currently twenty to. They had time. The Galeries couldn't be too far.

"Just hold on a second," Carrie said as she moved to the edge of the sidewalk and reached for her phone. She pulled up her navigation app and searched for the Galeries.

"I can't believe we got lost," her mother said. "We're going to miss the class."

"Mom, we're not going to miss it. It'll be fine. We have plenty of time."

Carrie focused on her phone, but out of the corner of her eye saw her mother tapping her foot. Her anxious buildup only tensed her in turn. She intentionally took a deep breath, reminding herself this wasn't a huge deal and they'd find their way. Trying to reason with her mother when she was like this was a fruitless endeavor, so she'd just focus on figuring out where they were and how to get back to where they needed to be.

"I knew we should have left the cafe earlier."

"You're the one who had to use the bathroom," Carrie pointed out.

"We should have left earlier," she repeated.

The directions loaded and Carrie bit the inside of her cheek. "Okay, this way," she said. "We went left when we needed to go right back there."

She began walking and her mother followed, letting out a loud sigh. She ignored her and kept moving.

"There it is," Carrie called out when the Galeries was

within sight.

"There's only a few minutes before it begins."

"We'll be fine. If we miss the first couple of minutes, I'm sure it won't matter."

"We're just going to walk in while the class is going on?" her mother asked, her eyes practically bulging from their sockets.

Carrie drew another deep breath. "Yes. It will be fine."

They made their way across the street and through the main entrance of the Galeries. Once inside, Carrie stepped to the side and pulled out her phone. "Okay, where exactly is the class?" she asked as she scanned the confirmation email for the location information.

Her mother checked her watch again. "It's four o'clock."

"Mom!" Carrie shouted. "I know the time. But you constantly shouting it out isn't helping anything."

Her mother leaned back slightly, her mouth slightly open and her eyes wide. Carrie wasn't usually so harsh with her, but this was getting ridiculous. The more she obsessed about the time, the more stressed Carrie became, and the longer it would take them to get to the class.

"Okay, it's on the third floor." She pointed to the escalator in the middle of the store. "This way."

Instead of following, her mother remained frozen in place, her lips tight and her eyes narrowed, like she was about to cry. "This never would have happened if your father were here."

Carrie whipped around, walked a couple paces, and looked right in her mother's eyes. "You honestly think I don't also wish I were here with Dad instead?" she asked, her voice much louder than she'd intended.

Her mother looked around, her face turning red. Other shoppers turned their heads towards them, clearly checking out the commotion.

Carrie regretted the words instantly, but her mother had

pushed her. Again. How did she live with this level of anxiety all the time? Still, they had a class to get to. Carrie would be the bigger person. As usual.

"Mom, I didn't mean that. I'm sorry. I'm just stressed too and was trying my best to get us here on time. It will be fine to walk in a couple minutes late, I promise."

Her mother cleared her throat but kept her head down. "It's fine. Let's just go."

They took the escalator up to the third floor and found the hidden room tucked into the back corner where the class was being held. Sure enough, one of the chefs greeted them at the door. The class hadn't yet started.

Such a waste of energy.

———

"It was absolutely ridiculous," Carrie said later that evening to Jack as she relayed the macaron class incident. Her mother had already gone to sleep for the night, but she wasn't yet tired. Instead, she'd gone for a walk and Jack had called her on his way home from a happy hour with his coworkers. She had found a bench near a statue and watched a group of local teens skateboard while she talked.

"It sounds like it," Jack said. "I can't imagine getting so worked up about being a few minutes late for something."

Carrie chuckled. "Says the man who's always early for everything."

"Fair enough."

"I didn't even know what to say to her. And then I just lost control." She felt terrible for basically telling her mother she wished she were dead rather than her father, but she'd only been able to hold in so much. "I tried so hard to get us there as quickly as possible. She just didn't understand her anxiety was actually making it take longer. Then she comes at me and tells me that wouldn't have happened if my dad had been there instead? Honestly? He'd have taken even longer trying to navigate the GPS!"

"I mean, you're not wrong." Jack's voice trailed off, the way it did when he had more to add but wanted permission first.

"But..." Carrie prompted.

He sighed. "I guess I feel a little bad for her," he said. "She's on this trip with you but she must be constantly thinking what it would be like if your dad were there instead. It must be really hard for her is all I'm saying."

"You're supposed to be on my side, you know," Carrie teased.

"I'm always on your side." Jack paused. "But your mom *is* your only family now. I completely understand your reasoning for pulling away from her before, but she needs you now, and whether you want to admit it or not, you could use her too."

"You're my family," Carrie said, then regretted the words instantly, trying to be cognizant of not unintentionally leading him on.

He was quiet again. "I'll always be here for you, Carrie. You know that. But you're on this trip with your mom. Maybe just ask her how she's doing? Give her the opportunity to be open with you rather than the two of you constantly having your guard up with each other."

She looked around at the other tourists walking by, several couples walking hand in hand. They were in one of the most romantic cities in the world, and Carrie could imagine being here with her daughter rather than her husband had to be difficult. Still, her mother's anxiety was so unbearable.

But she loved how Jack cared about her—truly cared—even after how terribly she'd treated him just a week ago, and it killed her to still have this awkwardness hanging between them.

Carrie sighed and cleared her throat. "Jack?"

"Yeah?"

"I'm sorry."

"Um..." He paused. "What for?"

"I shouldn't have come over there the other night. I'd had too much to drink, and I wasn't thinking clearly. I messed up, and I'm sorry."

Jack was silent, and Carrie's mind raced wondering what he was thinking.

"Jack?"

"I'm here. I'm sorry too."

"What are you sorry for?"

"I shouldn't have put this on you, not now. You have enough going on and I just added to it all."

"You don't need to apologize. I'm glad you finally told me."

"You are?"

"I mean, yes, it does complicate things, but if that's how you feel, I'm glad you told me."

"But you don't feel the same, do you?"

Carrie opened her mouth to speak, then closed it again.

"It's okay," Jack said. "I didn't really expect you to love me back. Okay, I mean, maybe partly I hoped you would. But I get it. We're friends, and that's good enough."

"It's not...it's not that I don't love you," Carrie said. "It's more that I don't know if I love you in the romantic kind of way. And with just losing my job and everything being such a mess right now...I just need some space to sort things out."

"Fair enough," Jack said. "I'm always here for you if you need me. But really, try talking with your mom."

"I'll give it a try," Carrie conceded.

"Good. Night, sunshine."

She smiled, pleased they'd cleared the air. "Good night, Jack."

Chapter 15

As they left the Louvre the following evening, the pyramids out front sparkled with light. Had Carrie known there were three of them before today? Maybe. Somewhere in the back of her mind, she vaguely recalled knowing that. Her father had probably told her. It seemed a fitting end to their final day in Paris to spend it at the behemoth museum he had been most excited for.

While inside, she'd imagined him beside her, filling her in on the history of the museum that used to be a castle and giving her little bits of trivia about the art they viewed. She would have rolled her eyes, of course, and pretended not to care, but she'd always been grateful for his tidbits of historical knowledge. Lord knows she didn't have the time to learn such things for herself.

Carrie glanced at her mother, whose eyes were glazed over as she stared at the central pyramid. She'd seemed distracted inside, like she was hunting for something specific but didn't know what. Carrie's conversation with Jack the previous night ran through her mind, and her heart softened a bit. Of course the Louvre had been difficult for her. It had been hard for

Carrie, and she wasn't the one who'd been planning a trip here with her father for years.

She walked over to her and bumped her lightly with her elbow. "Dinner?" she asked.

Her mother nodded, and they began walking in silence, leaving the glowing pyramids behind them. There was bound to be a restaurant close by. The city was packed with them, much like at home, and Carrie marveled that so many were able to stay in business.

Sure enough, around the corner they found a cafe with a mostly empty outdoor section and a menu that was agreeable, and they took a seat and waited for their server. Carrie felt a twinge of guilt at not putting more thought into their last dinner in Paris, but they'd had some amazing meals this week. Tomorrow, they would be on to Barcelona. Two weeks down, two more to go.

"That was harder than I expected," Carrie ventured, opening the door for her mother to share her experience. It was strange making space for such a vulnerable, honest conversation with her, but Jack was right. They both needed someone to talk with about their grief.

Her mother nodded, her eyes still glassed over. "I thought it would be the same as the other places we've gone, but this was tough."

"It's because the entire place screamed Dad. I kept expecting him to come up behind me with some corny history joke."

Her mother laughed. "Is it weird I was kind of hoping he would?"

Carrie opened her mouth, but the server approached and interrupted. "Bonsoir," he said as he handed each of them a menu.

"Bonsoir," her mother replied. She sounded much more natural, more comfortable than just two weeks ago.

Carrie looked around and took a deep breath. She would miss Paris, its classic architecture, the smell of cigarettes and coffee that mingled throughout the streets. She generally found cigarette smoke appalling, but for some reason, here in Paris, it didn't bother her.

They each ordered a glass of wine, a blush for Carrie and a white for her mother, and when the waiter walked away, she set down her menu and looked directly at her mother.

"So, how are you doing?" she asked.

Her mother took a sip of wine and squinted at her. "I'm okay," she said, though it came across as a question more than a statement.

"No, I mean, how are you really?" Carrie leaned in a bit. "Like, how are you handling...missing Dad."

Wow, she was horrible at this.

Setting her wineglass back on the table, her mother ran her fingers around the stem, her eyes trained on the glass. "It's been hard," she admitted. "I've just been hoping for some sign he's here with me, but so far nothing."

Carrie nodded. "It was weird for me going back to Buffalo," she admitted. "Being at the house without him...it made it real, I guess. If that makes sense?"

Her mother tilted her head. "It does."

She looked at the empty table beside them and swallowed hard. "Mom, I'm sorry I didn't come back to visit after the funeral."

"It's okay."

"No, but it's not. I should have been there for you, but instead I threw myself into my work to avoid the reality of Dad being gone." She paused and took a breath. "I think it affected me more than I wanted to admit."

Her mother looked at her for a moment before the waiter came back. This man had impeccable timing.

"I'll have the beef bourguignon, s'il vous plaît," her mother said

"And for you, mademoiselle?"

"I'll do the same," Carrie said. "And a cheese platter to start."

The waiter left, and she turned back, uncertain how to continue the conversation.

Her mother grabbed her wineglass again. "This wine is wonderful," she said. "I imagined the wine would be good, but I really haven't had a bad one yet."

Carrie nodded, mentally preparing to shift topics and move away from their discussion of Dad and their grief. It made sense to do so. They'd never been good at talking about tough things with one another.

But then her mother set down her glass and folded her hands on the table. "Carrie, I don't know that I've properly thanked you for coming on this trip with me." She paused and fiddled with her napkin. "I know how important your work is to you, and it means so much to me that you took this time away to come with me. I've been grateful since you told me you got the time off, but I realize I haven't actually told you that. So, thank you."

A stab of guilt hit Carrie, and she struggled to take a breath. She should come clean, tell her the real reason she was able to get away from work. Right? Or would that only make things worse again? Was a small lie—though, one could argue this lie wasn't quite so small—worth it to maintain the peace between them? If she told her mother she'd had no intention of ever asking her boss for the time off, that she was only here because she'd been humiliatingly fired, wouldn't that only create more issues than it resolved?

Carrie forced a smile. "You're welcome," she said simply, then reached for her glass and took a large gulp of wine. Another time. Maybe.

———

After dinner, the rain had cleared, and they strolled along the Seine, taking in their last sights of Paris after dark. They paused for a minute when they glimpsed the Eiffel Tower between buildings and trees at the top of the hour, twinkling away more magnificently than Anita could have imagined before seeing it in person.

They moved on, strolling past tourist shops and closed-up book stalls. They stopped at an Amorino for gelato. Though they were both full from dinner, there was always extra room for gelato. Victor insisted there was a special dessert pocket, and Anita thought of him as they leaned against a railing overlooking the Seine, cups of gelato in hand.

"Look," Carrie said, pointing to their right. "Notre Dame."

"Oh, I hadn't even noticed it," she said. Since the fire, it wasn't lit up at night and blended into the darkness. Victor had been so looking forward to going inside the cathedral, and seeing it so dark, trying not to draw attention to its devastated remains, stirred sadness in Anita. Another reason not to put off adventures. She'd finally made it, but the world didn't wait for you to get your shit together. It simply marched on as it always had.

They finished their gelato and made their way to the metro station around the corner. Before they descended the stairs, Anita took one final glance around at the Île de la Cité. She felt she'd made progress this week, allowing herself to relax more and enjoy the experience, and Paris now held a special place in her heart. Maybe she'd make it back here someday. Maybe when the repairs to Notre Dame were completed. She hoped so.

Anita followed Carrie into the metro and through the turnstiles. Though the metro had overwhelmed her their first day, they'd mastered it quickly and no longer paused at the signs to determine which direction they needed to go. They waited only a couple minutes for the next train, then boarded as several people raced off. The seats were full, so she and Carrie took a spot standing by the central bars. Anita took a breath and waited for the train to depart, then startled at a thud on the platform.

She looked back to the door where a man lay face down on the platform, his leg caught between it and the train.

"Oh my God!" a woman screamed.

Anita was still processing what she saw as the signals sounded that the doors were closing, the train about to leave. A young man pushed past her and yanked the man's leg out of the gap, but he remained unmoving.

"Monsieur?" the young man asked, but there was no response.

A few people bumped into her as crowds formed both inside and outside the train. Anita stared in horror, saying a prayer the man was all right. She looked again at the large gap between the train and the platform. How could that be allowed? It certainly wasn't safe.

A man in a police officer's uniform approached and knelt beside the man. After a brief time that seemed to last forever, the man pushed himself up and hobbled off with the officer. The young man who'd helped him hopped back onto the train, and the doors closed. The train departed and the crowd dispersed, everyone going back to business as usual. But Anita couldn't get the image out of her mind. What if the train had left before the young man intervened? What if that had happened to her?

"You okay, Mom?" Carrie asked, her voice quiet and reassuring.

Anita nodded, though her reflection in the metro's window was ghostly white. *It all turned out fine*, she reminded herself.

They arrived at their stop and she and Carrie walked through the tunnels until a gust of wind greeted them as they reemerged onto the Paris sidewalk. They crossed the street, walking around the corner and back to their hotel, a route now so familiar Anita could do it in her sleep.

"I'm going to take a quick shower before bed," Carrie said once they were back in their room.

"Okay. I'll start packing for tomorrow."

Carrie disappeared into the bathroom, and Anita swung her empty suitcase onto the bed. It might have been more work to unpack and repack her bag each time they changed locations, but Anita never understood how people could live out of suitcases. She needed all her belongings organized and accessible.

She found the folder with their travel reservations and pulled out the train tickets for tomorrow. This next week would be a tough one. The anniversary of Victor's accident was coming up in six days, and Anita wondered once again if spending it at the Sagrada was only going to make the day that much harder. But then again, the cathedral was the place Victor most wanted to see. If he was going to find her anywhere on this trip, that was likely where he'd be.

Setting the tickets down on the bed, Anita grabbed her purse. She reached for the zipper and froze. It was almost completely open. Had she forgotten to close and lock it after dinner? She plunged her hand in, searching for her passport, but the pocket she kept it in was empty. Her stomach clenched, and she felt like she was going to pass out. She violently shook the bag upside down, hoping to see the navy-blue booklet fall onto the bedspread. Several things fell out, but not the passport book.

Shit.

The bathroom door opened, and Carrie came out, wrapped in a fluffy towel. "Is everything okay?"

"I...I can't find my passport."

She narrowed her eyes, and her eyebrows scrunched together. "What do you mean?"

"I forgot to lock my purse after we left the restaurant, and my passport isn't in here." Anita threw the empty purse on the bed beside scattered receipts and euro coins.

"Are you sure you brought it with you today?"

She nodded, but she scanned the room in case she was wrong. She remembered grabbing it this morning. "I had it," she said with certainty. "What are we going to do? We're supposed to leave for Barcelona tomorrow morning!"

Carrie tucked the top of her towel into itself, freeing her hands. "It'll be okay," she said. "Do you still have your credit cards?"

Her credit cards. Anita looked at the bed. They hadn't fallen out with all her shaking, but she thought she remembered seeing them in there. She scooped the purse back up and looked inside. There were the cards, still tucked into the side pockets. "Yes," she said. "They're here."

Carrie visibly exhaled. "Okay, that's good. Double check the safe and make sure you didn't leave your passport in there this morning. I'm going to get dressed really quick."

She grabbed a pair of sweatpants and a T-shirt out of her dresser and went into the bathroom again.

Anita rushed over to the safe and entered the four-digit passcode, her fingers stumbling over each other. After entering the code incorrectly twice, the door popped open, revealing only the photocopies of their passports, a few credit cards they left behind, and Carrie's iPad.

"It's not in here," she called out.

"Okay, give me one minute."

Anita's heart rate took off and her vision blurred. She'd been doing so well, her last panic attack in the airport prior to their flight to London. *Damn it.* She crossed the room and sat down on the bottom edge of her bed. She stared at the ceiling, blinking to ward off the tears.

The bathroom door opened, and Carrie emerged in her sweats, her wet hair framing her face.

"I'm such an idiot," Anita said, trying to catch a full breath.

Carrie shook her head. "You're not. This happens. It'll be okay."

"What are we going to do about our train?"

Carrie grabbed her phone from her dresser and tapped away at the screen. "We'll figure it out. The embassy opens at nine a.m. We'll get there right when they open and find out what we need to do."

"But our train leaves at seven!"

"Mom!" she shouted, dropping her phone to her side. "It will be fine. We'll change our train tickets. It's not the end of the world."

But it felt like the end of the world. This was precisely what Anita had feared. She'd been careless, letting her guard down, and now she was paying the price. She recalled the shove she'd felt on the metro when that man was lying helpless on the platform. Had that been when her passport was stolen? What an idiot she was.

Now her passport was just out there somewhere, with God-knows-who, and who knew what they were planning to do with it. It would probably end up in the hands of some criminal who'd go on to commit horrible acts in her name. And what then? Would she end up being charged with a crime she truly didn't commit? Or what if she was asked for her passport tomorrow morning before they made it to the embassy and she didn't have it? Would she be arrested for not having proper identification?

Anita brought her hands to her cheeks. "I can't believe I let this happen," she said, staring at the carpet.

"Mom, calm down. Seriously. This happens all the time. It's not a big deal."

"Easy for you to say. You're not the one who's going to end up responsible for some terrible crime being committed."

Carrie raised her eyebrows at her, and Anita looked away. She hated that look, the one that meant she was being ridiculous and Carrie wanted nothing to do with her irrational thoughts.

"Do you want a Xanax?" Carrie asked.

She did, but she also resented being treated like a child by her own daughter. "I don't need a Xanax! I need my passport."

"I know, Mom. But there's nothing we can do about this until the morning. So, let's just get some sleep and we'll sort it all out tomorrow."

"But what about Barcelona?"

Carrie drew a deep breath before responding, her face turning red. "Barcelona isn't going anywhere. If we need to post-pone a day or two, we will."

"But that will affect all of our other plans."

"Mom!"

She was right: there was nothing they could do about this until tomorrow. And yet, Anita couldn't stop. The what-ifs kept cycling through her mind.

Carrie went into the bathroom and came back with the orange pill bottle and a glass of water. Anita grabbed the bottle and shook a pill into her hand, refusing to look her in the face. She swallowed the pill and waited for the effects to kick in. Her thoughts slowed down along with her heartbeat, and after several minutes she was able to get up and change into her pajamas.

"Get some sleep," Carrie said, then turned out the light. "I promise, everything will be fine tomorrow."

In the darkness, Anita let the tears slip down her cheeks. She was no longer worried about the passport. They'd figure that out. What bothered her now was the fact she was so reliant on these stupid little pills. Would she ever be able to live her life again without an orange bottle on standby?

Chapter 16

The following morning, Carrie and her mother rose early, showered, and took the metro to the American Embassy. They'd been right in front of it a few days prior on their way to see Monet's waterlilies and hadn't noticed the building. Now, it seemed like an intimidating fortress. Beside her, her mother clenched her fists, her body stiff. She'd been on edge all morning, despite Carrie's attempts to convince her this wasn't that big of a deal.

She had been trying to put herself in her shoes since last night, but she couldn't understand what had her so frazzled. Sure, losing her passport was an inconvenience and the timing wasn't great, but if the worst-case scenario was they had to postpone their train to Barcelona and spend a little extra time in Paris, that didn't seem so bad. At least it wasn't their flight back to the States they had to rearrange. Carrie cringed to think how much that rescheduling fee would be.

The argument she'd had with her dad the night before he died kept replaying through her mind all morning. For the past year, she'd carried guilt over their last conversation, over the fact the last words she spoke to her father had been in anger. The harsh words she said that night haunted her, but watching her mother freak out about something so small reinforced she'd been right.

They entered the embassy and went through the security inspection, Carrie taking the lead. She glanced back at her mother. Her face was pale, and her hands were shaking. She looked like she was on trial for murder rather than here to replace her passport. The security guard collected their cell phones and directed them to the appropriate room, and they stood in line behind several other U.S. citizens unfortunate enough to be in the same position. Still, none of them looked as distraught as her mother, except perhaps the young girl there with her parents.

"I can't believe I let this happen," her mother said for the thousandth time that morning.

"Mom, you have to stop. It's going to be fine. I promise."

She nodded but remained tense. She clutched the folded papers in her hand, the photocopy of her passport they'd brought with them and the directions to the embassy the hotel had been kind enough to provide for them.

"This isn't that bad," Carrie reiterated. "It could have been worse. They could have taken all your credit cards as well."

Her mother's eyes widened. "Oh my God, but they could have!"

Carried tipped her head down and rubbed her temples. They hadn't stopped for coffee on the way, on a mission to get this taken care of as quickly as possible, and Carrie longed for the convenience of countless takeout coffee chains back home. She'd need to find some caffeine soon if she had any hope of getting through this day.

"Next!" the man behind the counter called, reminding Carrie of the DMV.

"Bonjour," Carrie greeted him automatically, then briefly

wondered if she should have spoken English instead. "My mother's passport was stolen last night, so we need to get a replacement."

The man nodded, then handed her two forms to complete. "How quickly do you need it?"

"Well, our train was supposed to leave a couple hours ago. I saw there's another train at noon with availability, but will that be too tight?"

The man pulled his lips into a grimace. "We can have it ready today, but noon might be pushing it."

Beside her, her mother deflated.

"That's fine," Carrie said. "We'll reschedule our train for tomorrow."

The man gave them directions for getting passport photos from the photo booth and their payment options. The cost was much lower than Carrie expected for an emergency passport, which was a pleasant surprise. They collected the paperwork and took a seat against the wall along with those who'd been in line ahead of them.

Carrie handed the clipboard to her mother and stood up. "You fill these out, and I'll step outside to reschedule our train tickets and arrange an additional night at the hotel."

She took the clipboard but made no move to work on the forms.

"Mom?"

Her mother's head snapped up. "Hmm?"

"The faster you do the forms, the faster we can get out of here."

"You're right," she said. "Go on. I'll be fine."

———

Anita let out a long sigh after Carrie left the room. She looked down at the clipboard in her lap, but she could barely make out the words on the forms. Her right hand shook as she lifted the pen, and her heart rate was through the roof.

All morning, Carrie reminded her this could be worse, that rescheduling their train wasn't the end of the world. Of course it could be worse. Of course her endless worrying was irrational, but she couldn't control it. This was simply how her brain worked. If only she could make Carrie understand.

"Is this your first time in Paris?" the young woman next to her asked. The man beside her had his own clipboard and was furiously filling out the forms, a reminder to Anita she better get moving or all these people would be ahead of her.

Anita nodded and smiled cordially, hoping that would be the end of it.

"Ours too," the woman continued, bouncing her leg up and down. "Just got in yesterday, and my husband here was so cocky thinking his passport would be safe in his back pocket on the train from the airport." The woman rolled her eyes and then smirked over at the man. "Just one more check in the 'wife is always right' column."

"Yeah, well, you're lucky I love you," the man answered, his head still down as he continued to write.

Anita smiled back at the woman, feeling like she was on the inside of a joke. "How long have you two been married?"

The woman raised her left hand, showing off a solitaire diamond and a white gold band. "Newlyweds," she said with a giant smile. "This is our honeymoon."

Just as she'd suspected. "Congratulations."

"Thanks. Do they learn with time to accept you know better than them?"

Anita laughed. "Oh, if only."

The woman pulled her long brown hair into a ponytail and

wrapped a hair tie around it. "How about you?" she asked, eyeing the rings on Anita's left hand. "How long have you been married?"

Anita straightened in her chair. "Oh, um…" She placed her right hand over her wedding ring. "Well, it would have been forty-one years this year. My husband passed away last year."

The man's head popped up from his paperwork, and the woman's smile turned to a look of pity. "I'm so sorry to hear that," she said. "Forty years, though. Wow." She looked over at her husband. "That's hard to imagine right now."

"Oh, the time will fly by." Anita paused and looked down at her ring. "We'd always talked about going to Paris, but we never managed to get here."

"I'm sure he's here with you now. I'm Megan, by the way." She motioned towards her husband. "And this is Jim."

"I'm Anita."

"Anita. That's our cat's name!"

She chuckled. "Good name."

Megan shrugged. "I don't know why we picked it. She just seemed like an Anita. Are you here by yourself?"

She shook her head. "No, my daughter's with me. She just stepped out to change our train tickets. We were supposed to leave for Barcelona this morning."

"Oh, I've always wanted to go to Barcelona," Jim said. "It was the runner-up for our honeymoon, actually. But this one won out." He pointed a thumb at Megan. "Said the Eiffel Tower was the most romantic place in all of Europe, so how could we not go to Paris?"

"We have plenty of time for Barcelona," Megan said. "But I wanted our first vacation together to be Paris." She looked at Anita as though expecting back up.

She sighed, remembering a time when she'd thought the same. In her twenties, her sixties seemed so far away. Victor's retirement was an abstract idea, something she couldn't picture in any substantial way. But since his accident, she realized time really did go too quickly, that there were no guarantees of tomorrow. Did this new perspective make her wise or cynical? Perhaps it didn't really matter. Even if she said anything, these two lovebirds wouldn't believe her. How could they? People didn't vow their lives to someone while believing the worst. To believe in a life together, there had to be some level of ignorance to the realities that life could bring.

Carrie came back into the room, her pace quick and deliberate. "Okay, the train tickets are rescheduled for tomorrow, and I've booked us another night at the hotel here and let the one in Barcelona know we won't be there until tomorrow."

"Tomorrow?" Anita asked, trying not to sound overly agitated. "But the clerk said my passport would be ready today."

Carrie pulled off her crossbody purse and sat beside her. "The tickets for later today were ridiculously expensive, so this seemed to make more sense." She eyed the clipboard. "Um, how's the paperwork going?"

Anita bit her lip, her hand hovering with the pen over the blank forms, trying to wrap her mind around all the changes she was talking about. *This* was why she was so upset this morning. Carrie wanted to believe it was so simple to rearrange their plans, but now they'd lose time in Barcelona. Which meant they'd miss out on something. Seriously, how could she have been so careless?

"Mom?"

"Oh, I got distracted talking," she said, snapping out of her ruminations and motioning towards Megan and Jim. "We really couldn't get a train for today?"

Carrie pursed her lips together and looked up at the ceiling. "The tickets were expensive, but we can look into it more later if you want. For now, can we please get these forms completed so we can work on getting out of here?"

Anita put her head down, trying to focus on the questions, but her mind wouldn't stop spinning with all the chaos her idiocy caused. Why hadn't she kept better watch over her passport? The incident on the metro was the exact thing she had been warned of, the exact reason she'd been so cautious of where her passport was at all times.

She wanted to stop worrying about this, to take her mind off it and move on, but how? "I'm just worried we won't have enough time in Barcelona now. Why did I have to be such an idiot?"

"Mom!" Carrie shouted.

The other people in the room were all watching them now, and Anita wished she could run out of the building. But she needed her passport.

"I wish your father were here," she said softly, tears burning the corners of her eyes. Victor would reassure her, would already have a revised plan for Barcelona to walk her through.

"Well, this is exactly why I *didn't* want Dad here with you."

Anita narrowed her eyes. "What's that supposed to mean?"

Carrie's face reddened, clearly debating whether to keep going or not. Whatever she was holding back, Anita sensed it would change things completely.

"Tell me," she demanded.

Carrie stared at her. "He'd been to the doctor about two weeks before you were supposed to leave. His blood pressure was through the roof, but he didn't want to tell you. He didn't want to stress you out any more than you were or risk you trying to cancel the trip."

Carrie took a deep breath, maintaining eye contact. Though every part of Anita wanted to scream at her to stop, to not say another word, it was too late to stop her.

"The night before...before he died, he called me, and we argued about it. I wanted him to tell you so you wouldn't stress him out on the trip and risk his health any further. But he insisted he had it handled." Carrie paused and tilted her chin up. "The last conversation I had with my dad was an argument. Because of you."

Anita's vision blurred slightly, and she had to work to catch a full breath. Victor hid this from her? He'd wanted to go through with the trip despite the risk to his health? There were no words, nothing she could say to defend herself. None of it made sense.

She cleared her throat, and as she turned away from Carrie, several other people quickly looked back at their own clipboards. "I have to finish my paperwork," she said. What else could she say?

Carrie clicked her tongue. "Whatever." She grabbed her purse and dashed back out of the room.

Anita watched her leave while the world collapsed around her. To her left, Megan offered a slight smile, but she couldn't summon one in response. She put her head down and began writing. The faster she finished, the faster they could get out of here.

———

Carrie collected her phone from the security guard and stepped outside of the embassy. A couple passed by her, and cigarette smoke wafted her way. It had been years since she'd smoked while studying in Australia, but the smell combined with her current stress level triggered a cigarette craving. There was a *tabac* nearby—she'd seen it as they walked over from the metro— but she didn't need another reason for her mother to get on her case. Instead, she crossed the sidewalk to a small green space and sat on a bench.

Her phone pinged, and she pulled it out. It was an email from Kate Blinker, one of the contacts she'd emailed. Carrie didn't need to add to her shitty morning if it was a no, but she couldn't not read the email either. She took a breath, then clicked on the message and skimmed. The words "sorry to hear" and "absolutely love to meet" jumped out at her, and she squealed. She forced her eyes back to the beginning and read the entire email.

It was an opportunity. Not a solid offer, but that was okay. All she needed was one person willing to give her a shot. She could work with that. She tapped out a response, explaining to Kate she was overseas but hoping they could set up a meeting when she returned in a couple of weeks.

Carrie blew out a breath and set her phone in her lap. Jesus. Two more weeks with her mother, and she'd just blown everything up between them. Anything that might have been improving between them, Carrie had just taken out in the matter of thirty seconds.

She hadn't meant to hurt her, but watching her freak out over something so trivial had brought back too many memories from her childhood. All the times she'd nagged her about folding laundry the "right" way. Getting after her for not putting the cap back on her toothpaste and leaving her paper cup on the sink.

While she may have been right to worry about her dad taking this trip and angry with him for not seeing her perspective, in the end, none of it mattered. Whether she'd voiced her concern about his health or not, there would never be a chance for her to be proven right or wrong. Instead, she would forever harbor the guilt of arguing with her dad the night before he died and be haunted by the fact she argued with him in much the same vein she'd fought with her mother over the years: about something that wouldn't matter a few days later anyhow.

Across the street, a woman emerged from the embassy building. Carrie recognized her. She'd been sitting beside her mother inside. The woman scanned the scene in front of her, then locked her eyes on Carrie. She crossed the street and headed right towards her bench, and she groaned.

"May I?" she asked, motioning towards the empty spot beside her.

"Um, sure," Carrie said.

The woman sat down and took out a pack of cigarettes. "Want one?"

Carrie glanced up. She did, but she didn't want to give this woman any more reason to hang around. "I'm good, thanks."

The woman shrugged, then lit her own cigarette and took a long drag.

"I'm Megan."

"Carrie."

Megan kept her eyes straight ahead as she talked, taking slow puffs of her cigarette. "Listen, I don't know you or your mother. But I feel for her."

"What you saw in there..."

She waved a hand at Carrie. "I know. It's none of my business. But I was talking with your mother a bit while you were outside before, and she mentioned your dad passed away this year." She paused. "Are you married?"

Carrie shook her head.

Megan waited a moment before continuing. "My fiancé died a few years ago, three months before our wedding. Completely unexpected. He had a stroke at the gym one day, and that was it."

"That's terrible."

She looked down at her wedding ring. "It was really rough.

Jim has been a lifesaver, and I can't believe my life is what it is today. But that first year after Greg died? That was the worst year of my life. I acted in ways I never thought I would. I was difficult to be around."

Carrie's knee bounced up and down. She felt for this woman, but was she really using her personal tragedy to teach her some lesson about being nicer to her mother?

"All I'm saying," Megan continued, "is maybe cut her some slack?"

Carrie pulled her purse onto her lap and stuffed her phone back into it. "I appreciate your concern, but you know nothing about me or my mother."

"I know, I just—"

"No, you don't know. You witnessed one argument between us and made this generalization about who we are. I'm sorry for your loss and all, but please stay the hell out of our business."

Carrie stood and stormed off towards the embassy, her arms crossed. Apparently, there *were* worse places to be than stuck in a room with her mother.

Chapter 17

After Carrie fell asleep that night, Anita lay awake staring at the swirls on the ceiling, replaying her bombshell from this morning until she wanted to scream. Out the window, the city lights shone brightly, and the urge to venture out, to get some air, overtook her. She peered over at Carrie's bed to confirm she was truly sleeping, then quickly wrote out a note on the hotel stationery, changed into a pair of jeans and a sweatshirt, grabbed her purse and phone, and headed out of the hotel.

The streets were lively for almost midnight on a weeknight. The joys of city living—always something to do, no matter the time. A group gathered at an outside table with their drinks across the street, and Anita watched them for a moment. She'd imagined that was what Carrie's life in LA was like—surrounded by friends, out having a good time without the burden of a family waiting at home. But it was beginning to appear her vision of her daughter's life was wildly off base. Rather than the confident, carefree go-getter Anita always pictured, Carrie seemed burdened by all her life was and wasn't at the moment. And while they'd skimmed the surface of that topic the past week, Carrie still had her held at a guarded distance.

Anita shook off the thoughts and kept moving down the sidewalk, clutching her purse closely. Wandering Paris by herself, especially so late at night, intimidated her, but the room felt hot and stifling and she needed to think through what Carrie had shared with her.

She'd felt numb ever since they left the embassy, going through the motions simply to avoid inviting any further discussion about the matter. But how could Victor have hidden something so important from her? She'd thought they communicated well, thought they'd shared their lives with each other, and yet he'd kept this secret from her.

Even worse, he'd shared it with Carrie.

Of course he had.

She kept walking and stumbled upon a McDonald's. She laughed. As much as she and Victor planned their trip to ensure experiencing as much local cuisine and culture as possible, he insisted he wanted to visit a McDonald's at some point on the trip.

"They're all over the world for a reason," he'd argued. "And Frank at work told me McDonald's overseas is different. Something about their food quality expectations being higher."

Anita had simply nodded and agreed, happy to indulge his small request in exchange for the trip of a lifetime. Of course, McDonald's had been one of the first things to be cut from the list this go around. And in light of recent news, Victor shouldn't have been anywhere near a McDonald's in the first place. But everything else was closed, and the warm glow of the arches reminded her of home, so she crossed the street and stepped inside the restaurant.

"Different, my ass," she whispered to herself with a smile. The inside looked exactly like any McDonald's she'd walk into back home. The same signage—although upon further inspection, the menu items were listed in French—the same tiled walls, the same easy-to-mop flooring. The one difference she saw was an interactive menu board where you could place your order yourself. No need to speak with a cashier and navigate potential language barriers. Perfect!

Anita walked up to the board and ordered Victor's favorite—a Big Mac and a medium fry with a vanilla milkshake. Once her order was ready, she collected her tray and walked up to the empty second floor. She took a seat and tried a fry. It tasted exactly the same as back home. Anita shook her head and unwrapped the Big Mac. She had no idea what Victor was talking about. McDonald's here seemed identical to back home in her estimation.

She set down her sandwich, pulled out her phone, and began looking through the photos she'd taken since their trip started. Photos of places she had only dreamed of seeing in person years ago. They weren't the photos she'd imagined, of course. Victor was nowhere to be found among them.

And yet, had they been able to follow through on their original trip, what might have happened? Was his high blood pressure concerning enough he was truly putting himself at risk by following through with their plans? Or was Carrie overreacting? Would he really have put this trip ahead of his health?

Why hadn't he just told her?

She could wonder on this all she wanted, but she knew the answer, didn't she? If he'd told her, she'd have called the trip off immediately. Whether or not she really believed his health would be in jeopardy if they went, it would have been another excuse not to go, another excuse to sit home and continue in her safe bubble where her anxiety was manageable. Victor knew that. He wanted more for her. He wanted more for them both.

Of course there'd been obstacles preventing them from

taking this trip all those years, but how many of them were true impediments and how many had she exaggerated simply to avoid stepping out of her comfort zone?

The truth was, *she'd* been holding them back all these years. Her anxiety after Carrie was born crippled their opportunities to do new things, to explore the world, to venture beyond what they were familiar with. She'd known this all along, but Carrie's revelation that morning hit her in the face with it. Anita may have wanted this trip, but Victor *also* wanted it. And she'd held him back.

Her anxiety had run her life for too long. But she wouldn't live the rest a slave to it.

Victor wanted more for her.

Chapter 18

The smell of fresh baking breads and pastries. That was what Carrie would miss most about Paris. Waiting in line at the small boulangerie down the street from their hotel, she tried committing the scent to memory and vowed to come back to Paris sooner than later.

"Bonjour," Carrie greeted the cashier. She ordered two *pain au chocolat,* handed over a few euro, then met her mother at the small table outside where she'd waited with their suitcases. This was their last stop before they headed to the train station, finally on their way to Barcelona.

"So, we have one and a half less days in Barcelona," her mother began the moment Carrie sat down. "Are you sure we shouldn't consider staying an extra day?"

She took a bite of her *pain au chocolat* and shrugged. "We could," she said, repeating the same thing she'd told her on the walk over here. "But that would just mean less time in Rome, and I don't see how that's a better solution. We don't want to pay to rebook our flight home."

Anita took a bite of her own croissant, but her face remained scrunched in worry. "I guess that makes sense."

It did make sense, but that didn't stop her from constantly harping on it. A buzz from Carrie's purse pulled her attention, and she dug inside for her phone. An email from Kate Blinker, short and sweet. She was pleased to hear Carrie had a chance to get some "R&R" and she'd love to meet with her when she was back. Just let her know when.

Carrie rolled her lips in to disguise the smile she felt bursting across her face. Just one bite. That was all she needed.

"I'm going to miss Paris," her mother said, interrupting her joyful reprieve.

And yet you've been so eager to leave. "Me too," she agreed. She watched her finish up the last bite of her pastry, and Megan's words came back to her. Was she being too harsh with her mother? Maybe. But the issues between them weren't new since her dad's death. Still, perhaps she could lighten up with her, try to understand where she was coming from. Maybe.

They finished their final Parisian breakfast, then collected their bags and walked across the street to the metro station. From there, they took the metro to the train station.

Gare de Lyon station bustled with people hustling to their trains, but they still had time to spare before they needed to board. "Coffee?" Carrie asked as they approached a Starbucks.

"Sure," her mother said. They wheeled their suitcases into the line, but the smell of espresso was so heavy, and Carrie's stomach churned. She cleared her throat and held her breath a moment, hoping the nausea would pass, but it didn't.

"I'm good, actually," she said, trying not to draw attention. She pointed at a bench a little farther down. "I'll wait over there."

"Are you okay?"

Carrie waved a hand. "I'm just feeling a little lightheaded all of a sudden."

"Do you want me to get you a coffee? Or some food maybe?"

She shook her head and rushed out of line. Dropping onto the bench, she put her head down in her hands, closing her eyes. The smell was gone, but the incessant urge to throw up wouldn't leave. She hadn't felt ill this morning at all; she was fine until she smelled the coffee, an aroma that was usually a Godsend to her. There was only one other time she recalled when the smell of coffee had put her off so badly.

Carrie's eyes flew open. She scrambled in her purse for her phone, then pulled up her calendar and desperately counted the days. In the craziness of traveling, she'd lost track, but she should have been due for her period yesterday.

Shit.

It was possible she was wrong. With all the stress the past several weeks, her cycle could easily be off. But she didn't have the usual pre-period cramps, and the coffee thing was definitely new.

And she and Jack had forgotten protection.

How could she be so stupid? She'd gone off the pill a few months ago, wanting to give her body a break from the many years of hormonal birth control. Clearly, she hadn't been thinking at all that night. This seemed to be a trend with her lately.

Her mother walked towards her, rolling her suitcase with one hand and carrying a tray with two coffee cups in the other. Carrie sat up, blew out a puff of air, and attempted to wipe the worry from her face.

"Are you sure you're okay?" her mother asked. "Your face is very pale."

She stood up and steadied herself on the handle of her suitcase. "I'm fine now. Just a weird little spell."

Her mother pulled a venti cup from the tray and handed it

to her. "I figured you might want something for the train," she said.

Carrie took the cup and thanked her but left the stopper in and kept it as far from her nose as possible. She forced a smile and motioned toward their gate. "Shall we?"

———

The train from Paris to Barcelona was the longest seven hours of Carrie's life. She tried to sleep, but her mind wouldn't allow her to. She got up to use the bathroom at least a dozen times, each time praying to discover her period had started, but no such luck. Babies and pregnant women seemed to overrun their train, constant reminders that the possibility of returning to her life as usual back in LA may be in serious jeopardy.

"Are you sure you're all right?" her mother asked as they waited for a taxi outside of the train station in Barcelona.

Carrie rubbed at her temple. "I'm fine. Just tired." Her act was unconvincing, but it was all she could give at the moment. Her mind was preoccupied trying to determine how to find and take a pregnancy test immediately without her mother noticing. At this point, the only thing that would ease her mind was a negative test.

The man running the taxi stand ushered them into a cab. While Carrie longed to look out the window and take in the scenery with her mother, even being in Barcelona wasn't enough to take her mind off this potentially disastrous situation. What was wrong with this picture that her mother was the calm one while Carrie's own mind raced a mile a minute?

They checked into their hotel, each minute excruciatingly slow, and after setting the bags down in their room, Carrie blurted out that she needed to pick something up from the corner store.

Her mother checked her watch. It was already past four o'clock, and Carrie's own stomach rumbled, but she couldn't hold off any longer.

"Do you want me to go with you?" She eyed her up, clearly wondering what was going on with her. Exactly what Carrie did not need.

"No, I'll be fine. You can relax. We'll head out for food when I get back."

Carried raced out the door before her mother could interject further, over to the store she'd seen a few doors down as their cab pulled up to their hotel. She found the pregnancy tests nestled beside the condoms, a joke Carrie found particularly cruel in this moment. She knew nothing about brands or accuracy, and she certainly wasn't going to figure that out with the boxes in Spanish, so she grabbed the most expensive one and hurried to the register.

"Bonjour," Carrie said, then shook her head. "I'm sorry. Hola."

The cashier smirked and reached for the box to scan. Though she probably wasn't, Carrie imagined she was judging her purchase. But she wasn't a teenager anymore. For all this cashier knew, this could be a joyous occasion for her. Carrie straightened and plastered a smile on her face.

As she was about to walk out the door, she remembered she needed a decoy to bring back for appearances. She dodged down the nearest aisle, searching for anything that might be worthy enough of ducking out to the store the moment they entered their room. Deodorant! Perfect.

She hustled back to the register, even more thankful she'd never see this woman again, tucked the box inside her purse, and raced back to the hotel.

"There you are," her mother said as she entered the room. "Did you get what you needed?"

Carrie pulled the deodorant out of her purse, holding it up like her most prized possession. "Just give me a few minutes to freshen up and we'll head out."

She locked the bathroom door behind her just in case and pulled the other box from her purse. Pulling the thin, wrapped package from the box, she stared at it for a moment, horrified she was reduced to this again. It had been over a decade since she'd last needed a pregnancy test, and the memory of that day hung over her now.

After awkwardly peeing on the plastic stick, Carrie replaced the cap and set the indicator on the sink. She started the timer on her phone for three minutes, then looked in the mirror, willing herself not to look down until the timer buzzed. She tugged at her hair tie, letting her hair fall from its messy bun, and brushed out the mess. She retied it into a more presentable ponytail, then rinsed off her face and threw on some foundation and mascara. Regardless of the outcome, she'd have to suck it up and go for dinner with her mother, and she needed to at least look presentable.

Her phone vibrated on the counter, and Carrie closed her eyes. She drew two deep, slow breaths, and opened them.

Two pink lines. One in each window.

She sunk onto the toilet and clasped her hands over her mouth. What was she going to do? Her whole life was already in shambles; did she really need something else added to the chaos?

She reached for her phone and opened a new text message to Jack, then closed out of it. In any other circumstance, he'd be the first person she'd reach out to. But no matter how unplanned this situation was, she wouldn't drop the bombshell he was going to be a dad via text message, especially an impromptu, hastily written one.

A gentle knock on the door pulled her from her thoughts. "Carrie? You okay?"

Carrie looked back at her phone. She'd been holed up in here for fifteen minutes. "I'll be right out," she said, trying not to let her voice crack with emotion.

She forced herself up and checked herself over in the mirror. Her eyes were still slightly red from fighting back tears, but hopefully her mother wouldn't notice. She swiped on a fresh layer of deodorant, threw her jacket back on, then looked around for what to do with the test stick and box. Without another option, she emptied her toiletry bag onto the counter and stuffed the box and test inside.

She swung the door open and smiled as best she could. "Dinner?"

Her mother looked her over, likely trying to piece together what was so off with her today. "Sounds great," she finally said.

With her eyes on her, Carrie felt like a child concealing a secret again as she stashed the toiletry bag with her suitcase, trying to behave as casually as possible. The words were on the tip of her tongue, waiting to be released, looking for some outlet so she could talk this through and somehow determine this wasn't *actually* the end of the world, but Carrie forced herself to stay quiet. Until she knew how she was going to handle this, until she'd discussed this all with Jack, she couldn't say a word to her.

She threw her purse over her shoulder and followed her mother out of the hotel room, coaching herself into a positive mindset. One way or another, she'd get through this evening and as many more as needed until she figured out what to do.

———

Her mother chatted away as they walked to the restaurant, one from the original list her parents had put together, as though she'd been waiting for the opportunity to spew out all the history and random facts she'd absorbed about Barcelona over the years.

"Did you know Barcelona was offered the Eiffel Tower before Paris, but they turned it down?" her mother asked. Any trace of the anxious individual who'd been on the verge of a meltdown due to the change in their plans just yesterday was long gone, and she was now fully back into ecstatic tourist mode.

More than anything, Carrie wanted to be consumed by the magnificence of Barcelona. She spotted the top of the Sagrada Familia as they walked, complete with construction cranes as the basilica was still some years from completion. Traffic whizzed by, and Carrie feared being run over by a moped when they attempted to cross the street. With the sun now fully set, the Catalonia capital seemed more energized than when they'd arrived only an hour ago.

Carrie longed to join her mother in enjoying the sights, but she couldn't focus on anything other than the two pink lines that were now burned into her brain. All she wanted was to travel back to a week ago when her biggest concern was whether or not her career was forever derailed. She wanted to go back to stressing over whether she and her mother would have enough topics to fill a dinner conversation, back to when any decisions she made affected her and her alone. The idea of being responsible for another individual was beyond her comprehension.

Her mother ceased talking suddenly, as though she'd run out of words. The silence was welcome, but a glance over at her mother confirmed that she was not okay as her eyes glossed over and her eyebrows pinched with worry.

"Mom?"

"Sorry," she said. "It's just...your father was most excited for Barcelona. And with the anniversary coming up...it's hard not to think about it."

Carrie swallowed hard. In the day's chaos she'd forgotten how close they were to the anniversary of her dad's death. It felt like an eternity and only a few days at the same time since she'd last spoken with him, last told him she loved him, last joked with him.

"It's just going to be a tough week," her mother said.

You have no idea. "It will," she agreed. She looked at her mother, who'd turned ghostly white thinking about the upcoming day, and suddenly her own problems seemed small. Yes, an unplanned pregnancy was life-altering. But she hadn't lost her husband. She hadn't lost the person who mattered most to her in this world. Her thoughts briefly turned to Jack and how devastated she'd be if she lost him. Was that love? Carrie shook away the question. "But it'll be okay," she continued. "We'll get through it together."

They found the restaurant and followed the hostess to their table. As they sat down, Carrie took in the atmosphere. The restaurant was dimly lit with flickering candles on each table and was filled almost exclusively with couples. She looked at her mother, who seemed to notice the same thing.

"I don't think we did enough research on this one," Carrie teased.

Her mother's bottom lip quivered. "I forgot. We'd chosen this place for our anniversary dinner. We were supposed to spend our fortieth anniversary in Barcelona."

"We could go somewhere else if you want. But I'm okay here if you are."

Unsurprisingly, she opted to stay. Getting up and leaving would embarrass her mother more than dealing with the awkwardly intimate setting. They ordered a plate of stuffed olives to share and looked over the menu.

Just as Carrie thought the evening might take an upturn, her head began throbbing with a headache, stress induced no doubt. She rubbed her temples, and her mother noticed.

"Carrie," she said, her tone soft and serious. "I know you've been telling me all day everything is fine, but I'm sorry, I don't believe you. What's going on?"

Carrie stared at her, and despite years of experience telling her the opposite, she saw someone she could talk with, someone who loved her in her own obnoxious way but might be able to offer some support in this moment.

"I just have a lot on my mind," she started, testing the waters. Her mother had been different the past week or so, less critical and more open. But Carrie was so used to keeping her guard up.

"I'm here to listen," she said. "I know you always shared these things with your dad. But I'm here for you."

Carrie bit her lower lip. She needed to unload some of this weight or she was going to explode. Maybe her mother was right. Maybe she could trust her with this. *Just do it. Just rip off the bandage.*

"So, the real reason I got the time off from work for this trip is because I was laid off." Carrie closed her eyes instinctively, then forced them open and looked at her mother.

Her eyes widened, and Carrie could see the pieces falling into place for her. "Laid off?" Her voice was full of disbelief. "How come?"

She grimaced. "Well, fired would be a more accurate description."

"Fired?" Her mother leaned back in her chair. "Carrie, what happened?"

Her tone felt critical, but Carrie reminded herself she was

likely just surprised, just trying to comprehend how her workaholic daughter had been fired.

She played with her fingers and forced herself to continue. "Remember the night you called me about the trip? It was the premiere for Adam Hartley's new movie? Well, things got a little out of hand, and I ended up filling in as his date." She paused and took a deep breath. *Just get the rest out there.* "Long story short, I went home with him that night, which is against the agency's policy."

Her mother's mouth fell open a bit. "You mean to tell me you slept with *Adam Hartley* and got fired for it?"

"Um, yes." Carrie bit the inside of her lip, then leaned back as the waiter placed a basket of bread on the table.

"Do you still need a minute?" he asked.

"Si, por favor," Carrie said.

Her mother blinked several times, then continued. "So, are you in a relationship with him?"

Carrie winced. She didn't know which was worse—admitting to her mother she'd had a one-night stand or admitting she'd been fired. It was a close call but being fired probably won out. "Not exactly," she said.

Her mother placed her napkin on her lap and fiddled with her silverware, refusing to look at Carrie.

"Mom?"

"Hmm?"

"Say something."

"I don't know what you want me to say."

"Just say what you're thinking." Did she really want to know? Maybe not, but she *needed* to, needed to know where this left them.

Her mother shook her head and looked off to the side. "I guess I'm disappointed you hid it from me. But it does explain the lack of work you've been doing." She paused, and sadness passed over her face. "And it explains how you got the time off to begin with."

Guilt stabbed at Carrie's heart. Had she only come on this trip because it was a convenient getaway from the chaos she'd created at home? Yes. But now that she was here...she might have made a different choice had she known how much it meant to her mother to finally follow through on this trip.

"I'm sorry I didn't tell you. I was embarrassed and disappointed in myself, and I'm still trying to figure out why I did it."

"You did seem rather frazzled when you got to Buffalo. I assumed you were tired from the plane ride, maybe grieving without your dad there. But this makes more sense. You just seemed so...fine. Until today."

Carrie froze, put on the spot. She couldn't continue, couldn't tell her about the pregnancy test hiding in her suitcase back in their hotel room. Revealing she'd been fired had been enough of a bombshell for one dinner. Even if she wanted to, she needed to tell Jack first. He at least deserved that from her.

Carrie opened her mouth, trying to find some excuse for today's odd behavior, but her phone vibrated and lit up on the table. She lunged for it, grateful for the distraction.

"Who's that?"

"Jack." Her voice cracked over his name, so many emotions hitting her all at once. Jack, her best friend, her rock. Jack, the man she'd slept with on a drunken whim and ruined everything.

Jack, the father of her child.

Carrie cleared her throat and read the text message. "He wants to meet up with us while we're in Barcelona."

Her mother's face brightened. "That would be wonderful. I didn't get to see him while we were in London."

Carrie smiled half-heartedly. She wanted more time to process all of this, to figure out how she felt before letting others in on the news. But she needed to face Jack at some point, and as much as she wasn't ready to share this news with him, something tugged at her. She wanted to see him, no matter how complicated things were. She needed her best friend. She needed Jack.

She looked back at the text message, then began typing. *That would be great.* She hit send and reached for the breadbasket, bracing herself for the chaos.

Chapter 19

The following night, after a flamenco dance performance, Anita and Carrie scoured the town for a restaurant for dinner, but finding a place they both agreed on was proving impossible. Everything she suggested, Carrie scrunched up her face at, and her ideas all offered limited menus with nothing Anita found appetizing. She had been acting odd all day, back to the highly reserved version of herself who'd first landed back in Buffalo. Anything Anita said was met with a grunt or one-word answer, and she'd even seemed distracted throughout the flamenco performance. Just as she was about to give in to one of Carrie's choices just to save the peace, they stumbled across a small little Mexican restaurant. The bright and cheery décor welcomed them after a long day of walking, and while it seemed odd to go all the way to Spain for authentic Mexican food, they both agreed tacos and guacamole hit the spot.

After they ordered, Carrie pulled out her phone and began snapping photos of the restaurant. "This is a pretty neat find," she said.

Anita nodded. It wasn't what she'd expected from

Barcelona, but she had to admit it was a fun little restaurant, and at least she understood the menu.

Victor would have loved it.

She turned away and bit her lip. She'd been doing surprisingly well today, but they had been on the go since this morning, moving faster to fit as much as they could into their shortened time in Barcelona. But with the break in momentum, all the sadness caught up with her again.

"Mom?" Carrie asked.

She cleared her throat and shook her head. "Sorry," she said. "I got distracted."

Carrie leaned towards her. "Missing Dad?" she asked, her voice quiet.

Anita nodded, though it wasn't the whole truth. She missed him, yes, but there was a newfound anger since Carrie told her about his blood pressure that she couldn't shake. And yet, being angry with her deceased husband felt wrong.

"Just thinking about how much he'd have loved this place," she said, trying to keep things light. "He was always such a sucker for homemade guacamole."

Carrie chuckled. "He definitely was." Her eyes drifted away. "I've been missing him a lot today too."

"Grief's fun," Anita said, trying for a lighthearted joke, but Carrie turned back with watery eyes, a major departure from her guarded demeanor earlier.

"What's wrong?" she asked, leaning in slightly.

Carrie shook her head. "I just wish Dad were here." She paused, and her eyes grew wide. "I don't mean I wish he were here instead of you. I hope you didn't—"

Anita waved her hand. "No, I understand."

"It's just so unfair." Carrie's shoulders slumped.

It was the same sentiment she had ruminated on for the past year. She'd often told Carrie as a child that life was unfair. It was one of those platitudes parents pulled out for their kids when they whined about not getting a candy bar in the checkout line or that some other kid got the lead role in the school play. It seemed trite and cliché, but Anita felt every word deeply. Nothing about her life these days felt fair.

She bit the inside of her cheek. While the restaurant buzzed with happy, tipsy tourists, her mind spiraled down a rabbit hole of grief. Looking at Carrie, a fresh wave of guilt overtook her. Had she not been so forgetful, Victor might still be here with them. Had she gone to Walmart instead of him, Carrie might still have her father.

"It was my fault," she said, her voice barely audible in the noisy restaurant.

Carrie's eyebrows furrowed. "What's that?"

"It was my fault that your dad...that he was at Walmart that night."

"What do you mean?"

Anita blinked to stop the tears that threatened and shook her head, the night still vivid in her mind. "I'd forgotten to pick up an extra voltage adapter. I was going to run to the store, but he offered to go instead. That's why he was there." She swallowed hard and looked towards the bar. "If I'd just remembered the adapter, he'd still be here."

Carrie reached her hand across the table and placed it over Anita's. "Mom, it's not your fault Dad died. You couldn't have known. People forget things all the time. You can't blame yourself for what happened."

It was exactly what Meredith had been telling her for a year, and, logically, it made complete sense. It *was* silly to assume the blame for such a careless accident. But emotionally, Anita didn't think she'd ever relieve herself of the guilt.

"It's not your fault I argued with Dad the night before his

accident either," Carrie continued, looking down at the table. "I'm sorry I put that on you. I was wrong."

She smiled, but she couldn't help thinking Carrie was letting her off the hook too easily. It *was* her fault they'd argued. If her anxiety hadn't ruled her life so thoroughly for so long, Victor may have felt he could tell her about his blood pressure without fear of her canceling the trip. Since her miscarriages, she'd leaned on Victor to get through the tough times, the times when her anxiety was too overwhelming and rendered her paralyzed to do things on her own. It just hadn't occurred to her the toll that had taken on Victor or the things he'd given up to support her.

Still, this was the most honest, open conversation she and Carrie had ever had with one another. Maybe she hadn't been so delusional after all in hoping this trip would bring them closer together. And yet, it was an odd feeling to know this was only possible because of the tragedy they'd endured. That if it weren't for the loss of Victor, they might still be essentially estranged.

Maybe some things weren't ever meant to make sense.

Chapter 20

The next day, Carrie mentally berated herself for agreeing to let Jack meet up with them for the weekend. As she and her mother walked to the restaurant they were meeting him at for lunch, her stomach ached. Though whether that was due to morning sickness or anxiety, she couldn't be sure.

Of course, the situation could be a lot worse. She could be sixteen years old and knocked up by her homecoming date. The baby's dad could be some no-good idiot Carrie had a one-night stand with. Her situation wasn't ideal, but there were far worse ones she could be in. And yet, that knowledge did nothing to fend off the nausea she felt thinking about sharing this with Jack and, eventually, her mother.

One step at a time. Telling Jack would be difficult. Seeing him again after all that happened in London might be strained and weird, but he deserved to know she was pregnant. And hopefully once he knew, they could figure out the next steps together.

Her mother kept glancing at her as they walked, likely trying to gauge her mood about meeting with Jack after their encounter in London. Carrie was certain her face was ghostly white, but to her mother's credit, she didn't ask a single question.

Jack was already seated at a small outdoor table beneath an umbrella when they arrived, his carry-on bag tucked between his chair and the building behind him. Even arriving from a different country, he was still more punctual than Carrie. He looked amazing—the perfect amount of stubble on his face, his smile wide and inviting. As Carrie sat beside him, the smell of his cologne washed over her and she had an urge to grab his shirt collar, pull him towards her, and kiss him as though it were the most natural greeting for them.

Was that love or hormones?

"Hi, Jack," her mother said as she settled across from him beside Carrie. "Long time no see."

"Too long," he replied, eyeing Carrie. "It's great to see you again, Mrs. Lorello."

"Oh, you're as sweet as always. Please, call me Anita."

"Anita," he repeated. "I'm sorry we didn't get to see each other while you were in London. If I'd had more notice, I'd have taken the week off and shown you ladies around properly."

"That would have been lovely. It was just such a spur-of-the-moment plan. I'd actually forgotten you were in London now. How is the job going?"

Jack nodded, though his attention was now on Carrie. "It's going really well, thanks."

He tried catching her eye again, but she buried her face in the menu. If she looked at him, he'd know something was up with her. What had she been thinking, letting him come here?

"I'm starving," Carrie said, though she had no appetite. "What's good here?"

"I've never been here, so don't ask me," her mother teased.

Jack was silent a moment, just long enough for the space

between them to feel uncomfortable. "Well, I've never been *here*, but you can't go wrong with paella in Barcelona," he said.

"You've been to Barcelona before?" her mother asked.

He sipped his water and nodded. "A couple of times. Once during my study abroad while I was staying in Paris and again a few months ago with a friend from work. It's so easy to get to these places from London. It's unbelievable how inexpensive it is."

Something about the way Jack said 'a friend from work' triggered something in Carrie. Was that jealousy? Had he been seeing someone over here and not told her? He couldn't *still* be seeing someone, could he? No. Jack wouldn't do that. He was too honorable to cheat.

"I didn't realize you studied abroad as well," her mother said. "Such a great opportunity study abroad is, don't you think?"

All thoughts of Jack's love life were now replaced by annoyance at the small dig in her mother's words. She kept her eyes on her menu, but her heart rate sped up and her cheeks warmed.

The waiter came to the table and Jack took it upon himself to be the connoisseur, ordering a bottle of wine for the table. Carrie swallowed hard. She didn't know much about being pregnant, but she knew alcohol was a giant no-no. But how could she avoid drinking a glass of wine without drawing attention?

After their glasses were filled, Jack lifted his in a toast. "To spending a wonderful weekend in Catalunya with the two most beautiful women I know."

Her mother blushed and lifted her glass to join him. Carrie grabbed hers, then paused midway to her lips. Jack looked at her and smiled, and she took a small sip, then set the glass down. A tiny amount wouldn't cause any harm, right?

She set the glass down and cleared her throat. "Just a tad dry for me," she said.

Jack's smile fell.

"I'll order something else. Something sweeter?" He turned his head and put his hand up, signaling to their waiter.

"No, it's fine," Carrie said, louder than she'd intended. "I'm okay, really."

Jack locked eyes with her, and her stomach turned. This had been a mistake. She'd been naive thinking she could hide something this big from him, even for a day. She'd hoped to have some time with Jack before telling him to sort out her feelings about him, about the baby, about what all of this meant. As of now, she had no idea what would come next. But it was only a matter of time before he caught on, and she needed to tell him before he pieced it together on his own.

Maybe it was for the best. Jack always seemed to have the answers. Maybe he had the answer for this.

———

They grabbed a cab back to the hotel after lunch so Jack could check into his room and drop off his bag. He and Carrie shared the backseat, but she didn't dare look at him. She felt his eyes on her, likely trying to sort out her odd behavior. She hoped she could pass it off as feeling awkward in front of her mother, but at some point, she would owe him an explanation.

After a couple of awkwardly silent minutes, there was a gentle tap on her knee. She turned to face Jack, whose face was scrunched with worry. "Is everything okay?" he asked. His voice was barely above a whisper, but there was no radio on in the cab.

Carrie opened her mouth to reply, but her mother turned her head just slightly.

Instead, she nodded, then tilted her head towards the front seat.

Jack's hand inched closer to hers on the empty seat between them, resting just shy. Carrie wanted him to take her hand, to tell her everything was going to be okay. Or at least, she wanted to want that. What an easy, movie-perfect ending to decide she loved him after all, move to London, and start a family together.

But real life wasn't a movie. What about her career? Would she have to move to London? Or would Jack move back to LA?

And then there was the small matter of the fact she didn't even know if these feelings for him were real or just the hormones talking.

Or was all this just her commitment issues flaring up?

She moved her hand into her lap, tucking it between her legs, and flashed an apologetic smile at Jack. She should have arranged a private meetup for his arrival. What part of her thought lunch with her mother had been the best idea?

When they arrived at the hotel, Carrie and Jack led the way into the lobby.

"I'm just going to run up to the room real quick and grab some ibuprofen," her mother said. "I'm starting to get a headache."

Carrie caught the slight look of mischief in her eyes as she headed for the elevator before she could join her, then followed Jack to the empty reception desk. Standing beside him, she swallowed hard, trying to get rid of her nerves. This was just Jack.

"What do we think the odds are your mum actually has a headache?" he asked while they waited for someone to greet them at the desk.

Carrie stifled a laugh, some of her nerves disappearing. "My mum?"

He closed his eyes and smirked. "British influence."

"Of course. You're a true Brit now."

Jack reached for her hand. "My vocabulary might lean that way, but my heart is very much still in California."

Carrie cleared her throat and tucked her hair behind her ear with her free hand.

"Jack…"

"I'm sorry," he rushed to say, then dropped her hand. "I told myself not to come on too strong my whole way here this morning. But then I saw you and I just…I'm sorry."

"It's just that…"

"I know. You're still upset about what happened in London."

Carrie blinked at him, unsure how to respond.

"That's why you've been acting weird all day, right?"

"It's not that," she said automatically. Was that it?

"Then what is it? You can't tell me it's nothing. You've refused to look at me since I got here."

Carrie took a deep breath and tried to gather her thoughts, but the desk clerk appeared from the back room.

"Hola," he greeted them. "Reservation for two?"

Carrie blushed.

"Just myself, actually," Jack said, reaching into his pocket for his wallet.

While he checked in, Carrie breathed in his cologne and blinked to prevent tears. She wanted to go back to a year ago, back to when everything made sense in her life. When her father was still alive, her mother's anxiety wasn't her concern, and she and Jack were best friends without the question of whether she wanted anything more looming.

The clerk handed Jack his key card, then disappeared again.

"We need to talk," Carrie said. "Alone."

He raised his eyebrows. "We are alone."

"When we have more time," she clarified, eyeing the elevator.

"Okay. Just tell me one thing." Jack placed his hands on her shoulders and looked her square in the eyes. "Are you okay?"

Carrie cleared her throat and struggled not to break eye contact. "I am," she said. "We'll talk."

"When?"

"Tonight? Mom usually goes to bed somewhat early."

"Okay," Jack agreed.

Carrie closed her eyes. The pressure was on now. She had to tell him tonight whether or not she was ready. Whether she had answers or not.

Chapter 21

By the time the check arrived at their table, Anita was exhausted from trying to keep a conversation going throughout dinner amid the silence and strange looks between Carrie and Jack. What the heck was going on between them, and why had she invited him for the weekend if she was going to be cold to him the entire time? But it was none of her business. She'd stay out of it and hoped Carrie would see she was trying to do better.

They walked out of the restaurant, and Anita pulled her sweater a bit tighter around her. The sun was almost set, and a crisp, autumn chill greeted them. "If you two don't mind, there's a place nearby I wanted to visit by myself," she said, trying to sound nonchalant. They'd passed the secondhand bookstore Victor had been so enthused about on their way to the restaurant, and it was clear from dinner these two needed some time alone to sort out whatever was going on.

"You don't have to leave on our account, Mom." Was she imagining it, or was there a pleading tone to Carrie's comment?

"No, it's okay. Tonight seems like a good time to go. I'll be fine on my own." Fine might be stretching the truth a bit, but she was comfortable she could at least make it to the bookstore and back to the hotel on her own. Besides, Carrie was only a call away if something went wrong.

"Jack," she continued. "It's great to see you again. I'm looking forward to continuing our adventure tomorrow."

"Likewise," he said with a smile.

Anita walked away, leaving them to whatever hashing out they needed to do. She came upon the Sagrada Familia, illuminated against the darkening sky, and paused to take in its incredibly detailed exterior. Even with construction cranes parked beside it, it was one of the most remarkable pieces of architecture she'd ever witnessed. Her heart grew heavier as she stood there. She'd hoped to sense Victor with her at some point on this trip, desperate for any connection to him she could get, but so far, she hadn't. The trip was more than half over, and she worried she would leave for home without the closure she had hoped for after all.

She moved on and found the bookstore, an English secondhand shop she'd stumbled across in her research and excitedly shared with Victor. He loved secondhand stores, always said they were like a treasure hunt where he didn't know what he might discover.

The shop looked dim and empty inside, and given it was already a few minutes past eight o'clock, she worried it might be closed despite the open sign in the window. But when she pushed on the door, it opened, and bells signaled her arrival.

"*Bona nit,*" a man greeted her from behind the counter. He was about her age with a full head of gray hair and a pleasant smile.

"Hello," Anita said, then quickly corrected herself. "I mean, *hola.*"

The man smiled and the lines around his eyes deepened the

way Victor's had in recent years. "Anything I can help you with tonight?"

"I'm just browsing for now but thank you."

"If you need anything, my name is Enric."

Anita slipped down the nearest aisle. Books filled every crevice of the shop, and she ran her fingers down their spines, inhaling the musty smell of dust and ink and leather-bound editions. She closed her eyes. Victor would have been in heaven here. She could almost see him, plucking book after book from the shelves, marveling at the yellowed pages, checking for hidden notes. He had a thing about collecting handwritten notes left behind in secondhand books. She imagined him finding one and looking up at her with an expression like a child in a toy shop, his eyes saying, "See? Isn't this amazing?" And she'd smile back at him, just as she was now.

She opened her eyes. The dim aisle was empty. Victor was gone. Really, really gone.

"Everything all right, *senyoreta?*"

Anita jumped at Enric's voice behind her and spun around, swiping beneath her eyes. "Oh, I'm so sorry," she said. "I'm fine, *gracias.*"

Enric studied her a moment as though trying to determine if he believed her. "American," he said. "Where are you from?"

"Buffalo, New York," she said, forcing a smile. "Near Niagara Falls."

"Ah, Niagara Falls. *Magnific.*"

"Have you been?"

Enric pulled a book from the shelf beside him and slipped it into a different spot. "No." He turned back to Anita with a devilishly handsome smile. "Someday, si?"

She chuckled. "You sound like me."

Enric tilted his head. "How is that?"

"I've dreamed of coming to Europe 'someday' for so long." She spread her hands, motioning around her. "Now here I am."

Enric leaned against the bookcase, and they locked eyes. "Here you are."

Her heart sped up, and she looked away, simultaneously uncomfortable with the attention yet feeling a connection with Enric she couldn't put into words.

"What brings you to my little bookstore your first time in Barcelona?"

"My husband."

He looked around as though expecting to find a man he'd overlooked.

"He passed away," Anita clarified.

"I'm sorry to hear that." His sparkling eyes darkened subtly, but enough that she knew he was also a widower.

"Gracias."

"How did he bring you here?"

Anita fiddled with her wedding rings. "It's a long story."

"I have time," he said, glancing around the empty bookstore. "Would you care for some wine?"

Anita considered telling him she had to leave, that someone was waiting on her, but she *could* use a glass of wine. And something niggled at her, telling her she could really talk with this man. "That would be lovely," she said.

She followed Enric, pausing for him to flip the open sign to closed. His office was tucked into a small room behind the cash register. Clutter littered the space, just as Anita imagined a bookshop owner's office to be. He picked up a pile of books from his desk and placed them beside another stack on the floor, then opened a small cupboard, producing a bottle of red wine. From the shelf above his desk, he grabbed two wineglasses and set them on the desk.

"Do you always keep wine in your office?"

Enric looked at her, his expression serious. "Si. You never know when a beautiful *senyoreta* will come in needing a glass of wine and a friend."

Anita straightened but said nothing.

"*Perdó.*" Enric handed her a filled wineglass. "That was rude of me."

She waved a hand. "You're fine," she said, curious about this man who was quick to call himself her friend and seemed to know exactly what she needed.

"I lost my wife not that long ago," he said, his voice softer and more distant. "It is hard." He sat at his desk and motioned to a chair across from him.

Anita sank into the chair. "It is."

"What happened to your husband?"

She took a long, slow sip of her wine. "A car accident. He was coming out of a store, and a young man hit him in the parking lot."

"That's horrible," Enric said. "I'm sorry."

Anita looked out into the empty store, her eyes filling with tears. "We were supposed to leave for London the following morning. I'd forgotten a voltage adapter and he ran out to pick one up." She paused and took a deep breath. "If only I'd remembered that damn thing, he'd still be here."

Enric was silent, not rushing to offer comfort where there could be none. Most people became uncomfortable when she alluded to it being her fault and quickly offered assurances that she was wrong. But, somehow, he understood she wasn't looking for such platitudes.

"My wife died almost two years ago now," he finally said. "Cancer."

Anita frowned. "I'm so sorry."

"I watched her suffer for months, wishing I could trade places with her. I would have done anything to take that pain away from her"—he raised his hands in a shrug—"but that is not how life works."

"I can't imagine how awful that was." She leaned back and sighed. "It sounds terrible, but I wish I'd had the chance to say goodbye like you did."

Enric nodded and sipped his wine. "I've heard that before. 'Oh, you are lucky you had so much time.' But no amount of time prepares you for that final moment. And no amount of time makes it easier."

"Oh, I'm sure. I didn't mean to say it must have been easier. It's just...I keep thinking about what I would have said to Victor that night if I'd known we wouldn't see each other again."

"I still think about." He reached over and poured more wine for each of them. "I go over and over our last moments in my head, wondering if I told her I loved her enough, wondering if I should have said something different. The truth is, she was so delirious by the end, I don't know she understood a word I was saying anyway."

Anita swallowed sadness and looked out the office door at Enric's shop. "How did you get over your wife's death?" she asked, speaking softly as though she were asking him to reveal classified intel.

He shook his head. "You never get over it. It will get easier to find other things to be thankful for and to fill your days with, but the pain never goes away. It becomes a part of you, and you learn to live with it."

"I just can't believe it's been a year already. And then other times I can't believe it's *only* been a year."

Enric nodded. "I remember when Alba first passed, that first year. There were many days I did not get out of my pajamas. I only got out of bed to use the bathroom and maybe grab a slice of bread to eat. I would not even butter it. Alba was dead, so what was the point in eating anything more than unbuttered, cold slices of bread? I was alive, but I was not living."

Anita's eyes widened as Enric spoke her own thoughts aloud. "How long did that phase last for you?"

He shrugged. "It came and went. There was no magical date I woke up and moved on. It happened slow, then I would be better for a time, but always I would go back to being sad. Each time it gets easier to pull myself out of the sadness, but it is always there, trying to make me give into it."

"You still struggle with it?" She'd been searching for words for encouragement, some tidbit of hope she could hang onto like a beacon shining into her grieving darkness. Yet all she heard was this was a wound that would never heal.

"It has become easier over the years, but not a day goes by that I do not think of my Alba and miss her, wonder what we would be doing if she were still here with me. I would not have it another way, though. She is still in my heart, like Victor will always be in yours. But I found ways to create a new life without her physical presence, and you will find that too." Enric paused for a sip of wine. "I must say, I am impressed at your dedication. Most people would not travel to a foreign country to work through their grief."

Anita smiled and looked down at her hands. The compliment felt unearned. She was here, true, but she didn't feel she'd worked through much of anything yet. "This trip was something we'd wanted to do for so long, but there was always some reason we couldn't, or at least we told ourselves we couldn't. I hoped that following through on it would help me find some closure."

"And did you?"

She gave a small smile and shrugged. "Honestly? I'm not sure." She looked around at the piles of books in Enric's office and imagined Victor here talking books with him. "Victor always loved secondhand bookshops. I'd found yours mentioned online and he was so excited for it. I just had to come here for him."

"Well, I'm happy you did." From most men, the phrase would have seemed like a come-on, as a man preying on her vulnerability, but from Enric, she only sensed sincerity and comfort. She'd been hoping for some sign from Victor, something to let her know he was here with her. As unbelievable as it seemed, Anita sensed this man was it.

"I feel so guilty being here without him, though. Victor should be the one here with Carrie. God knows they'd have had a better time together."

"Who is Carrie?" Enric asked.

"Oh, my daughter. She came with me."

He tilted his head. "And things are not going well with your daughter?"

Anita let out a puff of air. "They're fine, I guess. Better than I expected, honestly, but tense a lot of the time. She told me a few days ago that Victor's blood pressure was high right before his accident. The doctor was concerned, but he didn't tell me about it. He still wanted to go through with the trip. He didn't want to give *me* another reason to back out."

"He didn't want to worry you." Enric was so confident in his statement that Anita wondered if he'd done something similar with his wife.

"But he told Carrie." That was what it ultimately came down to, wasn't it? She understood why he hadn't told her. And besides, she hadn't told him everything throughout their marriage either, kept her own small secrets. The real issue was Victor and Carrie confiding in one another over her. Always. Anita was the third wheel in her own family, there but often not seen or included. And for him to have told Carrie then justified not telling her by citing her anxiety made her feel like a child rather than his life partner.

She loved her husband, but he hadn't always been perfect.

Anita glanced at the clock, suddenly feeling claustrophobic in the small, cramped office. "I should get going," she said. "Carrie will be wondering where I am."

"I am happy to have met you, Anita," Enric said as she stood up. He grabbed a scrap piece of a paper from his desk drawer and scribbled something on it. "I hope I am not being too forward, but here is my phone number. In case you need a friend."

Anita took the paper and stared at it a moment. She should offer hers in return, but that felt too much like an invitation for him to keep in touch. She'd appreciated his company, but she had no intention of speaking with him again.

She tucked the paper into her purse and stood up. "It was lovely meeting you as well," she said, then left the store and rushed back to the hotel.

Chapter 22

Carrie had never missed her mother more. She bit her lip as she watched her walk away, Jack's expectant eyes on her. This was it. No turning back.

He shoved his hands into his pockets. "Do you want to go for a drink?"

She did, desperately, but she shook her head, trying to defog her brain and form a sentence. "How about some coffee and dessert?"

If her suggestion surprised him, Jack didn't show it. "I saw a place back that way that looked interesting." He pointed down the street where they'd come from earlier.

They walked the few blocks in silence to the Gaudí Bakery. The walls inside were a mural in the style of Antoni Gaudí, and Carrie's first thought was how much her father would have loved this place. It was empty except for one couple at a table near the door. The case by the register displayed several beautiful pastries and cakes, and Carrie wished she had an appetite. She ordered a Nutella cupcake and a cappuccino to keep up appearances, and she and Jack took their plates to the back corner.

"So," he said almost immediately after they sat. He peeled the wrapper off his red velvet cupcake and blew on his espresso. "What's up?"

. If Jack was anxious about what was to come, he didn't show it. Carrie wanted to spit the words out, to just get the information out there so they could move onto figuring out what came next, but despite ruminating on this conversation all day, she still didn't have the words sorted. Instead, she cried.

Jack set down his cupcake and stretched his hand across the table, placing it over hers. "Hey. Everything's okay."

"You don't know that."

"I'm sure whatever it is can't be that bad."

Carrie sat up straighter and swiped beneath her eyes. How awful was she making him comfort her after she'd been cold to him all day?

"Now, tell me," Jack said. "What's going on?"

Deep breath in. Deep breath out. "I'm pregnant."

Jack pulled his hand back and his eyes widened for a second before he caught himself and forced a neutral expression. Two small words, yet two of the most life changing.

"I...I don't...Is it mine?"

Carrie closed her eyes. She couldn't blame him for asking, for making sure he had his facts straight before reacting. She *had* slept with a celebrity less than two weeks prior to being with Jack. But she'd done the math and verified the timing. "Yes," she said.

His expression remained unchanged. Carrie focused her attention on his uneaten cupcake, the white frosting still perfectly placed, and felt a bit guilty it likely would go uneaten now.

"What are you thinking?" she asked. Not knowing his reaction was torture.

Jack pressed his lips together. "I don't know."

Carrie slid back in her seat and looked down at her lap. "I know. It's a lot to take in."

"I thought you were on the pill."

She shook her head timidly. "I went off it a few months ago."

"Shit," Jack said, leaning back and covering his face with his hand. When he dropped his hand, his face brimmed with hope. "So...what does this mean? For us."

Carrie shrugged, apologizing with her eyes. "I don't know," she whispered. "I'm still processing all of this."

"I don't know what there is to process, Carrie." His voice quipped with agitation. "You either love me or you don't."

"Is it really that simple, though?" She truly wanted to know. Part of her wanted to collapse into him and agree to be with him. But a larger part of her hesitated. Was the hesitation because she didn't love him, or because she was afraid to love him?

"It should be," Jack said.

"To be fair, you did just drop this on me a couple of weeks ago."

He nodded and looked away. They sat in silence for a minute, then he swung his head back to her.

"Are you going through with the pregnancy?"

Carrie leaned farther back, the accusation like a physical push. "I..."

Jack ran his hands through his hair and let out a sarcastic laugh.

"What?"

"I'm not stupid, Carrie. I know a baby would hinder your life right now."

"I didn't say I wasn't keeping it."

"But it would tie you to me, something I'm not sure you want. And we both know you're not against abortion."

Carrie's cheeks burned. "Seriously? You had to go there?"

She couldn't imagine how painful this must be for Jack, to be so close to having everything he'd dreamed of, yet knowing she was still unsure. But to throw her past in her face like that—that was low.

He looked down at the table and stayed silent far longer than Carrie was comfortable with, though she was afraid to hear what he had to say.

Finally, he spoke, though his eyes remained down. "Was there any part of you that was excited when you found out?" His voice was quiet and small, not typical, confident Jack. "Any part of you that felt happy instead of like your life was completely over?"

Carrie turned her attention to the mural on the wall. Had it only been impending doom she'd felt when both lines appeared on the test stick? Had there been any glimmer of joy? All she remembered was the overwhelming anxiety of not knowing what to do next.

"I don't know," she said, turning back to him. "I want to say yes, but I...I don't know what to do, Jack. I didn't plan for this. My life was already a mess and now this? I'm scared, and I feel so helpless right now. And I'm trying to be honest with you, but it kills me that my uncertainty is hurting you."

Jack sniffled, and Carrie thought she saw a tear in the corner of his eye before he shook his head. "I know what I want," he said. "I very much want this baby, and I want to be with you. But you're the only one who can decide what *you* want." He pushed his chair back from the table and stood up.

"Jack."

"I'm sorry, Carrie," he said, not meeting her eyes. "I just need some time."

He walked away, leaving her alone at the table. She let her head fall into her hands and exhaled. That had gone even worse than she'd anticipated.

Anita wondered only briefly where Carrie might still be when she returned to their hotel room, relieved to have the room to herself for a bit to process her evening. As she washed the tears and makeup from her face, she reminded herself she had nothing to be ashamed of, nothing to feel guilty about. Everyone needed a friend to talk to, and that was all her conversation with Enric was. And yet, she couldn't stop feeling like she'd betrayed Victor, as though she'd crossed a boundary that may have been imaginary but felt real, nonetheless.

She turned the faucet off and stared at her reflection. She looked tired and aged, but there was a spark of hope within her. Enric's story and his understanding of her situation inspired her. He'd carried on without his wife, continued to run his bookstore and make new friends. Maybe, just maybe, life had something good in store for her yet.

Beauty products cluttered the bathroom vanity, most of which belonged to Carrie. Anita tried each morning to make some sense of the chaos, but it was a futile effort. Each of their shared bathrooms so far ultimately wound up a tangled mess of cosmetics despite their pristine conditions upon arrival.

She searched the mess for her ibuprofen, moving things around but to no avail. She went back into the room but didn't see the bottle on the nightstand or table. She riffled through her suitcase, but no luck.

Carrie's carry-on sat on the chair by the table. It wasn't likely it ended up in her bag, but Anita was running out of places to look. She opened the bag and pulled out Carrie's makeup bag. She unzipped it, then stared a moment, unprepared for what she found.

She pulled the box out of the bag and set it on the table. Spanish words covered it, but the photo was clear. The top had been opened, and Anita swallowed hard before pulling out the contents, a pregnancy test kit and the plastic wrapper.

Carrie's strange behavior since they'd arrived in Barcelona suddenly made sense—her aversion to coffee, her desperate need to get to a corner store alone, her awkwardness with Jack. How had Anita not pieced it together before?

She stood, dumbfounded, with the test kit in her hands. *In and out. In and out.* She didn't need to look at the test kit to know it was positive, but she forced herself to pull it out of the plastic wrapper anyway.

Positive.

And she'd said nothing to her mother.

Chapter 23

Carrie woke to an empty room and a pounding headache. Pieces of the previous night danced around her mind until the grogginess cleared and she put them in order, remembering everything.

Her heart sank as she recalled Jack's broken face as he left her at the bakery last night. She'd walked back to the hotel alone, unsure how to fix what she'd broken. Perhaps she should have waited until she was more certain of what she wanted, but she still wasn't convinced she had been wrong to tell him so soon. He was the father of this baby; he deserved to know it existed.

Instinctively, Carrie reached for her stomach. Could she go through with this pregnancy given her mess of a life at the moment and how unprepared she was? The thought of becoming one of those mothers who neglected their child because they couldn't figure out their own issues horrified her. But if the alternative was an abortion? She didn't know she could go down that path again.

She forced herself out of bed and into the bathroom. After washing her face and brushing her teeth, she called her mother's phone, but the phone's ringtone chimed from the nightstand. She threw a sweatshirt over her T-shirt and headed down to the breakfast bar.

She found her mother at a table in the corner, sipping coffee and staring out the window. "Hey, Mom," she said as she sat down across from her, trying hard to sound cheerful.

Her mother turned to face her, but her expression remained neutral, a far cry from her jovial mood the day before. "Oh, good morning."

Carrie swallowed hard. Something was up. "What are you doing down here?"

"I needed to get out of the room."

The iciness in her mother's tone brought her back to being in high school, to all the days she'd arrive home from school to her upset about something but waiting for Carrie to figure out what rather than just tell her. But she didn't have any more mental energy to expend. Whatever her mother was upset about, she'd have to deal with it on her own.

"How was your evening with Jack?"

Carried shrugged. "Fine."

"Is he joining us today?"

Okay, what did she know? The plan was for Jack to join them. Why would she think any differently? Had he booked it out of the hotel already and her mother saw him? "I'm not sure," she admitted.

"Hmm."

Oh, for the love of God. "What is it, Mom?"

"What?"

Carrie rolled her eyes. "Don't play that game," she said. "Clearly I upset you somehow, so just tell me what I did."

"You didn't do anything." Her mother paused and leveled a gaze at her. "I just thought Jack would be ecstatic to learn he was going to be a dad."

Carrie's jaw dropped. "I...how did you..."

Her mother smiled smugly. For once, she knew something Carrie hadn't intended her to. She picked up her coffee mug and shrugged as though playing detective was an everyday occurrence for her. "I found the pregnancy test in your makeup bag last night."

"Mom, I..."

Her hand went up, silencing Carrie. She said nothing further, just stood and headed to the elevator.

Carrie sunk back in her chair and sighed. Was there any way for her to screw things up even more? If there was, she'd certainly find it. She snatched her phone off the table and called Jack.

"Hello?" His voice was scratchy, freshly awake.

"Are you coming with me and Mom today?"

"I don't know, Carrie." He sighed. "I don't think that's such a great idea after last night."

"My mom knows."

Jack laughed. "Yeah, I think that's my cue to head home."

"Please? You can't leave me alone with this right now." She hated groveling, but what other choice did she have?

"I don't know what you want from me. You drop this all on me last night, but you're still not sure what you're doing or what you want. But now you want me to play buffer between you and your mom?"

Carrie let her head fall back. This was too much. "I can't deal with her on my own. Not like this, not when she thinks I purposely withheld something this big from her."

"But you *did* purposely withhold it from her, didn't you?"

"I mean, yes," she admitted. "But only because I thought you had a right to know first. Was I wrong for that?"

"Not necessarily. But I can see why she would be upset."

"Okay, great. So why don't you and her go exploring today

and talk about how badly I messed up, and I'll stay here and sleep?"

Jack sighed. "I'm sorry. I just...I don't know what I'm supposed to be thinking or feeling right now." He paused. Was she was supposed to say something? Before she could, he continued. "I've loved you for a long time, Carrie. But I can't hang out on the sidelines anymore while you figure out your life and what role I play. And now there's a baby—*we* have a baby—on the way? It's like everything I ever wanted is dangling right there, but it's just out of my reach while you decide what you want."

"Don't you think you're being a little unfair here? You *just* told me how you felt a couple weeks ago. Don't I get some time to play catch-up?"

"I'm sorry, Carrie. You know I've always been there for you, but right now I need some time alone to figure this out."

The line went silent before she could say anything else. She stared at the phone, and her lips quivered. Jack was the one person she could count on, and he'd just hung up on her when she needed him most. The only other person she had ever been able to rely on had been her father. And he was gone.

She wasn't in the mood to head upstairs and deal with her mother, deal with another slew of unfair accusations being thrown her way. But with Jack bowing out for the day, she saw no other choice. Sitting around downstairs was only prolonging the inevitable. She took the elevator back up to their fourth-floor room, relieved each time it paused to let someone on or off.

She entered the room to find her mother straightening up, which Carrie knew from experience she did to distract herself from being upset. "Mom," she said, trying to keep the edge from her voice. "Can we talk?"

"I don't think there's much left to talk about."

"There is, though." Carrie sat on her bed, her mother's back to her as she continued cleaning. "I'm sorry you found out like that, but you have to understand why I didn't tell you yet."

"No, I get it. You wanted to tell Jack first."

"Exactly." Carrie frowned. If she understood, why was she so upset? Carrie's head throbbed, and she feared a migraine was starting. "I wanted Jack to be the first person to know. I thought we should figure out what we're doing before telling anyone else."

Her mother dropped the towel she'd been fussing with and whipped around. "What is there to figure out?"

Carrie squirmed under her eyes. "I mean, there are options. Neither of us planned for this."

"Are you having an abortion?"

The straightforwardness of the question surprised Carrie, even though she and Jack had been discussing this possibility just minutes ago. "I...I don't know..."

Her mother snatched her purse off the dresser. "I need to get out of here." She headed for the door, but before leaving, she turned back to Carrie. "And for the record, I'm not 'anyone else.' I'm your mother. And we both know damn well if your father were still here, you'd have told him before Jack without a second thought."

The door slammed shut, leaving Carrie frozen on the bed, her mother's final sentence reverberating through her mind.

Was she right? If her dad were still here, would she have gone to him immediately before even telling Jack?

She cringed to admit it, but yes, she likely would have.

Carrie fell backward on the bed and let the tears stream onto the bedspread. She picked up her phone and scrolled through pictures of her and her dad. She'd created the album on her phone shortly after his death, but she hadn't looked at it often. It had been easier this past year to throw herself into her work and ignore her grief than to confront it head-on. Which was, she realized now, how she dealt with most things in her life.

But look where that had gotten her.

She'd read once that to put yourself in a more positive mindset, replace the word "problem" with "opportunity." In that vein, Carrie had an opportunity here to redefine herself, to shed the bad habits of her old life and move in a new direction. She wanted desperately to figure out her next steps, to decide what she actually wanted from her life and how she was going to proceed, but to do so, she needed space.

Carrie sat back up, and nausea overwhelmed her. She ran into the bathroom and tried to throw up, but nothing came. As she stood back up, her chest was heavy, and she struggled to catch her breath. The room felt as though it were caving in around her, and she began hyperventilating. She grabbed her phone, ready to dial 911, but that wasn't right. What was the emergency number in Spain?

Then, a memory came back to her, and she tossed the phone back on the bed. She didn't need a hospital. It had been years since her panic attacks in Australia, but she remembered this feeling now, how her brain convinced her she was dying despite any evidence to the contrary, how she felt powerless and weak.

She'd forgotten just how terrifying it was.

She raced back into the bathroom and riffled through her mother's toiletry case. The Xanax bottle had to be here somewhere. After pulling everything out with no luck, she stuffed it all back and went out into the room. She swung her mother's suitcase onto the bed, searched through every pocket, and finally found the bottle. She unscrewed the cap and tapped a pill into her hand, but then the warning label caught her eye.

Do not use if you think you may be pregnant.

Damn it.

She threw the bottle back into the suitcase, but as she went to zip it back up, she noticed a small notebook. She pulled it out and stared at its water-colored cover for a moment. She shouldn't open it. Whatever was inside had been hidden for a reason. And yet, the possibility of learning something that might help her understand her mother intrigued her.

She flipped the cover open, and a loose sheet of paper fell to the floor. She grabbed the paper and unfolded it. Inside, all that was written was, "Improve my relationship with Carrie. Have a meaningful conversation."

Carrie stared at the words for a minute, trying to decide how this discovery colored the interactions between her and her mother over the past few weeks. Her mother was trying. Actively trying. The fact that she was attempting to reconcile their relationship while Carrie had been deliberately avoiding opening up or getting close to her made her heart ache.

A part of her wanted to call her and tell her she loved her, tell her they could fix whatever was broken in their relationship. But a bigger part of her was mentally exhausted, unable to contend with anything more. Besides, goals or not, it was her mother who'd just stormed out on her, not the other way around.

Carrie ripped a piece of paper from the notebook, grabbed a pen off her nightstand, and scribbled a note to her mother. She jammed her belongings into her own suitcase, watching the door and holding her breath that her mother wouldn't return, then zipped up her bag and left.

Chapter 24

Anita left the hotel and walked with no destination in mind, just indiscriminately crossing streets and turning corners. It was cooler this morning than the past few days, and she wished she'd grabbed a sweater on her way out. But who remembers a sweater when they're storming out of a room?

Spotting a gift shop across the street with souvenir sweatshirts in the window, Anita waited for a break in the traffic, then crossed. She grabbed a gray zip-up sweatshirt from the rack with "Barcelona" spelled out across the front in dark green, paid the cashier twenty-five euro, and continued on her way.

She ended up on La Rambla, amazed at how empty it was. There were still many people around but compared to just yesterday when she'd walked this sidewalk with Carrie and Jack amid throngs of other tourists, it practically felt as though she were alone now. The trees flanking the sidewalk enveloped her, as though she were in her own little bubble in the heart of Barcelona.

And yet, with all the beauty around her, all her brain wanted was to ruminate on her argument with Carrie.

Theoretically, Anita considered herself pro-choice. She

believed women had the right to choose what to do with their own body and whether or not to carry a child to term. But after suffering three miscarriages, after grieving three babies she'd never had the chance to hold yet had loved with everything she had, she couldn't fathom how her own daughter could *choose* to lose a child, as though she could erase the evidence and carry on like nothing ever happened. Wanted or not, that wasn't how it worked. That unborn child would leave a mark forever.

But Carrie didn't know about her older siblings. She didn't know the toll it had taken on her mother to lose her children.

She thought back to the moment the delivery nurse handed Carrie to her, a perfect, healthy little newborn, and yet all she could think of was what might still go wrong. She'd thought getting through the delivery and seeing that pristine infant in her arms would be enough to curb her anxiety, but in that moment, all she saw was a lifetime of potential disaster ahead. The trauma of her miscarriages had left a permanent mark on her, and by proxy, Carrie as well.

Anita found a bench along the sidewalk and took a seat. She reached into her purse and pulled out her phone, and a small piece of paper fell onto the sidewalk. She bent over and picked it up, then recognized the handwriting. It was Enric's number.

She stared at the paper for a moment, anger building in her chest. She ripped the paper in half and stuffed it back into her purse. She'd gone to Enric's bookstore because of Victor. She was on this trip to grieve her husband, not to look for a new man to spend her time with.

But that wasn't the whole truth. Of course she was here to grieve her husband, but the next step was to make her peace with the past and move forward. She'd made a new acquaintance last night, nothing more. If the bookshop owner she had struck up a friendly conversation with had been a woman, she wouldn't feel guilty over it. Enric was an ear to listen when she needed it, someone who understood what she was up against and could offer wisdom and advice, and someone she'd likely never see again after this week ended. But she needed a friend right now, someone to talk this all through with and make sense of her emotions.

Without allowing herself another moment to change her mind, she pulled the piece of paper back out and called Enric.

———

The smell of espresso and pastries greeted Anita as she entered the small cafe. She glanced around and found Enric waving to her from a table by the window. His smile widened as she sat across from him, and the knots in her stomach settled. He had a way of putting her at ease. Just like Victor.

"I am glad you called," he said. "I worried I was too pushy last night."

Anita waved her hand and set her purse on the table, now hypervigilant about keeping her possessions in view at all times. "No, you were fine," she assured him. "Thanks for meeting me."

"My pleasure," he said.

"I needed to get away from my daughter for a while, actually."

He frowned. "What happened?"

The waiter interrupted them to take their order. Enric ordered a black coffee, which matched his no-frills personality. Victor would have liked him. She looked to the empty chair beside them, picturing him there.

"And for you, miss?"

Anita snapped her head back to the waiter. "Oh, a cappuccino, please."

"Would you like a pastry? They have wonderful *xuixo*," Enric said.

"What is that?" she asked.

"Oh, they are delicious," Enric said, his eyes shining. "They are like a fried croissant with sugar and filled with cream."

"Sure, that sounds good." Anita didn't have much of an appetite this morning, but she didn't want to seem rude by declining.

"Dos, por favor," Enric said to the waiter.

Once the waiter left, he turned back to Anita. He didn't have to repeat his question for her to know he was waiting on her reply. But how much did she want to tell him? She barely knew him, but perhaps a fresh perspective made him the perfect person to weigh in on her situation.

Her shoulders rose and fell, then she laid it out. "I stumbled across a pregnancy test in our hotel room last night when I got back. It was my daughter's, but she didn't tell me." She filled him in on their argument, concluding with her storming out of the room.

"This must be difficult for both of you," he said after she'd finished.

Anita leaned back in her chair, the words hitting her hard. She hadn't actually considered how Carrie was feeling about everything. She had been so focused on her own feelings.

"I..." she started. "You're right. Wow, I'm awful. I haven't even asked how she's handling it."

"You are not awful," Enric said, then pulled back to make room as the waiter came back with their drinks and pastries.

"No, I am." Anita shook her head. "What mother finds out her daughter is unexpectedly pregnant and doesn't even ask how she's doing? It's just...I know I shouldn't feel this way, but I know if her father were still alive, she'd have told him immediately." Anita paused and sighed. "It's been a year, and I'm still jealous of their relationship. Is that awful"

"Deceased parents are forever a threat to those of us still

living. They are saints and can do no wrong. How can us humans compete?"

Anita smiled, amazed at Enric's ability to put her feelings into words when she couldn't. "I've been trying to do better, trying to listen and understand her. I thought things were getting better, but then I found out she'd been fired from her job before we came here, and she'd hidden that from me too. It was the only reason she came on the trip at all, actually. I felt like an idiot thinking she'd gone to some great effort to get this time off work, but it turned out she just had nothing better to do."

He leaned towards her. "She still chose to be here with you," he said. "She could have stayed home or gone somewhere on her own. But she came with you."

Anita tapped her foot on the floor. "I should have known something was up from the beginning. She'd never take a whole month away from her job, especially not to go on a trip with me."

Enric shrugged. "Sometimes people do things we don't expect them to. Sometimes people surprise us."

Anita looked out the window, cradling her cappuccino in her hands as she waited for it to cool down. "She might not keep the baby," she said, unable to look directly at Enric for fear of her emotions letting loose. "And I just lost it. She doesn't know this, but we had three miscarriages before her. Three children I never held in my arms but loved so much." Anita sniffled and looked back to him. "The thought of her ending her pregnancy willingly just kind of set me off."

"Why did you not tell her?"

Anita shrugged. "Victor didn't want to dwell on the past. He didn't want her to feel burdened, like she had to make up for the children we couldn't have. I know he had good reasons. I understood them at the time. But it always felt like we were keeping this giant secret from her. Any time she asked why she was an only child, we told her we only ever wanted one. It hurt every time I said those words."

"Of course it did," Enric said. "Alba miscarried our first time. It is hard."

"I'm so sorry. I had no idea."

He nodded and looked down at his mug. "It's not something you get over, but you learn to live with it. Just like losing a spouse."

Anita ran her finger along the coffee cup handle. "I loved Victor, but we always disagreed on how to handle the miscarriages. I think he needed to forget about them, but they affected me differently. And I always thought Carrie needed to know about them to understand me. Maybe if she knew, my reactions to things would make more sense."

"Men and women, we handle our grief differently. Your husband needed to forget, but you need to remember." He paused and looked her in the eye. "You should tell your daughter what you think she needs to know."

"I wouldn't even know where to begin. It was all so long ago now. She'll probably just think it's an excuse at this point."

Enric reached across the table and placed his hand over Anita's, surprising her. It was an unexpected gesture given they'd only met last night, and yet given the connection they'd developed, it seemed natural. She didn't completely mind his hand there, and she didn't know if that bothered her more or less than the fact he had put it there to begin with.

"Tell her what you told me," he said. "Word for word. She will understand."

Chapter 25

Anita returned to the hotel filled with a mix of anxiety and hope. Talking to Carrie about her miscarriages would be hard, but maybe it would make her see how much she'd struggled to have her. And why she was always so afraid to lose her.

The room was empty when she entered. Carrie's bed was made, her things gone. There was only a note in her handwriting propped in front of the television. Anita picked it up, and her heart sank.

Mom -
I need some space to sort everything out. I'm renting a
room elsewhere for the time being.
Carrie

She crumpled the note and threw it nowhere in particular, then sunk onto her bed. She'd never felt like such a complete failure as a mother, and she certainly had a vast backlog of incidents to choose from.

She hadn't been the perfect mother, but who out there could claim to be? Motherhood, she had learned, was merely a setup for making mistakes over and over again in front of a tiny person who expected you to be God. She'd read once that parenting was less about the mistakes you made but more about the way you handled them. If that were true, Anita was doubly screwed since she seemed even worse at handling her mistakes than at making them in the first place.

She grabbed her phone and called Carrie, but it went straight to voicemail.

"Carrie, it's Mom," she said after the voicemail greeting. "I'm sorry about before. Call me back. Love you."

The words felt inadequate, but they were all she had. She set the phone down and stared out the window, counting all the ways she'd messed up with her daughter. Just the past few weeks alone, she ran out of fingers to count them off on.

She'd resolved to change so much during this trip, but who had she been kidding? The trip was quickly winding down, and she felt worse off than before they'd arrived in London. She was old, set in her ways. She had thought if she set her mind to it, she could change, but she failed at every turn. All she'd done was push Carrie even further away, and she still felt terribly alone and isolated in a world where her husband no longer existed. Anxiety still consumed her, and she was always worrying the next awful thing was just around the corner. She was exactly where she'd been before leaving home.

Okay, so maybe that wasn't entirely true. There'd been small changes the past few weeks. Maybe not on the scale she had envisioned, but some small progress. She'd learned she could survive having her passport stolen overseas, that changing their travel plans at the last moment wasn't the end of the world. She'd willingly wandered the streets of Barcelona on her own last night and found Enric's store without assistance. And despite how angry Carrie was with her at the moment, this was the most honest they had been with one another in many years.

Not the progress she'd hoped for, but still, it was something.

And yet the anger overwhelmed her. She was angry with God for taking Victor from her too soon, angry with Victor for withholding his health issues from her and for leaving her, and angry with Carrie for loving her father more than she loved Anita.

But then it hit her. She was angry for so many reasons. But the person she was angriest with was herself. Angry that she hadn't been able to move past her miscarriages, that anxiety had ruled her life for more than three decades, so much so that her husband felt the need to hide medical concerns from her. She hated that she'd reacted so unsympathetically to Carrie this morning, that she'd been so focused on her own needs she hadn't even considered how she must be feeling. And she was angry that she'd turned to Enric this morning when she needed a shoulder to lean on, and even angrier that when he placed his hand on hers, she liked it there.

She'd thought this trip had been about getting over Victor, about grieving his death and coming to terms with it. But really, it was about redefining her life in this new chapter. She needed to gain control over her anxiety, she needed to rectify things with Carrie, and she needed to stop feeling guilty for enjoying her life because Victor could no longer experience it alongside her.

A conversation they had many years ago came back to her. They were driving home from a friend's house on New Year's Eve, and in true Buffalo fashion, a snowstorm caught them a bit by surprise. They'd expected it to hit the following morning, thinking they'd be safe for the drive home, but when they came out to their car at one in the morning, there was easily six inches already piled on top and more rapidly accumulating.

As Victor slowly but safely drove them home, somehow the

topic came up about what they'd want for the other if they were to die first.

"I want to go first so I don't have to live a day without you," Victor had said.

"That doesn't seem fair," Anita said. Though it was a sweet thing to say, it was also a cop-out. Going first might be easiest for the one leaving, but it was a self-centered notion to wish dealing with the fallout on your spouse.

Victor shrugged, his eyes glued to the road ahead. "Maybe not. But I guess we don't really get control over that decision anyhow."

They drove another minute or so in silence, then he continued. "But seriously," he said, his voice more somber. "If I go first, I want you to find happiness. Whatever that means, I want you to be happy. And I don't want you to feel like you owe me anything."

Anita shook her head. "I can't imagine being happy without you."

"I know. But, if it's possible, I want you to be."

Had Victor somehow had a crystal ball and seen her future? Had he known how difficult it would be for her to find happiness without him? Of course Victor would want her to be happy. He wouldn't want her to be miserable forever just because he was no longer here. In fact, if he were watching her right now, he probably wanted to lecture her for spending so much time this past year sulking and pitying herself.

If Victor were here, what would he tell her to do about Carrie? He'd been the logical side of her brain when emotion overwhelmed her, the antidote to her anxiety. With him gone, she needed to be her own logical guide.

As much as it hurt to acknowledge, her daughter needed space. No matter how good Anita's intentions, Carrie never responded well to being pressured into something she wasn't ready for. She needed to make decisions on her own, in her own time. The best thing she could do was give her the time she needed to sort out her thoughts and trust she'd come back to her when she did.

In the meantime, there was a giant, beautiful city outside her hotel waiting to be explored. The thought of carrying on alone terrified her, but she didn't come all this way to sit in a hotel room and wait for her daughter. Victor wouldn't forgive her if she finally made it here only to squander her time in self-pity.

Anita pulled her suitcase from the closet, the guidebooks clunking to one side as she swung it onto the bed. She grabbed the Barcelona guide and paged through it, pausing to read some of Victor's scrawled comments. A tear fell and marked the page, blurring some of his writing. It was a fitting, albeit heartbreaking, addition to the narrative contained within the outdated books. This was how their story ended.

But it wasn't the end of Anita's journey.

Knowing she had to continue on without Victor stung, but wasting the rest of her life tied up in grief would be worse. She stared at the travel guide in her lap and resolved to find her new purpose, beginning with not wasting a moment in this glorious city.

She closed the book and set it aside, then opened the map app on her phone. She plugged in Park Guell, started the navigation, then left the room, this time full of resolve and determination.

Chapter 26

Park Guell was a bit of a hike from the hotel. About thirty minutes walking according to Google Maps. She could walk it, but the distance meant a higher chance of getting lost. Her other option was navigating public transportation on her own, and that intimidated her far more. The possibility of taking the wrong train and ending up on the completely wrong side of town scared her more than being one or two streets off.

Anita pressed her lips together and started the directions on her phone. She paused a moment, deciphering which direction she needed to head towards to begin. The phone shook a bit in her hands, and she reminded herself to take a deep breath. Everything would be fine. She'd found her way to Enric's shop last night, back to the hotel, and to the cafe this morning. This was the same concept, just traveling farther.

She checked her phone for the next cross street, then checked the street sign to make sure she was going the right way. She headed towards *Carrer de Provenca*, along with other pedestrians, and tried to project confidence.

She made her way through the center of Barcelona, a swirl of Spanish and Catalan surrounding her as she took in the unique Gaudí architecture that made this city so special. She passed street-side markets with fruits, vegetables, even fish on full display right in front of her. She passed businesspeople out for lunch, couples walking hand in hand, and other tourists with their own phone maps glued to their palms. She checked her phone at each intersection, reassured each time she verified she was still on the right path.

After about fifteen minutes, she stopped at a corner and waited for the signal to change as traffic raced past. A car horn blared, and Anita jumped back, then realized it wasn't meant for her. Her heartbeat raced, the incident at the Chinese restaurant just a few weeks ago playing through her mind, once again triggering thoughts of Victor's accident. She struggled for a breath, and her vision blurred slightly. The signal changed and pedestrians on either side of her rushed across the street, but she remained planted in place.

She turned around and saw a cafe on the corner behind her, then ducked inside and sat at an open table beside the window. She dug through her purse for her Xanax bottle and tapped out a pill, but she hesitated before tossing it into her mouth.

How had she become so reliant on these little pills? She'd gone so many years with severe anxiety not needing them. She had Victor. She requested the Xanax initially only for their flight to London, a special circumstance she'd been willing to make an exception for. It was never intended as a long-term solution or a regular fix.

She set the pill on the table in front of her and stared at it. She focused on her breathing, concentrated on slowing it down one breath at a time. The symptoms would pass. They always did. They weren't life-threatening, even though they felt like it. She would be fine. She just needed to get through this episode. And she needed to prove to herself she could do it without the magic pill.

The panic passed, but anger replaced it as she stared at the pill. She had relied on her Xanax prescription too heavily this past year. She'd used them to mask her grief, to mask her pain, but all she had really done was sabotage her ability to move on, to create any life for herself going forward. As long as she'd had the pills nearby, she didn't have to work to resolve her anxiety— she just popped a pill and the symptoms magically vanished.

But suppressing the symptoms was not the same as addressing the root of the issues. Losing Victor had meant more than just losing her husband. She'd lost the person who kept her grounded, the person who often shielded her from the harsh realities of life. She lost her sole connection to her daughter. Any sense she'd previously had that her anxiety was under control had only been a guise.

Victor had been her Xanax.

She stared once more at the small pill before her. She picked it up and held it in her palm, this small little drug she'd allowed herself to become enslaved to.

It's in your head, Victor had told her more than once throughout the years. She'd brushed off his comments at the time, but she finally understood what he had meant. The symptoms weren't posing a threat to her life; they were simply a manifestation of her anxiety. But if she could learn to control the anxiety on her own, she'd no longer be at the mercy of a pill to live her life. And she'd just proven to herself she could make it through an attack without the medication.

She pulled the orange bottle back out of her purse and tossed the lone pill back in. She stood and walked to the back corner of the cafe where a restroom sign hung. Closing herself in a stall, she opened the bottle and dumped the remaining pills in the toilet. Then she flushed.

———

Anita headed back out amid the groups of tourists, rejuvenated and ready to conquer her fear. She could do this.

She restarted the directions on her phone and reoriented herself. She approached the corner once again, reminding herself not to let the traffic rattle her.

The light changed, and Anita was about to cross the street, but instead she paused. Park Guell could wait. She didn't know where the idea came from, but if she'd learned anything the past few weeks, it was that she needed to trust her gut. And her gut insisted there was somewhere else she needed to go first.

She moved towards the edge of the sidewalk and hailed a taxi. After a minute, a black-and-yellow cab pulled to the side of the road, and she climbed into the backseat.

"Can you take me to Tibidabo?" she asked.

"Si," the driver said, then merged back into the traffic.

The ride to Tibidabo was about twenty minutes, which gave Anita plenty of time to reconsider what she was about to do. But while she expected to talk herself out of it, surprisingly, she didn't.

The cab finally pulled up to Tibidabo, where people milled about the terrace. She swallowed hard, then paid the driver and got out. The cab drove off, and Anita walked towards the railing of the platform, looking out over the edge at all of Barcelona below.

Tibidabo was the highest point in Barcelona, up on a hill with a beautiful church and a small amusement park with carnival rides. It had been on her and Victor's secondary list, the list they made of places they wanted to visit if time permitted. Being so far from the city center, they weren't sure they'd make it, but the area promised incredible views of the city. Particularly from the Ferris wheel.

Anita turned and set her eyes on the ride, its rainbow-colored seats impossible to miss. Victor never would have expected her to go on the Ferris wheel, but somehow it seemed like exactly what she needed to do to move forward, to prove to herself she would no longer allow anxiety to rule her life. To most, it may have been a simple carnival ride, but to her it was so much more.

The line was shorter than Anita expected, and soon she was next up. The young girl ahead of her climbed into a bright green bucket with her father, and her mind drifted to Victor and Carrie all those years ago.

"Next," the operator called out.

Anita walked to the next open bucket, this one sunshine yellow, and climbed in. With a small lurch, the wheel took off, propelling her slowly into the air. Instinctively, she closed her eyes, then forced herself to open them. She didn't come this far to ride with her eyes closed. Besides, it made her more nauseous not to see where she was going.

At the top of the wheel, she looked out across the amazing city she'd spent the past few days exploring and falling in love with. Although this Ferris wheel was smaller than the one in London, being up on a mountain made it seem as though she was higher off the ground than she was.

"I did it, Victor," she whispered.

She smiled as the wheel lifted her up and around once more. She *had* done it. She made it to Europe, made her way to Tibidabo on her own, and conquered her fear of Ferris wheels.

But there was still work to be done.

Anita had crossed the Atlantic with two goals: to mourn the loss of her husband and the life they'd shared and to improve her relationship with her daughter. She'd forced herself to follow through with this trip in the hope it would kick-start her back into the realm of the living, but no matter how amazing and beautiful Europe was, it couldn't solve her problems for her.

Her thoughts switched back to Carrie, her beautiful

daughter who seemed at a crossroads of her own. Somehow, they had spent the last several weeks living in the same room and still avoided getting too involved in each other's lives, just as they'd done Carrie's entire life. She always went to Victor with updates, and Anita maintained her distance under the guise of respecting her daughter's wishes. But that had merely been an excuse to avoid taking action, to avoid looking herself in the mirror and determining what needed to change.

She had been the adult in their relationship all those years; if she'd wanted something to change, she'd needed to do something about it.

And yet, all these years of wisdom and experience later, and she was still waiting on Carrie to change for them both. Taking that first step towards change seemed scary and far beyond her comfort zone, but so had traveling to Europe and she'd made it here, alive and well. She had missed too much of her daughter's life out of fear of being vulnerable, but soon there would be a grandchild, God willing, and she'd be damned if she was going to miss out on that child's life as well. Anita owed it to Victor to step up and be the best parent and grandparent she could be in his absence.

And she owed it to herself to be happy, whatever that looked like. The only thing holding her back from a beautiful life right now was herself.

The ride came to a stop at the bottom, and Anita unbuckled and scooted out. She turned around and took one more look at the Ferris wheel, at how high she'd gone despite her fear.

She found a bench nearby and sat down, then fumbled through her purse for her phone. She stared a moment at the lock screen photo of her and Victor, then opened her messages.

Carrie, it's Mom. I'm sorry about earlier. I reacted for reasons that had nothing to do with you. I'd love the chance to explain when you're ready.

She sent the text, staring at the screen as if doing so would summon an instant reply. It was likely Carrie would take some time to respond, and Anita reminded herself that was okay. She'd put her apology out there rather than sitting back and waiting, and that was progress.

Chapter 27

Everywhere Carrie looked, there were pregnant women or babies. She'd come to the beach to get away from the crowded city center, to clear her mind and figure out what came next for her. But what was with all the babies?

She found a cafe along the boardwalk with tables overlooking the beach. She bought a bottled water and sat down, the table's umbrella offering a welcome relief from the direct sunlight. Though the morning had started chilly, the sun came out in full force a bit ago, and all the walking had Carrie sweating through her T-shirt.

Today would have been the perfect sightseeing day. Why had she gone and ruined the day for them?

No, her mother had ruined the day. She'd been the one freaking out about something that was none of her business.

But that notebook. She had been trying.

Why were mother-daughter relationships so complicated?

Carrie pulled out her phone, but no messages awaited her. She should call her mother and apologize, but what would she say? She wasn't sorry she'd held off sharing the news with her. She needed to sort her feelings and thoughts around her pregnancy before involving her in the discussion. And though her mother may have been right that if her dad were still alive, she'd have shared the news with him immediately, that was beside the point. She and her dad shared a different relationship. Did she really need to continuously apologize for that? Even a year after he'd passed away?

The panic attack from this morning had her shaken, though. Since Australia, she had successfully avoided them. She'd seen the counselor her dad arranged for her a few times, but then stopped going. She didn't need it. She wasn't like her mother, whose anxiety controlled her life. She'd just had a rough patch. Anyone would have reacted the same given the circumstances.

When her dad passed last year, she'd gotten away with only mild anxiety when Jack dropped her off at the airport. He had offered to go back with her, and for a moment she almost agreed, but she restrained herself. In all the years they'd been friends, she never brought him home to Buffalo with her, worried what kind of message that would send to her parents, her mother in particular.

And, truthfully, she hadn't wanted to send the wrong message to Jack either.

On some level, she'd known he had feelings for her for a while. Maybe not early on, but as the years passed, there were subtle hints she brushed off but now recognized. Certain looks he'd give her, his lack of romantic relationships or willingness to talk about those he did have, his open invitation to her to crash at his place whenever she needed. Even if she hadn't consciously admitted knowing this, she had. She'd kept him at arm's length romantically, telling herself she only saw him as a friend. But really, admitting that she might have feelings for her best friend opened the possibility to something she wasn't emotionally ready to handle. If things went badly, she lost not only a boyfriend but her best friend as well.

But now she had really tangled everything up, and there was no way to avoid addressing her feelings for Jack once and for all.

Which left her with the question she'd been avoiding answering: did she have feelings for Jack?

She remembered the first time she met him back in their sophomore year of college. They were at a birthday party for a mutual friend, and after about an hour, they were the only two remaining who weren't completely drunk, including Carrie's ride home. Jack offered to drive her home, but they decided to go to a diner around the corner instead. They stayed and talked for a couple hours, and she distinctly remembered thinking how much Jack reminded her of her dad. He had a steady, confident presence, and he made her feel comfortable, willing to open up about things she never talked about, including her dreams for her future and her odd relationship with her mother. He listened without judgement, and from then on, they were inseparable.

Carrie's friends nagged at her often at the beginning, wondering why they weren't dating. She brushed them off, insisting she didn't have those kinds of feelings for Jack, but now she understood. Even then, even before Australia, even before her career ambitions truly took hold, she'd been afraid to put herself out there. She'd never felt so herself with any guy she'd dated, never felt so comfortable, and the possibility of losing that with Jack terrified her. So she dubbed him the brother she never had and left it at that. Never going all in, but never risking what she had.

But the sadness in Jack's eyes when she told him about the baby, when she told him she still hadn't sorted her feelings for him, showed her just how deeply she'd hurt her best friend by refusing to take action. In trying to prevent her own heart from breaking, she'd instead been chipping away at his little by little.

She was in a period of transition, one of those rare opportunities in which she could recreate her life in any manner she wished, an opportunity many coveted but squandered if actually presented to them. Though Carrie always wanted to think of herself as someone who met change head-on, she could admit she tolerated it a hell of a lot better when given a chance to plan for it. Spontaneous change, the story of her life this past month, she didn't fare so well with. And impulsively sleeping with her best friend while in a foreign country and becoming pregnant while overseas with her mother hadn't been on her list of scenarios to prepare for.

So where did that leave her? She could go back to LA, fight for her career and reputation and hope someone would give her a second chance to...what? To work ridiculous hours with an unpredictable schedule for little to no recognition? Actually, the entire point of her career was to go unnoticed, to work magic without being given credit for any of it, other than the rare occasions where the Adam Hartleys of Hollywood shouted out your accomplishments and lulled you into torpedoing your entire life.

Or she could face her fears, take a risk, and maybe, just maybe, end up happier than she'd ever dreamed.

Her phone rang, breaking her away from her thoughts. She checked the screen, then took a deep breath.

"Hello?" she answered.

"Hey, it's me. Can we get together for dinner?"

———

Carrie shouldn't have been surprised Jack was already at the restaurant when she arrived, and her stomach clenched when she saw him.

Here goes.

The restaurant Jack had chosen was rather romantic, a beachfront location with dim candles for light and small, cozy booths. She hoped his choice hadn't been intentional, but perhaps it was fitting.

He watched her as she approached the table, and Carrie wondered what was going through his mind.

"I'm surprised you came," he said as she scooted into the booth opposite him.

Carrie tilted her head and blinked. "Come on, Jack. Can't we be adults about this?"

He leaned back and his shoulders slumped. "I'm sorry. I didn't mean to start out in attack mode."

"But you were leading up to that possibility?" Carrie raised a playful eyebrow, trying to diffuse the lingering tension.

Jack stared at his hands, folded in front of him on the table. "You took me by surprise the other night is all."

"Well, I didn't exactly plan for this either."

The waitress came over with his drink, a double scotch.

"Anything for you, *senyoreta?*"

"Just a water, please."

Jack sipped his scotch, then set it down and looked at her sheepishly. "I'm sorry. Was it rude for me to order a drink?"

"You're fine," she said, though she wished she could also partake. "So, I was surprised you hadn't hightailed it back to London yet."

"I thought about it," Jack admitted, then his eyes softened and his shoulders slumped, relaxing into the conversation. "But I couldn't let yesterday be your last impression of me before making this decision."

"I know that wasn't the real you," Carrie said, though his accusations still stung.

"I was unfair to you. And I'm sorry."

She smiled. "Apology accepted."

"I know you don't feel the same way about me as I feel for you. That's not your fault. It just makes this new situation...well, more complicated."

Carrie leaned over the table, closer to her best friend. "Jack..."

He shook his head. "No, it's okay. I understand. You need some space to sort this all out, and I'm going to give that to you. Take as much time as you need, Carrie. I'll be here when you're ready to talk about it."

There he was, the Jack she knew and loved. The man who put everyone else's needs before his own even to his own detriment, who tried his hardest to see situations from all perspectives before deciding anything.

"So, you asked me to dinner to tell me you're leaving me alone?" Carrie teased.

Jack smiled and shrugged. "I suppose so."

She broke eye contact and looked around the restaurant at all the other couples snuggled up. What she wouldn't give to trade places with one of them, to be in a position to simply enjoy a romantic dinner out with a partner without the pressure of life-altering decisions weighing her down.

"I'm keeping the baby," she whispered, so quietly she had to look to Jack for confirmation she'd spoken aloud.

A smile broke across his face, and his eyes gleamed. "You are?"

While keeping the baby felt right, acknowledging it aloud did nothing to relieve her fear. In fact, she felt more uncertain now than a moment ago. "I have no idea how to be a mother," she admitted. "I don't even know that I deserve to be a mother after last time."

Jack took her hand and looked her square in the eyes. "You absolutely deserve this. And you will be an amazing mother."

Carrie shook her head. She wanted to believe him, but

saying the words aloud filled her with fear. "How can you know that?"

"Because the situation last time was entirely different. You were young, you weren't ready, and *he* was a complete ass. But you've got this. I know you do. And I'll be here for you, whatever you need. We'll figure this out."

Carrie looked at Jack's hand on her own, and something clicked. This situation *was* entirely different than before. She was a grown woman, fully capable of raising a child. And Jack wasn't some jerk who'd played games with her heart. He was her best friend, the man who knew her best other than her dad. And just like her dad had always been there for her, Jack would never leave her, never hurt her.

She looked up and blinked back emotion. "Well, I guess the first thing we need to figure out is how I get a work visa."

Jack squinted at her. "A work visa?"

"Well, I'm not keen on long-distance relationships, and you know I'm not just going to be the stay-at-home mom while you go off and make money. If I'm moving to London, I'm going to need a job."

"You're…"

"I love you, Jack," she said, entirely confident in the statement. "I'm sorry it took me so long to realize or admit that, but I do. You've always been the one."

Carrie watched as the reality of what she'd said sunk in and he smiled larger than she'd ever seen him smile before.

"Well, sunshine, I know you're going to love London."

Carrie squeezed Jack's hand. She had a strong feeling she would too.

Chapter 28

On the anniversary of Victor's death, Anita awoke alone in her hotel room well before the sun displaced the darkness. Before even opening her eyes, she was aware of the date and the pain and sadness awaiting her over the next twenty-four hours. She lay still, wanting nothing more than to will herself back to sleep for another few hours, anything to shorten this day. But falling asleep last night had been troublesome enough. Now that she was faced with this day, there'd be no more drifting back into her dreams.

She pushed herself up against the bed's headboard and stared at the wall, the quiet room grating. Since the accident, whenever Anita woke to find Victor's side of the bed empty, typically her first thought was that he was in the kitchen making coffee. She'd listen for sounds of him tinkering, then the grogginess would clear, and she would remember all over again. It had taken months before she was no longer terrified of falling asleep for fear of the nightmare that awaited the following morning.

Anita thought back to one year ago, one day before she and Victor were supposed to board their plane for London. The biggest worry on her mind had been the fact she'd be stuck in a plane high above the Atlantic for hours on end, and she prayed the Xanax her doctor prescribed her would be effective enough to ward off a full-blown panic attack. The journey was bound to be stressful, but she tried to picture them falling asleep side by side in their hotel bed, laughing over how silly her fears had been.

She'd taken for granted they would have that day, that he would be there beside her at the end of it.

The actual day itself was one big blur, but the emotional impact remained, the numbness only slightly less today than a year ago. And while all she wanted today was to forget the events of last year, that would be impossible.

Anita grabbed her phone from the nightstand and checked for messages. Still nothing from Carrie. She still intended to visit the Sagrada Familia this morning as they'd planned, and while she wanted to remain hopeful, she wondered if Carrie even remembered their plan at all.

Anita set the phone back down and headed into the bathroom. She dressed slowly, as though procrastinating leaving the hotel would ward off the emotionally draining day. She took a bit of extra time with her makeup but decided to forego mascara. Hers wasn't waterproof, and she'd rather not risk a mess of makeup streaming down her face while out in public.

A little after eight o'clock, she collected her purse and her phone. Before leaving the room, she opened her message thread with Carrie, as though perhaps she'd simply missed a response. Still nothing.

Anita's heart sank a bit further, but she reminded herself not to be discouraged. Instead, she sent another message.

I'm heading to Sagrada this morning like we'd talked about. If you're still up for it, call me when you get there. Love you.

She tucked her phone into her purse, then headed out of her hotel. She didn't need directions to get to Sagrada; it was only a few blocks away, and it was visible between buildings. Besides, she was in no rush.

She stopped across the street from the basilica and waited before crossing, taking in the architecture's magnificence. The ornately decorated exterior was so exquisite it took Anita a minute before noticing the cranes towering in the background. Standing before the place Victor was most excited to see, realizing once again how much he'd missed out on, Anita's knees shook, and she grabbed hold of a bike rack beside her to steady herself.

Had she been out of her mind suggesting they come here for the anniversary? As if the day weren't already destined to be the most difficult of the trip, she'd had to add even more weight to it by coming here?

Of course, when she had suggested it, she'd thought Carrie would be beside her to distract her and lighten the emotional burden. She'd even been delusional enough to think Carrie might need someone to lean on as well and they'd be here for each other.

Anita bit the inside of her cheek as she watched the sea of strangers milling about in front of the Sagrada, hoping she might spot Carrie mixed in with them, but no luck. This day was bound to be as difficult for her as it was for Anita, and her daughter's absence told her all she needed to know. Anita had screwed things up beyond repair this time.

She considered turning around and leaving, but today was her last chance. Besides, it was early yet. Carrie might still show up. And anything she did today would be an emotional roller coaster, so she might as well get on with it.

She crossed the street and worked her way through the crowd to the entrance, handed over her ticket to be scanned, and made her way up the stairs. Elbows and backpacks jostled her as she approached the basilica doors, everyone too distracted by the detailed exterior to watch where they walked.

"Excuse me, ma'am," someone said beside her. "Would you mind taking a picture of my wife and me?"

Anita turned to her right to find a man roughly her age, and she blinked to stop herself from seeing Victor. She nodded, unable to find her voice, and took the man's phone. It surprised her, actually, that this was the first time anyone asked her to take their photo on the trip. She was the type of person she and Victor would have searched out, a non-threatening older woman traveling alone. Heaven knows they wouldn't have been caught dead with those horrible selfie sticks street vendors chased them with everywhere they went.

The man scurried back to his wife and wrapped his arm around her waist as they posed in front of the entrance, their smiles radiant. For a moment, Anita disappeared into her parallel universe where she and Victor were the couple standing in front of a lonely widow taking their photo. A child bumped into her from behind, drawing her back to the present, and she snapped a few successive photos.

"They look great," she told the couple with a smile as she handed back the phone.

"Thank you!" the woman said, then they wandered through the doors.

Anita glanced around outside once more in search of Carrie before following the couple inside.

She'd read countless times over the years that the Sagrada Familia's beauty couldn't properly be portrayed in photographs, and upon stepping inside the basilica, she now knew this to be true. Standing in the middle of pillars that seemed to stretch to the heavens surrounded by stained-glass windows so clear she could have sworn the sun's rays streaming in were actually different colors, she choked back a few tears. She reached out to grab Victor's hand, genuinely surprised to find no one beside her.

The realization pummeled her, and her throat constricted. A panic attack was coming, and she looked around at all the people here to witness it.

Ahead of her were rows of pews sectioned off in front of the altar. She hurried over and sat in the closest one, the row farthest back from the altar. She rummaged through her purse briefly before remembering she'd disposed of her Xanax yesterday. Shit.

Victor wasn't with her; he was dead. But she was still here, and she'd proven to herself yesterday she could manage a panic attack without the medication. She would get through this just as she had gotten through so many before.

She focused her attention ahead at the altar, at the magnificent stained-glass backdrop and at the figure of Jesus hanging from the cross, looking upward as he surrendered to his fate. Anita folded her hands and closed her eyes as a few tears trickled down her cheeks. Her breathing slowly returned to normal, and a sense of peace replaced the panic.

She'd dreaded this day for an entire year, dreaded reliving the memory of losing Victor and her future as she'd planned it. She had been frozen in place for a year, afraid to take a step forward for fear of leaving Victor behind. But he was gone regardless of what she did now, and he'd want her to be happy. She knew that now without a doubt. He was beside her in this moment, assuring her she could let go. She'd grieved. She'd tried all she could to hold on to him, but she needed to close this chapter and move forward. His memory would never be forgotten.

Anita looked around the basilica, hoping to see Carrie wandering about, but no luck. She pulled out her phone, but still no calls or messages from her. But there was a message from Enric.

How are you holding up?

Anita stared at the message a moment, unsure how to respond. She appreciated his concern, especially knowing he'd been through this before himself. He understood her emotional roller coaster today better than anyone else she knew. And she could use some company. After all, today was their last day in Barcelona. She'd likely never see him again.

I'm hanging in there, she responded. *I'm at Sagrada. Care to join me?*

Her phone dinged with a response within thirty seconds. *On my way.*

———

With everything else she had going on, Carrie hadn't been prepared for the crushing grief that greeted her when she woke, intense grief like she hadn't felt since she'd been in Buffalo for her dad's funeral. She had tried convincing herself today was just another day, that her mother was being overly sentimental to treat it like some monumental moment. But the moment she opened her eyes, she knew she'd been deluding herself. Today was a really big deal.

She rolled over and looked at Jack, still passed out and oblivious to Carrie's grief. She swore he had a smile on his face still. What had he dreamt about last night?

Carrie pushed herself up against the headboard and grabbed her phone from its charger. There was a new message from her mother, letting her know she was heading to Sagrada and to give her a call if/when she got there.

She looked up at the previous message from yesterday, the one she hadn't yet responded to either. It was likely the most honest message she'd ever received from her, but she still didn't know how to process it.

"Morning," Jack said.

Carrie clicked her phone off and sunk back into the pillows. "Hey sleepy," she said.

He reached for her hand. "How are you?"

Carrie shrugged, unable to speak for fear of losing control of her emotions.

After a few moments of silence, she found her voice again. "Mom messaged me about Sagrada. I guess she's still going."

Jack nodded. "Are you gonna go?"

Carrie drew in a deep breath and stared at her phone in her lap. She'd officially be the worst daughter ever if she abandoned her mother today, though she didn't know which would be worse: the memories of last year that were destined to arise or watching her mother lose herself in grief all over again. Those days back in Buffalo for her father's funeral had been the hardest of her life, and she didn't know that she could handle watching her mother fall apart again. But that was the curse of being an only child: this was solely her responsibility.

"I am," she told Jack, trying hard to sound confident.

"Do you want me to come with you?"

Carrie smiled at the kind offer, but she shook her head. "Thank you, but I need to do this alone."

Jack patted her hand, then sat up. "Well, I'll get out of your hair then and get packing for my flight. But if you need me, I'm just a call away."

Carrie nodded and watched him get his stuff together to leave. They'd agreed last night that she needed to finish out this trip, both for her mother and for herself. Knowing she was trying, that she wanted to improve their relationship gave Carrie hope. With her father gone, her mother was all she had left. And she didn't want her child growing up without knowing his or her grandmother, no matter how strained their relationship had been in the past. Once the trip was complete and Carrie got back to LA, she and Jack would sort out their next steps.

After he left, she showered, letting the water wash over her for several minutes after she finished washing up. She couldn't bring herself to get out and face the day, but the water eventually turned cold, and she reluctantly shut it off and reached for her towel.

The hotel she'd checked into was only a few blocks from the Sagrada, and as she walked along the sidewalk on this warm, early fall afternoon, she envied the locals she passed. While they were in the midst of their normal weekday routines, side-stepping tourists without a second thought, it seemed strange to Carrie that the world continued on as though it was any other day when for her this date would forever be tinged with tragedy.

As she came to the front of the Sagrada Familia and really took it in for the first time, she understood why her father had been so excited to see it in person. No church she'd ever seen in the States could come close to this.

She considered calling her mother to find out where she was, but she needed a minute to herself first before assuming the role of the strong one.

Upon entering the basilica, Carrie couldn't believe it was more beautiful inside than out. She wandered around in a daze, admiring the endless details, but froze in her tracks as she approached the pews leading to the altar.

Her mother didn't seem to need any comfort Carrie might offer; she already had someone with her. A *male* someone. Who sat rather close to her mother, especially considering it was the anniversary of her husband's death.

Carrie's stomach clenched, and she wanted to run away, pretend she'd seen nothing. But her mother turned her head and saw her before she could. She waved Carrie over to the pew where she sat with the stranger.

"You made it," her mother whispered as she approached.

Carrie's eyes remained unwavering on the man beside her mother. "Hi." She extended her hand. "I'm Carrie. Anita's daughter."

The man, who appeared around her mother's age and was very good-looking, took her hand and smiled graciously. "I am Enric, a friend of your mother's," he said in a Spanish accent, emphasizing the word 'friend.' He looked back to her mother. "I should be going. Let me know if you need anything."

"Of course," her mother said. "Thank you for coming. I appreciate it."

Carrie watched Enric walk away, then spun back to her mother. "Are you *kidding* me?" she exclaimed in the loudest whisper possible.

"Carrie..." Her mother's eyes drifted to the couple two rows ahead who turned around at her outburst.

"I can't believe you. You moped around this entire trip, going on and on about missing Dad and how unfair his death was. Then the moment I'm gone, you're cuddling with another man."

"Carrie, sit down," her mother said, desperation in her voice.

"No, I don't want to sit down." It was mean, but Carrie enjoyed causing a scene and making her mother uncomfortable.

"Enric is only a friend. I met him at the bookshop the other night while you and Jack were talking."

"Oh, so blame it on me."

"I didn't say it was your fault. I just met Enric, and his wife died a few years ago and he understood what I'm going through." Her mother paused and looked around, then turned back to Carrie. "I was trying to let you have your space."

"Interesting time to start." She cringed. Her voice reminded her of a whiny teenager. What was wrong with her?

The vast walls of the basilica started closing in, and Carrie struggled for a full breath. Seeing her mother with another man, today of all days, triggered a million emotions she'd avoided for too long. She wanted to curl into her the way she'd done with her dad and cry until she ran out of tears, until her ability to breathe returned, but she didn't know how to be vulnerable with her mother.

She didn't know how to be vulnerable with herself.

"I need to get out of here," she said, looking down to ease the building nausea.

"Carrie."

She heard the disappointment in her mother's voice, recognized it from years of constantly letting her down. She shook her head as tears clouded her vision. She opened her mouth to say something, but she found no words. Instead, she turned and walked away, following the path Enric had taken moments ago out the door, leaving her mother alone again.

———

Anita watched her daughter storm away from her, dumbfounded and floundering to understand what just happened. Today of all days, Carrie accused her of absurdities and abandoned her. Again.

A few pews ahead, a woman sat with her infant daughter on her lap, holding the girl with one hand and fussing with her diaper bag with the other. Anita remembered those days, back when Carrie *needed* her to survive. She had a sense of purpose back then, and despite all the pain she'd endured, holding her baby in her arms eased her suffering. Looking at Carrie's chubby cheeks and almost-bald head, envisioning her future and the life she'd make for herself helped her make some sense of the previous losses. She had been given a chance to prove she was meant to be a mother after all, and she promised her little baby on numerous occasions she would always be there for her, that she would be the best mother Carrie could ever have hoped for.

How wrong she'd been.

Anita hadn't lived an extravagant life, but she thought she'd had a good one. Now she wasn't so certain. What had been the point of it all? Her husband was gone, and her only daughter hated her. Had Anita known her relationship with Carrie would turn out this way, what might she have done differently? Would she have convinced Victor to try for more children? Would she have pushed away her hypothetical younger children as she'd done with Carrie, or would she be sitting here with a larger support network on this difficult day?

The what-if game was a habit Anita had lived with her entire life. Tallying up the time she'd wasted over her lifetime worrying about things that never happened would have been a fruitless endeavor. But all this game amounted to was self-pity and anxiety.

Her daughter walked away from her just now over a misunderstanding. Okay. So what? She could sit here and wallow in the unfairness of it all, or she could take action.

Anita turned to the doorway Carrie had disappeared through moments before, and without another moment's hesitation, she collected her purse and rushed out after her.

Once outside, she scanned the crowd, now larger than when she'd first arrived. Down the steps, she finally found Carrie. Her back was to her as she was still on the move, but Anita recognized her hair and outfit, dark blue jeans and her black leather jacket, and she relaxed with relief that she hadn't lost her again.

"Excuse me," she called to the people around her, then pushed her way towards the steps.

"Carrie!" she called from the top of the steps.

She didn't seem to hear her as she kept moving.

Anita rushed down the stairs, her fear of losing her daughter again outweighing her concern of looking like a fool in front of these strangers.

"Carrie, wait!" she called again once she reached the bottom of the stairs.

This time, Carrie paused. She turned around, and her eyebrows scrunched together. "Mom?"

She must have looked ridiculous racing towards her, but she didn't care. She needed her daughter, and she had to put faith in Meredith's assumption that Carrie needed her too.

When she finally reached her, she threw her arms around her and pulled her into a tight embrace, the kind of hug she'd given Carrie as a toddler when she'd bumped her head.

To her surprise, she wrapped her arms around her as well.

"I'm sorry," Anita said into her daughter's ear. "Enric is just a friend. I would never..."

"I know, Mom. I know. I'm sorry I snapped at you. I just... the sight of you two...it was too much."

She pulled back and looked Carrie in the eyes. "I never meant to upset you. I love you more than anything, and I'm sorry I've been so terrible at showing you that."

Carrie shook her head and swiped a finger under her eye. "I love you too. And I'm sorry."

Anita's shoulders slumped as she released a giant sigh. "Can we go somewhere and talk?" she asked.

Carrie sniffled, then nodded. "That sounds great."

Chapter 29

They walked several blocks over to a small café Anita had seen on her way to Sagrada that had delicious-looking pastries in the window. If they were going to have a heart-to-heart mother-daughter conversation, Anita figured they would earn some pretty-looking pastries and perhaps some coffee.

They sat at an outside table beneath an umbrella. Pedestrians passed by on the sidewalk, and Anita's stomach clenched with nerves. This conversation could go one of two ways, and she wasn't sure she wanted an audience if it went poorly. But they were already seated, and she wasn't going to back out now. She'd come too far, physically and emotionally, to finally be in the mindset to have this conversation. No turning back. At least there were no other patrons on the patio.

A waitress took their order, then shuffled back inside.

"I've spent the morning trying to figure out exactly how to say what I want to say," Anita began. "But I'm afraid I still don't have the words figured out."

Carrie offered a slight smile. "I've had the same problem. Whatever it is, let's just talk about it, even if it comes off clumsy. We'll agree to cut each other some slack?"

She exhaled with relief and returned the smile. "Absolutely." She reached for the glass of water the waitress had left and took a small sip. "We've never been very good at talking to one another, have we?"

Carrie shook her head. "Why is that?"

"I wish I knew. You were the one thing I wanted most in life, and yet it wasn't long before you were a mystery to me. When they told me you were a girl, I pictured you as a mini-me, but you were so completely different from me." Anita shrugged. "And the older you got, the more anything I said was wrong. Somewhere along the line, I stopped trying and just accepted you only wanted to talk to your father."

Carrie straightened and shifted in her chair. "Dad and I had a very different relationship."

Anita waved a hand in front of her, wishing she could go back and rephrase. "I'm not intending to sound spiteful or jealous, though I'm sure I have been in the past. Believe it or not, I love that the two of you had such a special relationship. I just wish we could have had our own special one as well."

"It's not too late," Carrie said, her voice quiet and childlike.

The waitress came back with their pastries and coffee, and Anita tore open a sugar packet and dumped it into her cup. After waking so early this morning, she needed a caffeine jolt. And it wasn't even noon yet.

Carrie nudged her own cup away from her, her nose scrunched up. "I forgot," she said, motioning towards the mug. "Coffee's still not agreeing with me apparently."

Anita chuckled. "I guess we're both a bit sleep deprived, huh?"

"This whole being pregnant thing is going to take some getting used to, I guess."

Anita raised an eyebrow. "Does this mean…?" She ventured, trying not to sound too overly excited.

"I'm keeping the baby," Carrie said. She looked down at her plate, then back up. "And...I'm moving to London."

She coughed as her water caught in her throat. "London?"

Carrie shrugged and her smile twisted to one side. "Jack and I figured it made the most sense, given that he actually has a job here and I don't at the moment."

"So, you and Jack..."

Carrie nodded. "We're giving it a go," she said with a shrug. "Seems you were right all along. I did have feelings for Jack. I was just too afraid to admit to them."

"I...wow," Anita said, trying to find the right words. "That's amazing, Carrie. A new adventure!"

She squinted at her. "So, now we love new adventures?"

Anita's defenses flared up at the shift in Carrie's tone. "What do you mean?"

"You've never approved of my *adventures* before. Remember when I had to fight you tooth and nail to let me go to school in California? Or when you told me Australia was a terrible idea?"

She closed her eyes and pressed her lips together. "I know," she said. "Believe me, if you knew how many things I wish I could change—probably most of our interactions, to be honest."

Carrie leaned back and crossed her arms. "You wonder why I never want to tell you things, but that's why. Every time I told you something, you had something negative to say about it. Dad never did that. He believed in me. He trusted me."

Anita took a sip of coffee, deliberating her words and how best to explain everything. Finally, she looked at Carrie and set the mug down. "I don't have an excuse for any of it, and I won't make one up. All I can say is, it was my anxiety getting the better of me. And I need to explain to you why I was so upset the other day at the thought of you having an abortion."

"You don't need to explain," Carrie said, her tone softening.

"No, you deserve to know why you're an only child."

She tilted her head. "I thought you and Dad only wanted one child?"

Anita half smiled and spun her wedding rings on her finger. "That wasn't the full truth. You do have three older siblings," she said. "All lost before we had the chance to meet them."

Carrie's face crumpled. "Oh, Mom. Why didn't you guys ever tell me?"

"There were many times I wanted to. I hoped it would explain some of my anxiety, explain to you why I was the way I was. But your dad didn't want you to feel pressured to compensate for the children we couldn't have. He didn't like talking about it, to be honest."

"That must have been so difficult."

"It was. Absolutely. Other than losing your dad, the most difficult things I've ever had to get through. I just...I thought it was time you finally knew. I don't know if it changes anything or helps you to understand, but the reason I was always so protective of you, so concerned and worried all the time, was because I was just so terribly afraid to lose you too."

Carrie looked down at her hands resting on the table. "Mom, I need to tell you something."

"Anything," Anita said, eager to switch the attention off her.

"The reason I left Australia." Carrie paused and closed her eyes. "I started having panic attacks. I couldn't get them under control, so I begged Dad to let me come home early."

Anita narrowed her eyes at her daughter, her mind spinning trying to process this new information. "How come...your father. He never told me."

"I begged him not to. I knew you'd be upset with me for not finishing out the semester, especially after I harassed you to let me go and you spent so much money to send me. But I couldn't do it."

"But *I* have panic attacks. I would have understood."

Carrie cleared her throat and looked away. "I know that now. But then...I just couldn't imagine talking about it with you. Or anyone, really. Dad set me up with a therapist in California who helped me get past them. But we never talked about them again."

The thought of her fearless, brave daughter dealing with the same issues she struggled with shook her. You never did know what was going on in someone else's world. But the fact that Carrie felt she couldn't talk with her about the attacks made her feel like an even bigger failure of a mother.

"The panic attacks started because I'd been seeing this guy there," Carrie continued. "A TA, actually. But it turned out he was a liar and a cheater. I caught him with another girl."

"Oh, Carrie. That's awful."

"There's more." She looked off to the side, then brought her focus back to Anita. "When I called Dad, he wanted me to go home to Buffalo, but I begged him to let me go to LA instead. I told him it was because I couldn't be in the same house as you, but the truth was, I'd found out I was pregnant."

Anita's mouth dropped open. Her daughter had been pregnant all those years ago? And she'd had no idea?

"I never told Dad. I went back to LA and made plans to have an abortion. The appointment was set. Jack was going to take me." She paused and blinked back a few tears. "But two days before my appointment, I started bleeding. Jack took me to the hospital." Carrie shrugged. "I'd had a miscarriage."

"I...Carrie. I had no idea."

Carrie kept her eyes down on the table. "Jack was the only person I ever told. I couldn't imagine having a baby and becoming a mom then. But I'd started to question if I could follow through with the abortion. Then I miscarried, and all I could think was I'd caused it by not wanting the baby in the first place."

Anita reached out and held Carrie's hand in her own. "You did *not* cause it," she assured her. "Believe me. I wanted those babies more than anything. It still happened to me."

"I thought I was past it, but when I found out I was pregnant again, it just brought back all those guilty feelings. I didn't think I deserved to be a mom, not after what happened last time. And then the panic attacks came back."

"You had another panic attack?"

Carrie nodded. "After we argued yesterday. I went looking for your Xanax bottle because I didn't know what else to do. But instead, I found your notebook and the sheet with your goal to have a meaningful conversation with me. I felt so horrible reading that and knowing you were trying and I was being a shit daughter as usual. So, I ran away because apparently that's what I'm best at lately. Anyway, that's the reason I left Australia."

Anita stared at Carrie, suddenly seeing her in a completely different light than she'd ever seen her before. Where she'd seen a fearless, carefree, resilient woman, she now saw a fragile girl who'd been running from her feelings for too long. "I wish I'd known," she said. "I know I failed in so many ways as a mother, but all I ever wanted was for you to be happy. If I came across negative, it was only because I worried for you. Maybe now that you're going to be a mother, you'll better understand the love I have for you."

"I never doubted that you loved me," Carrie said. She swiped at her eyes and Anita handed her a napkin. "I just always felt like my choices were wrong in your eyes, so I stopped telling you about them. I know I broke your heart moving to California. The truth is, I'm not even happy there anymore. Probably haven't been for a while. Anyway, I hope you'll forgive me for moving to London. It's honestly not any longer of a flight, and I want my child to have their grandmother in their life."

Hearing Carrie extend this olive branch, hearing her offer an invitation to be the grandmother she'd hoped to be, meant more to Anita than she could possibly articulate. "I want that too," she managed to choke out through a throat full of emotion. "More than anything."

Chapter 30

Later that evening, while Carrie took a shower, Anita went for one last walk through Barcelona.

They'd stayed at the café for another hour, reminiscing about Victor and catching up on the past year, honestly this time. Anita told her how depressing it had been for her, how she'd barely left the house and instead lost herself in self-pity and pushed away her friends. Carrie shared how she'd buried herself even deeper in her career and then her life spiraled out of control right in front of her eyes. Her sincere desire for a stronger bond between them came as a surprise, but Anita was so pleased. She wished it hadn't taken the loss of Victor to urge them both to open up to one another, but better now than never.

But as hopeful as she wanted to be about the future, soon this trip would come to an end. Anita would return to Buffalo, Carrie would soon be moving to London, and she knew too well that words of good intention only got you so far. She'd been speaking them herself for years about this trip, her relationship with Carrie, her anxiety—but it took the catalyst of tragedy to force her to change.

But following through on this trip, coming here with

Carrie and finally saying everything she needed to say gave her hope that her future held more than only misery. She had the arrival of her grandchild to look forward to and a relationship with her daughter to nurture. She envisioned trips back to London to visit, holidays back in Buffalo with a little one running around again. And in Enric, she'd found a friend who truly understood what she was going through, and she had every intention of keeping in touch with him despite the distance.

Meredith had been right in suggesting she follow through on this trip. She'd gained the closure she needed, but more than that, she had found a reason to want to live again. *Reasons*, actually. To say this trip was life-changing was an understatement. It was lifesaving, really.

Taking a seat on some deserted steps near a small fountain, Anita pulled out her phone and sent a quick text to Enric letting him know things worked out with Carrie and thanking him for his support the past few days. Who knew someone she'd just met could have such a significant impact on her life?

She slipped her phone back into her purse and took in the city. The evening had taken over, and the streetlights illuminated the sidewalks while people passed by. On the street corner, a busker trio set up with a cello and two violins.

After a few minutes, the buskers began playing, and it took Anita a moment to recognize the song as Elvis's "Can't Help Falling in Love," her and Victor's first dance song from their wedding. A couple walking by paused and began slow dancing. Anita thought back to her wedding day, Victor holding her close for their first dance as he crooned the words in her ear.

"I've never been happier than I am right now," he'd whispered to her.

Anita closed her eyes and imagined him sitting on the step beside her. "I know you're here with me," she whispered. "I've missed you, but I hope you're proud of me. I'm doing my best. I'm ready to venture out again."

A tear slipped down her cheek. "I love you. I will always love you. But we'll be all right. *I'll* be all right."

The song ended, and Anita drew a deep breath. She felt Victor's presence leave her, but that was okay. What she'd said was true: she would be fine. She would keep living her life to make him proud, to honor him every chance she could.

Her phone beeped, and she pulled it back out of her purse. It was a text from Enric.

You are welcome, it read. *Please stop by to see me the next time you are in Barcelona. Or perhaps I will come see Niagara Falls someday soon.*

I'd like that very much, she replied, and she smiled to realize she meant it. So, this was what moving forward felt like. She'd never forget Victor, never fully leave him behind, but there was room for happiness in her life still if she was willing to allow it in.

Epilogue

The phone rang in the bedroom while Carrie finished up her hair, and she glanced up at the clock. She was running a few minutes late, as per usual, but her mother would understand. She rushed into the bedroom to check the missed call and saw there was a voicemail from one of her clients, but it would have to wait. She was officially on vacation.

She hustled into the adjacent room and looked down into the crib where her daughter slept, a rarity Carrie hated to interrupt.

"Come here, sweetie," she cooed as she lifted her from the crib. "It's time to go pick grandma up at the airport."

Victoria's eyelids lifted, revealing her stunning baby-blue eyes she'd gotten from Jack. Her lips turned upward slightly, and Carrie wanted to believe her daughter was excited about seeing her grandma.

She stepped out of her apartment building with the diaper bag that had replaced her designer purse slung over her shoulder and Victoria in her car seat carrier. The sun was shining, and the London traffic raced past her as she made her way to the parking garage. London had such a different energy from

Los Angeles, and though LA had long felt like home to Carrie, there was no question that this was now where she belonged, here with Jack and their daughter and a new career as a freelance event coordinator.

She secured Victoria in the back of her Volkswagen and headed for Heathrow Airport, thinking back to a little over a year ago when she and Anita landed there. So much had changed in just one year. The first anniversary of her father's death had been marked by uncertainty and instability in Carrie's life. Today, on the second anniversary, things were falling into place.

Carrie glanced down at the engagement ring on her left hand that in only a couple days would be paired with a diamond band and marveled at how sometimes the worst situations in life truly were only setting us up for better things to come.

Thirty minutes later, she pulled up to the arrivals section of Heathrow where her mother stood waiting with her baggage in tow. She looked every bit the confident international traveler, the anxiety that previously plagued her no longer apparent. They talked most nights by phone or FaceTime, and the only thing that saddened Carrie about her newfound friendship with her mother was that her father wasn't here to witness it. He'd have been so proud of them both.

Putting the car in park, she hopped out to help her mother with her bags. But first, they embraced, holding onto one another as only people who have lost someone unexpectedly do, savoring each second. As Carrie hauled the bags into her trunk, her mother opened the back door of the car and cooed at her granddaughter.

"How was your flight?" Carrie asked as they pulled away from the airport.

"Good. No turbulence or anything."

Victoria squealed from the backseat, and they laughed at her enthusiasm.

"And how was Barcelona?"

"Oh, just as beautiful as I remembered. It's amazing how much more there is to see and do than just a week allowed for."

Carrie raised an eyebrow and turned slightly towards her. "And Enric?"

Her mother blushed and smiled coyly. She was always discreet with the details, but Carrie gathered this trip was more than just another sightseeing adventure. While at first the idea of her mother traveling to a foreign country to visit a man who may or may not be her boyfriend had been a lot to take in, seeing the joy in her eyes at the mention of his name made her happy.

"He's good," her mother answered. "How is Jack doing? Any wedding jitters?"

Carrie laughed. "Oh, none at all. He'd have married me a year ago if I'd let him. He's eagerly counting down the minutes!"

"I bet!"

Her phone rang again, but she quickly silenced it. "Just a client," she said. "It can wait."

"I don't know how you do it. Raising this beautiful princess and running your own business, all while planning a wedding. In a foreign country, no less!"

She shrugged. "It's not really foreign anymore. This is home now."

"Home," her mother said and stared out the window.

Carrie glanced over at her, her heart full of love and joy. She was so proud of her mother for all the progress she'd made this past year. Despite her fears, she had embraced the changes and seemed to be truly enjoying her life again.

Sometimes, the most catastrophic circumstances created just enough space for something wonderful to take root.

Acknowledgments

I'm incredibly lucky to have so many people in my life who have not only supported but encouraged my dream of becoming an author since I first voiced that I wanted to write a book. Writing and publishing a novel is a challenging goal, and I truly couldn't have done it without the support of those close to me.

First, to my husband, Jon. Thank you for not only supporting my dream of being an author but for believing in me even when I didn't. When we first met and I shared with you that I was a writer, you earned major bonus points for thinking that was cool. And when I found out you'd been bragging about me writing a book to your coworkers after we were married, you earned even more. You're the best, and I love you more.

To my parents, bonus parents, and grandparents who have encouraged my writing since elementary school and never once made me feel as though this was a useless hobby, I'm thankful every day for your encouragement and love. Your faith in me throughout the years has meant so much. And to Daddy Bob who we lost too soon, I wish you were here today, but I know you're up there lovingly calling me a "dumbass" regularly.

And to the rest of my family and friends who have supported me over the years, thank you. Whether you read early copies of my work or simply cheered me on as I inched closer to becoming a published author, every ounce of excitement over my writing has meant the world to me.

I'm also grateful for the amazing writing communities I've become part of, particularly the Women's Fiction Writers Association. Joining WFWA was the best investment I made in my writing and myself as a writer. The resources and community I found there have been invaluable to me, and I'm so thankful to everyone there who encouraged me, offered feedback on this manuscript, or shared knowledge with me throughout the last several years.

To my amazing developmental editor, Lidija Hilje, I'm so incredibly thankful for your belief in this story and me as a writer. I was so nervous to send my book baby to an editor, but once we talked, I knew I could trust you to help me turn this manuscript into the story I envisioned. Your suggestions and guidance truly helped this story shine.

To my readers, thank you for picking up this book and giving a debut author a chance. A book is nothing without readers to enjoy it, and I'm so thankful for the opportunity to share my characters' journeys with you. If you enjoyed this book, please do consider leaving a review on Amazon or Goodreads. Reviews are the best support you can give any author, but especially a new one.

And finally, to my son, Logan. Thank you for letting me be your mama and inspiring me daily to keep chasing after my dreams even when it's challenging. Becoming a mother gave me a different perspective on this story, and I know it made it stronger. I love you more than anything, little man.

About the Author

Lisa Fellinger writes contemporary women's fiction with lovably flawed, relatable characters. When she's not writing her own stories, she's helping others achieve their writing dreams as a book coach and developmental editor. She lives in Buffalo, New York with her husband, son, and fur babies.

For bonus book club questions, author news, and more:
www.lisafellingerauthor.com/bonus-material

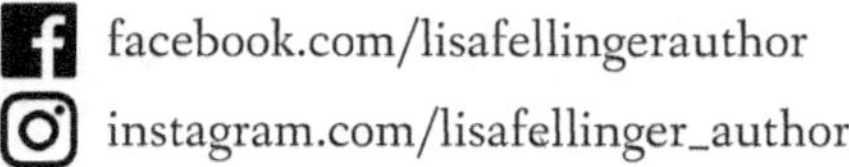
facebook.com/lisafellingerauthor
instagram.com/lisafellinger_author